The
GRACE
of
WILD
THINGS

HEATHER FAWCETT

The

GRACE

of

WILD
THINGS

BALZER + BRAY

An Imprint of HarperCollins*Publishers*

Balzer + Bray is an imprint of HarperCollins Publishers.

Library of Congress Control Number: 2022940749
ISBN 978-0-06-314262-6 (trade bdg.)—ISBN 978-0-06-331953-0 (special ed.)

Typography by Catherine Lee

22 23 24 25 26 LBC 5 4 3 2 1

First Edition

The
GRACE
of
WILD
THINGS

1

THE WITCH WITH THE SEASHELL HEART

On this long storm the rainbow rose,
On this late morn the sun . . .
The birds rose smiling in their nests,
The gales indeed were done . . .
—Emily Dickinson, "On this long storm the rainbow rose"

When Grace smelled baking bread, she knew she was nearing the witch's cottage.

It was her favorite kind of bread, she was certain. The kind she never had in the orphanage, where the bread was meant to be so filling that the children might as well eat rocks, for it wasn't as if they'd notice the difference in taste. No, the aroma drifting through the dark trees was from bread gone chocolaty brown on the outside and soft as a pillow within, full of gooey raisins that burst on your tongue.

Most children would have turned around when they smelled something like that, for it meant the witch was near.

The witch lived somewhere deep in the woods—she lured children in and ate them, and wasn't even a woman at all, for she could change shape into an enormous beast made of shadows. Those were the stories the children told, anyway.

But the witch didn't need to lure Grace. Grace was looking for her.

Grace paused to rub her aching feet. She didn't know how long she'd been walking through forest and pasture, but it had been dark when she'd left the orphanage and now it was dark again.

She stopped and looked about, not that it did much good. The moon was lazy that night, still asleep below the horizon, and the stars were all tangled up in the black boughs overhead like fish in a net.

Her stomach growled. She hadn't eaten anything since the stale crumpet she'd found in her pocket from days ago, because she'd forgotten that long journeys required food—not a good thing to forget, she knew, but she had no experience with running away, and if she had, she was certain she'd still be rotten at it just like she was at everything else.

If you'd only stop your daydreaming, Grace, Mrs. Spencer always said. She never finished the sentence, for Mrs. Spencer had no imagination. Grace, on the other hand, had too much, or so everybody told her. Her mind was always wandering off or drifting into her books and tales of magicians and quests. But whose mind *wouldn't* wander, she thought, if it had only the bare white walls of Rose & Ivy Home for Unwarded Children to occupy it?

Well, Mrs. Spencer's, she supposed.

As the smell of raisin bread grew stronger—raisin bread that, she was certain, would be glistening with honey and melted butter—Grace spied a gleam of light through the trees, and the little deer trail widened. The trees went from pine and oak to maple and cherry, and then she saw an apple tree, too, puffed up with its self-important blossoms. Her feet rustled through a pool of soft petals, white as little bones.

Then the path bent to the left, and there was the cottage.

On the surface, it was very cozy. Lonesome but pretty, tucked into a snug forest clearing, its white gables fresh with paint. It leaned its small face—only two windows to a story— over a stream glazed with petals and starlight. A willow brushed her branches over the stream, *shhh, shhh.*

But to Grace—to all children, probably—it looked . . . wrong. Like a smile on an angry face. The windows glowed golden, but too brightly.

If you were lost, though, Grace thought, scared and hungry, you might tell yourself you didn't notice any of that. You'd focus on the smell of bread or cookies or whatever you were hungry for, and march right up to the pretty red door. But Grace had heard enough stories about who was behind that door to know what was what.

She gazed up at that cottage, cozy on the surface but full

of magic and spookiness underneath, and fell in love with it right then and there. It was everything she'd ever hoped for in a home.

Windweaver settled in a pear tree, his black feathers rustling.

"What do you think?" Grace whispered.

It's definitely the witch. I asked the other crows. Windweaver spoke into her mind, a fluttery and slightly ticklish feeling like the brush of feathers. Windweaver was the name the crow had chosen for himself. Actually, he'd chosen Prince Windweaver of the Azure Bower, but Grace only called him that on special occasions.

Grace nodded. Crows knew all about witches, and magic in general. "Is she home?"

How am I supposed to know? he said irritably. Before he met Grace, Windweaver hadn't been able to talk—not to people, anyway; crows have their own secret language—and he still wasn't used to it. Then he sighed. *I suppose I could look in her windows.*

He soared into the night, just another shadow. Grace waited, her stomach in knots. It was in moments like this, when she wasn't watching for roots in the darkness or listening for the *clop-clop* of hooves coming up behind her—someone sent to drag her back to the orphanage—that she felt most afraid. What if she had to make her way back through that rough forest, along those country lanes gone ghostly in the darkness?

No. She set her jaw, and her hand tightened on her walking stick. Whatever happened, she wasn't going back.

She drew herself up and stood gazing at the cottage, imagining that she was a noble princess who had traveled through untold hardships to seek a favor from a wicked queen.

One of the curtains twitched, and she leaped behind a tree with a squeak.

Somebody's home, Windweaver said, settling noiselessly in the branches. *I saw a shadow moving behind the shutters.*

Grace drew in a deep breath, trying to be the noble princess again. But while she might have had the courage of a princess, she didn't have the knees of one—they were quaking like anything.

Are you sure about this? Windweaver said. *D'you really want to live with a witch?*

"I want to learn about my magic." Grace kicked a rock. "Besides, who else but a witch would want me?"

She tried to shrug as she said it, but it felt false. The truth was that Grace longed for a home more than anything in the world.

"It's not as if my parents are coming back," she added, looking at the ground.

Windweaver gave a soft croak and hopped onto her shoulder. He was Grace's dearest friend—well, actually, he was her *only* friend—and he always knew what she was feeling. *Maybe they will.*

 5

"No. Either they're dead or they're away across the sea, having adventures. Either they can't come back or they don't want to."

Grace kept her voice hard, to scare away the tears, but her eyes stayed dry. The only piece of her parents she had was a blurry photograph. She couldn't remember them at all—she'd been too little when they were *lost at sea*, as Mrs. Spencer said, a phrase Grace liked, for it made her think of desert islands and monkeys and lagoons. Though Mrs. Spencer had also said that Grace's father was a no-good sea captain who dragged her mother along with him on his fishing trips, sometimes even going past Cape Breton in the smallest, ugliest boat you ever saw, though everyone knew the sea was no place for a lady.

Windweaver cleaned a leaf from her hair. *I bet they're having adventures.*

"I think so too!" Grace said. "Mrs. Spencer knew them. She said sometimes they came back to shore without any fish, just these funny golden skins, like from an otter if otters came in gold, and wooden chests with symbols carved in them. And Mrs. Spencer said it, so you know it must be true. That's the benefit of having no imagination, isn't it? You can always be relied upon for plain facts."

Windweaver nodded. *I bet they became pirates.*

Grace pressed her lips together. She always tried not to think about the *other* thing that might have happened to her parents. Although she supposed that being lost at sea was a romantic way to die. After all, there were people like Sarah Haberdasher, whose parents got consumption and wasted away. There was no mystery in that at all, she thought, and you couldn't have a good story without mystery.

But she didn't believe everything Mrs. Spencer said. She had seen the sea when it was restless and roaring as the storms rolled in, and also when it lay still as a silver mirror for the stars to admire themselves. The waves coming in, full of secrets from distant lands, whispering them to the shore. She bet her mother had wanted to go.

She drew a deep breath, her bravery stirring again. "All right. I'm ready."

She lifted her battered carpetbag, which held only a few books. As she left the trees behind, the path grew wide enough for a carriage. Little lights dangled from the cherry trees—glass jars, their mouths wrapped in cheesecloth. But what was making the light?

"Oh!" Grace gasped. The jars were filled with fireflies, three or four in each. And there, growing next to the path, were wild strawberries like little red jewels. She wanted to stop and scoop some into her mouth, but she wasn't that much a fool.

She's clever, Windweaver said, perching on Grace's shoulder. *She knows what children like. D'you think the stories are true? That she—she eats them?*

"Sure," Grace said with a shrug. "What else do witches do? I bet she has a big oven inside that she roasts them in."

Windweaver tucked his head into her hair. *Be careful.*

"Don't worry. As soon as she sees me, we'll be safe."

She marched up to the door, which was as red as the strawberries, and knocked with a trembling hand. There was a long moment of quiet, though it was the sort of quiet that had eyes in it. Grace heard light footsteps within, and a shadow twitched under the door. Then the door slid open without even the slightest creak, and an old woman was beaming down at her.

She was a pretty old woman, comfortably plump with gold-streaked gray hair pulled back in a bun and floury hands that she was wiping on a tea towel. She wore an especially grandmotherly cardigan made of soft yellow wool, and her mouth was thin and a little stern, but with a lopsidedness that hinted at mischief. Her face was creased with what most people would call laugh lines, though Grace didn't take this as a friendly sign, for the old woman was a witch, and a lot depended on what she was laughing about. And Grace was sure she was a witch straight away, because her heart didn't beat.

Grace knew this because she could hear heartbeats—it was one of the three things she was good at, the other two being reading and magic (three wasn't a lot, she knew, but it was three better than none). The witch's heart was cold and empty, and made a sound like the whispered roar inside a seashell. What else could she be, given that all the stories said witches were heartless?

"Good gracious!" the witch said warmly. "Are you lost, poor child?"

Grace's stomach gave a rumble, for the smell wafting out of the witch's house was like an enchanted bakery. Not just raisin bread now, but apple tarts and sticky date pudding, maple gingerbread and pumpkin cakes, all hot from the oven. She thought about what the witch must see—a little girl, her black hair dirty and tangled with needles from the nap she'd taken under a pine tree, the front of her dress stained with huckleberry juice and her legs covered in mud. A wild thing from the forest, barely a girl at all.

The witch's smile grew as she looked Grace up and down, and Grace had the disturbing impression that the witch was measuring her against something. The bakery smell grew so delicious she thought she might faint from it.

"You can stop that," Grace said, trying for bravery when underneath she was terrified the witch would close the door in her face. "I know who you are."

The witch's smile didn't budge. She gave her floury hands another dusting with the tea towel. "Do you."

Grace looked up into that old face, and she couldn't stop herself from grinning. The witch's eyes narrowed ever so slightly, but Grace couldn't help it—she'd never met another witch before, somebody whose heart made the same seashell sound that her own did sometimes.

"There was a girl at the orphanage who told stories about you," she explained, talking fast now. "She used to live in the village down the lane—Brook-by-the-Sea. She said a little boy and his sister got lost in the woods near your cottage one night, and you lured them in. Then you ate the girl up, and you would've eaten the boy, too, but he escaped out the back door."

Grace ran out of breath. The witch gazed down at her, her happy-grandmother disguise not slipping an inch. For a moment, Grace almost believed this was just an old woman she had interrupted at her baking, one who might pat her on the head and tut over her scraped knees.

She's clever, Windweaver had said. He'd been right.

"My," the witch said calmly, "you're an imaginative girl, aren't you? Now, a little imagination's all right in a child, but too much can be a dangerous thing."

"You think you can eat me, too. But you can't." Grace gave what she hoped was a dramatic pause. "Because I'm a witch like you."

She was certain that the witch would gasp or at least blink in surprise, but instead she just looked at Grace blankly, as if she'd announced that she could knit socks.

"And, um, well," Grace went on after an uncomfortable silence, "I came to see if you'd teach me. Spells, I mean— proper magic. I can work for it," she added hurriedly. "I can cook and clean. Whatever you like."

She tried to keep the desperation from her voice, but desperation was a tricky thing to hide, like a bad odor. The witch paused, and then without warning, all her grandmotherliness fell away, and she *really* looked at Grace. Gazing into the witch's eyes felt like falling into an abyss so black and fathomless, you'd run out of screams before you hit bottom. Grace pulled her gaze away with a gasp, and when she looked back, the witch was smiling and folding up the tea towel, and Grace was half convinced she'd imagined it.

"A witch, are you?" the witch said, and Grace couldn't tell if she was pleased or not. "Well then, we must have a nice little chat, mustn't we?"

Grace let out her breath. She hadn't been sent away or called a liar. "Thank you," she whispered.

The witch smiled her secret little smile and opened the door wide. "Come in."

2

ALL THE GOOD THINGS IN THE WORLD

A Bird, came down the Walk—
He did not know I saw—
He bit an Angle Worm in halves
And ate the fellow, raw . . .
—Emily Dickinson, "A Bird, came down the Walk"

"Where are you from, Grace dear?" the witch asked. They were sitting in the witch's kitchen, which was wonderfully cozy, with a heavy oak table and pretty yellow curtains framing the two big windows, a potted geranium on each sill. Taking up almost an entire wall was a huge brick oven.

Grace was devouring a strawberry tart with whipped cream, raisin bread with butter and crab apple preserves, several chocolate crinkles, and a piping hot mug of tea with honey from the witch's own bees. Windweaver kept pecking at the window, but Grace ignored him. The witch wasn't going to hurt her. They were alike.

"Rose and Ivy orphanage, ma'am," Grace said around a mouthful of strawberry tart. "In Charlottetown."

"Charlottetown is over twenty miles away," the witch said. "That explains what a mess you are, I suppose. You've been through a trial, poor child."

Grace blushed. Her dress was one big stain, grass and mud mostly, while her hands were purple with blackberry juice.

The witch poured Grace another cup of tea and set a plate of lemon shortbread in front of her, still warm from the oven. Grace seized one and popped it in her mouth, almost fainting with happiness as the butter melted on her tongue.

"Now then," the witch said, "tell me about this magic of yours."

Grace looked down at her hands. She felt lost for words— not a thing that happened often.

"Can you cast any spells?" the witch pressed. She sounded irritated, but then she gave a warm, encouraging smile, so Grace thought she must have imagined it. "Perhaps you know how to fly? Or turn things to gold?"

Grace gave a surprised laugh. "I wish! If I could turn things to gold, I bet Mrs. Silverwood would have kept me."

"Ah." The witch leaned back. "This Mrs. Silverwood adopted you?"

"Yes." Grace looked back at her hands. "But then she found out I was a witch. She didn't want me after that."

"That must have been very hard," the witch murmured. "Having to go back to that dreadful orphanage."

"The orphanage wasn't so dreadful," Grace said. "Well, it was rather plain and worn around the edges, I suppose, and it was eight girls to a room—oh, some of those girls could snore up a storm, especially that Betsy Gulliver—but the food was all right and nobody was beaten or starved. Orphans are always being beaten and starved in stories, aren't they? So I suppose we were lucky. There was a beautiful green woodland out back, so green you could imagine any number of creatures living in it, but I always thought of elves—little elves that dart behind trees when anyone comes near, with footsteps that sound like raindrops—and also the library was *wonderful*. Twenty-four shelves full of books—I know because I counted—and you could read them as many times as you—"

"I see," the witch said, and Grace was certain she was irritated. Her smile had gone cold and hard.

Grace hurried to add, "What I mean is, the orphanage isn't a bad place to *live*. But it's a dreadful place to go back to." She swallowed. "I didn't know I was a witch before Mrs. Silverwood took me in. And after she sent me back, I wished . . . "

"That you weren't a witch?" the witch guessed.

Grace shook her head rapidly. "No, I *love* being magic. It's the best thing—the only good thing—" She stopped. "I just wish that I could be the good kind of magic, instead of the bad kind."

"And what makes you think you're the bad kind, Grace?"

Grace drew a breath. Then suddenly the story was tumbling out of her like a waterfall, unstoppable.

Mrs. Silverwood had come to Rose & Ivy when Grace was eight. She had needed a girl to help out with her babies—three of them, all born at the same time, plus two others who were barely walking. When Mrs. Spencer had called Grace into the parlor, Grace had thought it was because she was in trouble. She and Lily Reed had been sitting on her bed, eating a stolen apple pie with their bare hands—for pie, as Grace had told Lily, always tasted best eaten that way, devoured as messily as a bear devours a fish. When Mrs. Spencer walked in, Grace had hidden the pie under the pillow.

Mrs. Silverwood had been pale in a watery, washed-out way, with hair and eyes of an uncertain color. She reminded Grace of a mermaid forced into human form and stranded on dry land for years. Mermaids were much on Grace's mind then, for she hoped that was what her parents were, and that one day they would come walking back out of the sea, full of stories about underwater kingdoms.

Naturally, Mrs. Spencer had snapped at Grace for comparing Mrs. Silverwood to a mermaid, but Mrs. Silverwood hadn't looked upset. She'd smiled with a sort of surprised pleasure, as if she'd forgotten all about mermaids until Grace mentioned them, and a bit of the weariness had left her face.

Grace had lived with Mr. and Mrs. Silverwood for a day, the happiest day of her life. Everything was wonderful—even the name *Silverwood*, which had so much poetry in it, and was just the sort of name she could picture on the cover of a book. When it happened—the magic, that is—she was helping Mrs.

Silverwood pick apples in her garden (the Silverwoods had a beautiful garden, built into the slope of a hill with a brook running down it). Mrs. Silverwood had asked if mermaids liked apples, and Grace said that they probably had vast undersea orchards where the apples grew salty-sweet with slippery green skins. They laughed and chattered about all the things you would find in a mermaid garden—tulips with pearls in their mouths and roses tentacled like anemones.

Then one moment, she was looking at Mrs. Silverwood, and the next, she was looking *through* her. Not as if she were a ghost, but as if she'd clicked open like the door of a house. Mrs. Silverwood's gray eyes turned the gray of the winter dawn when her father had pulled her little brother, William, out of the lake. Mrs. Silverwood—who had been called Emily Brown back then, at sixteen—should have stopped her brother from wandering off that day, as she had been left in charge. But instead, she'd stayed in her room and read her books while he wandered out into the snow to look for frogs. Frogs freeze themselves in winter—Emily Brown had read that in a book. Then when a warm spring day comes, they melt and shake themselves and go back to their frog business. Emily thought of those frogs as she looked at her poor frozen brother, who would never shake himself back to life. Even after she became Mrs. Silverwood, she couldn't stand the sound of frogs croaking.

When Grace blinked and drew back, she saw from the expression on Mrs. Silverwood's face that she'd seen the exact same thing when she looked at Grace. Her face was white, and she stared at Grace with such a look of horror that Grace promptly burst into tears.

Grace never saw Mrs. Silverwood again, nor the house with the sloping garden and the brook. Somebody took her back to the orphanage, and when she got there, Lily Reed was gone, for the Silverwoods had swapped the two of them like pairs of shoes. Grace had dug around in the bed and found the cold, crushed pie still stuffed under her pillow.

"That's quite a tale," the witch said when Grace finished. "And is that the only time you've used magic?"

"Oh no," Grace said. The food had made her sleepy, and the cottage had that cozy, creaky quiet of old houses. "It happened twice more. Not one of those people ever told Mrs. Spencer why they were returning me—of course, she thought it was because I'm always saying unladylike things. Mrs. Spencer was forever saying that I have too much imagination, you see. Do you think one can have too much imagination? It seems to me it's rather like having too much lemon shortbread or too many flowers in your garden. After all, if you had too *little* imagination, you'd spend your life finding fault with everything, like Mrs. Spencer does, instead of noticing that there are beautiful things in the world alongside the horrible ones."

The witch's lips were pursed. "I wouldn't know about that. As for the rest of it, there's no need to mope—what you did is perfectly natural. All witches have that effect on people— we make them see their worst memories, the things they feel guilty about. We're what people fear, you see—we always have been. The thing lurking in the shadows. You know the funny thing about fear? It's usually mixed up with hate. Two sides of a coin. And the thing you hate most, the thing you fear, is often inside yourself. It's what you don't want anyone else to see."

Grace wasn't sure she understood any of this. "Can I stop it?"

"Oh yes." The witch gave a short, warm laugh. "You just have to learn how to disguise yourself. As I've done."

Hope fluttered in Grace's chest. "Then—then can I live here? And learn witchcraft from you?"

"I don't see any reason why you shouldn't stay here permanently," the witch said, which wasn't *quite* what Grace had asked, though she didn't notice it at the time.

Grace gave a cry of delight. "*Thank* you!" she said. "Thank you, thank you, thank—"

"That's enough," the witch interrupted. "You must be tired after all that walking. Why don't you—"

"How does magic work?" Grace demanded, leaning forward in her excitement. "I've always wanted to know. You mentioned spells, but I've never cast any. My magic just *happens*, you see."

The witch's mouth tightened. "Perhaps we can talk about that another—"

"I mean, I would prefer magic to be spells," Grace went on. "That's much more interesting. In some stories, magicians and sorcerers enchant people just by looking at them. That's dull, isn't it? Imagine if magic really came down to a lot of squinting. Although I suppose lots of things in life are like that—more interesting to imagine than they are to *do*." She paused, thinking. "But then, if magic is spells, why do I make people see the bad things they've done without saying a single magic word?"

"Magic is a complicated subject," the witch said. "Too complicated to get into this late at night. How about you get some sleep, hmm?" The witch took Grace's spoon and gently set it in the bowl. Grace followed her up the creaky stairs—her legs felt terribly heavy, and she stumbled a few times.

"Here we are," the witch said. The stairs opened onto a landing with a door on the left. The witch pushed it open, and Grace gasped.

The bedroom within was narrow, with just enough room for a bed and a chest of drawers, but oh! It was everything Grace had ever dreamed of. There was a patchwork quilt with a patch for every flower that grew on Prince Edward Island, from lupins to lady's slippers. The window overlooked an orchard of apple trees, their blossoms gleaming white in the moonlight like the umbrellas of little ghosts. The chest of drawers was a good solid thing of cedar planks that made the room smell like a summer forest, while a rug of blue-and-white wool spread softly at her feet like a pool she might dip her weary feet in. She thought of the long, narrow room where she'd slept in the orphanage—so narrow you had to turn sideways to get around the foot of the other beds to reach your own—with its plain gray walls and faint smell of cooking fat from the downstairs kitchen. The contrast between the two bedrooms was so great that for several moments Grace couldn't speak.

"Oh," she breathed finally. "It's as if all the good things in the world are here in this room."

The witch let out a sharp breath through her nostrils. "I've left a nightgown on the bed for you there. Good night."

Grace trailed a hand dreamily over the quilt. "Are there any witch children in the neighborhood?"

The witch stopped. "Witch children?"

"That I might be friends with," Grace explained. "I can't imagine how wonderful it must feel to have friends. At the orphanage, most of the other children were afraid of me—they guessed that I was Something Else. Children are better at spotting witches than adults, I think. Anyway, even the brave ones were never my friends for long, for they were always being adopted and leaving me behind. I was the oldest girl left—the next oldest was a whole two years younger. She only came up to my shoulder." Grace marked the height with her hand. "Do you know what it's like, to always be left behind? Well, there was a blackberry bush by the orphanage, and every season we would eat the berries, but there were always some that were too high to reach, and the longer they went unpicked, the more they shriveled up into husks. That's what it's like to be left behind—it fills you with a shriveled-up feeling. Mrs. Spencer said I shouldn't compare children to blackberries, or anything else, for that matter—she doesn't believe in comparisons, you see. But I think it's nice to find fellowship in the world, whether it's with another person or a blackberry bush."

The witch had that pinched look Mrs. Spencer wore when

one of her headaches was coming on. "To my knowledge, there are no witch children in the neighborhood. Now, get some sleep, dear. You must be exhausted after your long journey."

"Exhausted," Grace murmured. She tumbled into the bed, feeling as if she could barely hold her eyes open. "I do love that word, don't you? It just rolls off the tongue like a sigh. Isn't it perfect when words sound like what they mean?"

The witch was rubbing her eyes and did not reply.

"Why doesn't my magic work on you?" Grace said fuzzily. It was strange how quickly her sleepiness had come on! "Is it because you're a witch?"

The witch smiled vaguely. "Oh, I suppose it's because I don't have any regrets, that's all. Good night, Grace."

The last thing Grace was aware of before sleep swept her away was Windweaver frantically pecking at the window. She raised her hand to open it, but her arm was quite a bit heavier than usual and sagged back onto the bed. She tumbled into sleep.

3

THE WITCH IS SURPRISED

I caught a bird: She flitted by,
So near my window lifted high . . .
She fluttered, struck, and seemed to sing,
"Alas! I can't get out."
—Hannah Gould, "I Caught a Bird"

When she looked back on that night, Grace told herself she should have known better. After all, she'd read plenty of stories about witches. Enough to know never to fall asleep in a witch's house, especially after being stuffed full of sweets that made her feel sleepy in a way she'd never felt sleepy before.

When Grace awoke, she could hear the witch humming to herself. It sounded muffled, as if she was on the other side of Grace's window. Then Grace lifted her head and found that the window in question was actually the window of the witch's big oven, and Grace was inside it.

At first she could only blink, too stunned to move. Then—

"Let me out!" she shrieked, pounding her hands against the glass. "Let me out at once, or—or else!"

The witch snorted. She was standing by the stove, mixing something in a tall saucepan. "Given that I'm the one who put you in there, what are the odds that I'll let you out, you foolish girl?"

The witch stepped forward—and then she changed. She stopped being a plump grandmother with creases beside her eyes and became a towering shadow with teeth. She filled the entire room, and had no body anymore at all, just tendrils of darkness reaching out in every direction, like the threads of a spider's web. The shadow's teeth were long and sharp, sometimes here and sometimes there. The strangest thing about the shadow, though, was that it still seemed to be wearing the witch's clothes—the yellow cardigan, the practical boots, the locket and shawl. Somehow, they were stretched by the darkness.

It should have looked silly, a little voice in Grace's head thought. A shadow in stretched-out clothes. But it wasn't—the witch was *more* frightening that way, a hideous shadow dressed in an old lady's clothes, as if the shadow was part of the ordinary world and not some story—which, of course, it was.

Grace shrank back. "You can't *eat* me! I'm a witch, just like you—witches can't eat other witches!"

"True enough," the witch said. She turned back into her grandmother shape, quicker than a blink, though Grace could see shadows still lurking under the cuffs of her sleeves and around her collar, as if the witch had only bothered to disguise the parts of herself that were visible. She went back to bustling around the kitchen as if nothing had happened. "But I don't know that you're a witch."

"What? I—" At that moment, Grace brushed up against something sharp and let out a scream. There were *bones* in the oven—a whole jumbled pile of them. And worst of all were the two grinning skulls perched on top, like an audience waiting for a show to start.

"I told you about the visions!" she blurted. "You said they're normal for witches—how could I have known about that, if I was an ordinary girl?"

"Perhaps you stole the secrets of another witch. Who can say? Little girls like telling tales."

"But you *know* I'm a witch." Grace's eyes blurred with tears. She supposed anybody would weep if a witch decided to bake them, but that wasn't the full reason. She wept because once again, she was unwanted—as a *person*, that is, not as a meal.

"Perhaps I do," the witch said. "Perhaps I don't. In any case, killing you won't break any rules if you can't prove you're a witch. If the Halifax Council of Magic finds out, I shall tell them it was an honest mistake."

"But I thought this would be it!" Grace cried. "I thought if I could just find someone magic like me, I could have a home. But not even a hideous, evil old witch wants to keep me!"

And she collapsed onto her side in the grubby oven, crying

so fiercely she could barely breathe.

The witch didn't seem insulted, but she did seem annoyed. "Stop your caterwauling. The last person I put into that oven was so frightened he just sat there staring at me like a rabbit— very polite indeed. Be frightened, girl. You're about to be cooked, and then I shall gather up your bones and use them in a variety of spells. I'm going to fetch the wood now."

"It doesn't matter," Grace sobbed. "I'll never have a home! I'd rather be cooked than go back to the orphanage, where I will spend the rest of my life knowing just how alone I am in the world."

"Good grief," the witch muttered. She stomped outside, slamming the door behind her.

Grace kept on sobbing so hard that she didn't hear the tapping sound at first. Then came a small voice: *Grace! Look up!*

She looked. There was Windweaver, flapping frantically outside the oven. He must have snuck in through the kitchen window, which was open a crack. He was carrying a wooden ladle in his left foot, and it kept clattering against the oven door.

I think I can lift the handle with this, he said. *And if the witch comes back, I'll peck her good.*

Grace rolled over. "Go away," she said in a doomed sort of whisper.

What?

"Go away!" she cried. "Just go! I would rather be eaten by a

25

witch than live another day as a—a *spurned* orphan."

I don't know what that means, Windweaver said. *But if you don't get moving, I'll peck you too!*

Grace didn't reply. She appreciated her dear Windweaver's courage, but at the same time, in her misery, she couldn't help being annoyed at him, flapping around with that silly ladle—it wasn't at all an image suited to the tragedy of the situation. Of course, she would have called Windweaver to her as soon as the witch lit the match. She just wished he hadn't come to rescue her *now*, when it wasn't a proper rescue. In stories, proper rescues happened just in the nick of time.

Windweaver tried to hook the ladle around the handle of the oven, but it kept slipping off. *I'm going to get a twig,* he said. *If the witch comes back, shout!*

He flapped out the window. Seconds later, the cottage door creaked open, and the witch came in, her arms full of logs.

Grace sat up straight, tears dripping. "Wait," she said in her bravest, most noble voice.

The witch simply opened the oven and tossed in the logs, stirring up a cloud of ash that made Grace cough. She stopped at the sight of the ladle on the floor, shot Grace a suspicious glare, then shook her head and put the ladle back on its hook.

"Wait!" Grace repeated hoarsely. "You said I hadn't proved I was a witch. What if I could? You couldn't cook me then, could you?"

The witch paused. "And how will you do that? You only

have about three and a half minutes."

Grace swallowed, because of course the witch knew precisely how long it took for a person to burn up, and her hands went unconsciously to her hair—it was long and black and glossy, the only pretty thing about her. Her mind slipped back into her favorite stories, and she felt a flash of inspiration.

"I've got it! I shall make your cow give sour milk."

Grace grinned at her cleverness. In stories, witches were always making milk turn sour or fruit wither in orchards, so that their enemies would starve, she supposed. She had never understood why they did this, for in other stories witches were mostly concerned with fattening people up to eat them. Perhaps witches were simply contrary.

The witch wrinkled her nose. "I think that given the choice between cooking you and letting you ruin my poor cow, I think I know which way I am leaning."

But she didn't add more wood to the oven, nor light any matches. Grace said triumphantly, "You have to let me try, don't you? Otherwise your council will be mad at you."

The witch scowled. Grace didn't understand how some council would find out that the witch had eaten another witch unless she told them, but witches were magic, weren't they? Perhaps they would simply Know, with a capital *K*.

The witch folded her arms and smiled. "I'll give you one minute."

Grace realized her mistake then, which should have been

27

obvious—she didn't know how to turn milk sour. She didn't know how to turn anything sour, or sweet, for that matter. After all, she was a witch without any training.

"All right," she said, trying to sound confident, as if she put spells on cows every day. Then, not knowing what else to do, she *willed* the milk to sour.

She willed it very hard. She squeezed her eyes shut and put her fingers against her temples. She imagined the cow, who was surely asleep in her stall at that hour, dreaming cow dreams about sunshine and green fields.

"Oh noble beast," she chanted, "great cow, devourer of grass, black as night and white as snow; I will that your— that *thy* milk be sour as . . . as lemons. That's it, lemons. Not lemon tart, nor lemonade, but the sourest lemons that anyone ever—"

"Be quiet," the witch said. "That's not a spell, you imbecile. And anyway, your time is up."

Grace's eyes flew open. "But—"

The witch was already at the door. "If that milk hasn't soured yet . . ."

She left the sentence hanging in the air like a noose and vanished into the night. Grace collapsed and began to cry again. Unfortunately, only her nose would cooperate, running like anything. She wiped it on her sleeve, which was very unromantic and made her feel even worse. No tragic heroines ever got runny noses in stories. Come to think of it, no tragic heroine ever had to use the bathroom in stories, despite all the long quests they were always running off on. It was very odd.

Grace was approximately halfway through making a list of things that never happened to tragic heroines in stories—she'd just added *smelly feet*, for her own were terribly smelly after a long day of running away—when she heard the witch's footsteps returning, heavy and angry.

The witch banged through the door and threw a pail down by the oven, spilling its contents across the floor. It wasn't milk—it was far too thick. A few drops spattered on Grace's face through the oven grate. They were cold and wonderfully sweet.

"Ice cream!" she cried. "I made ice cream! How lovely—"

"It is not *lovely*," the witch snarled. "What am I to do with a gallon of ice cream, you wretched child?"

The oven door swung open and Grace tumbled out, too excited to notice the witch's anger. "It worked!" she cried. "I proved that I'm a witch!"

"You will fix my cow immediately," the witch snapped.

Grace faltered. "I—I don't know how I did that. But I'll work out how to fix her! That shall be my first task as your apprentice." Grace beamed at her.

The witch drew herself up and began to flicker back and forth between her grandmother shape and the fanged shadow. Grace gave a strangled shriek and leaped back, colliding with the pots and pans on the wall, which made an awful clamor.

"I do not require an apprentice," the witch said in a voice like the creak of winter trees. "And if I did, I would not choose a ridiculous, chattering brat such as yourself. Council law requires witches to offer hospitality to one another, so you may stay here for the rest of the night. But tomorrow you will go back to that orphanage, if I have to drag you there by your hair."

And then, in a swirl of black, she was gone.

4

A DOOR OPENS AND CLOSES AGAIN

There! where the flutter of his wings
Upon his back and body flings
Shadows and sunny glimmerings,
That cover him all over.
—William Wordsworth, "The Green Linnet"

It was impossible for Grace to sleep after that. She couldn't sob anymore, so she simply lay in a heap on the bed with the every-flower quilt, in the bedroom with the carpet that was like a pond and the chest of drawers that smelled of a summer forest. She had strewn her coat and shoes about the room, having decided that girls in the depths of despair couldn't be expected to care about tidiness.

She had thought she'd found a home—the perfect home. Now she wished she'd never left the orphanage, because having a home snatched away was a thousand times worse than never having one at all.

Tap-tap.

The sound came from the window. Grace rose and let Windweaver inside—he was in a panic, feathers fluffed and trembling.

I thought she'd eaten you! he said angrily.

"It's even worse than that," she said, slumping back onto the bed. "The witch doesn't want me."

Good! She's a nasty piece of work. Let's find another witch to live with.

"Unfortunately, I don't believe witches are very common on the Island."

Windweaver fussed over her, plucking oven ashes from her hair. *We can go live in the woods.*

Grace snorted, and Windweaver nipped her. *I will teach you how*, he said. *I will show you how to find berries and steal the eggs of smaller birds, and help you build a burrow to hide in.*

Grace sighed. Even though Windweaver could talk, he was still an ordinary crow in many ways, which meant he was self-centered and full of his own wisdom. Grace hadn't planned to give him the power to speak—indeed, she still wasn't sure how it had happened. She had found him in the woods behind Rose & Ivy when he was only a croaking baby barely the length of her thumb—he must have fallen out of his nest. She snuck him inside in her pocket and fed him scraps of bread soaked in milk. He had woken her the next morning, muttering *bread* in her ear over and over.

She petted him, and a tiny part of her misery dissolved.

Windweaver had always been there for her. As long as she had him, she would never be completely alone.

Read to me, Windweaver demanded. He loved poetry, and collected poems the way ordinary crows collected shiny objects.

"All right," Grace said. "I suppose that poetry is well suited to the tragic nature of the evening."

She fetched the book from her old carpetbag, a hardcover containing over five hundred poems that she had filched from the orphanage. She loved poetry as much as Windweaver did, though she rarely had any idea what those old poets were getting at. What she loved were the flashes of beauty in poems, the way the poet chose just the right word for a meadow or a river, one that made her realize there was more to meadows and rivers than she'd thought, that they had whole worlds hidden inside them. It was a different kind of magic, poetry. And she loved the strange words poets tossed about like enchantments. *Evensong. Darkling. Vernal.*

Read "To a Skylark" again, Windweaver said.

Grace sighed. The only poetry Windweaver liked was poetry about birds. "To a Skylark" by Percy Shelley had many beautiful parts. For instance:

All the earth and air
With thy voice is loud,
As, when night is bare,

33

From one lonely cloud

The moon rains out her beams, and Heaven is overflow'd.

When she read that, Grace liked to close her eyes and picture moonbeams falling out of the sky like rain. She wondered what they would taste like if you drank them. She thought they'd be sweet and cold, like milkshakes.

By the time she reached the fourth stanza Windweaver was already asleep, tangled in her hair. And Grace must have followed him soon after, for she didn't recall reading to the end.

When Grace went downstairs in the morning, trailing her hand along the beautiful wallpaper, which was patterned with dark green leaves and red and pink flowers, the witch was back in the kitchen, bent over the saucepan Grace had noticed yesterday. She was coughing so hard her shoulders shook, a handkerchief pressed against her mouth.

"Are you sick?" Grace asked.

The witch didn't look up. She was wearing a blue cardigan today, soft and every bit as grandmotherly as the yellow one. "That's none of your business, you ridiculous girl."

This seemed to be her favorite insult for Grace. Grace didn't actually mind it, for she had looked up *ridiculous* in her dictionary and it had said "absurd, fanciful." She had then looked up *absurd* and it had said "against reason and common sense." That was comforting, because magic didn't have anything to do with common sense. And as for *fanciful*, she couldn't imagine a lovelier word. It put her in mind of lacy parasols and gardens overflowing with flowers.

"What is wrong with you?" the witch said after Grace had explained all this to her. "Can you not be silent for one moment? It's like sharing a room with an oversized, freckled mosquito."

Grace folded herself into a chair in a miserable slump. She tried not to look at the oven, which had haunted her dreams. She had woken up with all the covers thrown off her, gripping her hair with both hands.

The witch plunked a bowl down in front of her. It appeared to be plain oatmeal, without even the dash of cinnamon they added at the orphanage. Also, it was cold.

"Eat," the witch commanded. "Then be gone. I've a busy day ahead of me, and I want no nattering children getting in the way."

That perked Grace up. "Are you busy with spells? I could help, you know."

The witch ignored her. She gave whatever was in the saucepan another stir, then suddenly doubled over, coughing into her handkerchief again.

"You *are* sick," Grace said in amazement. Who ever heard of a witch getting sick?

"Just a head cold," the witch snapped.

Grace wondered about that. She couldn't imagine the hideous shadow she saw last night coming down with the sniffles.

"I'll help you!" she said in a burst of inspiration. "I'm good at making people feel terrible. Perhaps my magic can also make them well."

"Brilliant logic," the witch said.

"Really?"

"No. You're more likely to turn me inside out than you are to cure me, you hopeless child."

But she paused ever so slightly after she said it. And in that pause, Grace saw a door open just a crack.

Grace leaped to her feet. "Of course I'll help you! Only show me where you keep your spellbooks, and I'll brew you a healing potion. We can do it together, for surely two witches are more magical than one. Or perhaps—"

The rest of that sentence turned into a squawk, for the witch had seized Grace by the scruff like a mother cat picking up a kitten. Then she marched her to the door and tossed her outside. A heartbeat later, Grace's shoes followed, tumbling off the step and down the lawn, and then her carpetbag. Then the witch slammed the door shut.

5

THE NINE-PETALED STARHOLDER

She caught the white goose by the leg,
A goose—'twas no great matter.
The goose let fall a golden egg
With cackle and with clatter.

—Alfred, Lord Tennyson, "The Goose"

Grace didn't know what to do with herself after that. She was used to wounds of the spirit, but she'd never been so mistreated in a bodily way. Well, one of the children at the orphanage used to pinch her, of course, and once she'd had a teacher who would wallop students on the head with a book if they misbehaved. But this was different. This was being thrown out of the only place that had ever felt like a home by the one person she had thought would understand her.

Eventually, she picked herself up and wandered away. The little stream that crossed the witch's front yard curled around the back of the house, too, before meandering off into the forest. She crossed a pretty white bridge, though she barely saw it.

The witch's garden flowed off the back of the house. It was an unusual garden, a mixture of flowers and bushes that Grace didn't recognize, many with lots of nasty thorns. She paused to reattach a wild rose to a trellis—it had fallen over and was starting to climb up a bush with sharp black leaves. She hadn't walked ten steps before she heard a *creak*, and then a *snap*. The roses had pushed the trellis over, as if out of spite.

Beyond the garden was an orchard of fruit trees, some still blooming even in August, scattered across a pleasant green field, and beyond that was the dark, wild forest. Grace crossed a third bridge. The witch's land was inconvenient in that sense, with the stream rambling through it in a very self-important way, and you had to cross at least one bridge if you wanted to get anywhere. She seemed to have a good acre of cleared land—grass and garden—and untold acres of forest. Lining the stream was a parade of cherry blossom trees.

Grace sat on a stump and watched the stream flow by. She felt horribly gray inside. What was she going to do? She would sooner climb back into the witch's oven than return to the orphanage *again*, which was the same as admitting to herself that she'd lost her last real chance at a home.

Tears rolled down her cheeks, and she pressed her face into her knees. "No one has ever wanted me," she murmured. "And now I am certain no one ever will."

Wind rustled the pines at her back. A spill of flowers drifted past, white and pink. Without noticing, Grace had sat down beneath a hibiscus tree.

She sniffed, feeling a little of her sadness lift. She had never seen such a romantic tree. It wore its blossoms like a fine lady wears silks, and they made the most wonderful whispery song when the branches moved.

Grace looked down at herself. She was a mess, still ashy from the oven and half covered in mud. What business did a ragged, unwanted thing like her have sitting under such a beautiful tree?

A terrible fury came over her. She would make the witch regret what she had done. And the witch would regret it most if Grace made her feel guilty.

Dashing the tears from her face, she reached into the branches of the tree and broke off a handful of blossoms. Then she tromped into the forest, looking in all directions.

There! Buttercups grew beneath a pile of ivy. She plucked a dozen or so, then turned her attention to the lady's slippers a little deeper in the woods.

Windweaver settled upon a branch. *What are you doing?*

"Help me," Grace said, snapping a foxglove in half.

He grumbled. But he plucked a beakful of late-blooming flowers from an apple tree and dropped them into her hand. *What are these for?*

"They're for the witch," she said. "I'm going to thank her for letting me stay the night. I'll be so nice about it that she'll feel ashamed for being cruel to me."

Windweaver shook his head. *It won't work*, he said.

Grace ignored him. She strode deeper into the woods,

hunting through the grass. It was one of those late summer days when the whole world felt lazy and slow, from the drifting clouds to the wind lounging in the treetops. Grace toyed with the leaves as she walked, using her magic to lift them into the air and swirl them around with a flick of her hand. It was the only magic she'd worked out how to do. She often fantasized about doing other kinds of magic—taming wild animals with a command (particularly bears, which she would ride around upon) and filling the night sky with shooting stars with a wave of her hand.

She played with the branches of a willow, making them toss about like a horse's mane. Beneath the willow was a circle of daisies—perfect for the bouquet, Grace decided, pushing aside the waving boughs.

That was when she saw the hand.

It was *just* a hand—which is to say, it was a hand that wasn't attached to a body. It was sticking right out of the tree, waving at her.

For a moment, Grace's breath froze in her chest. Then, before she was certain what she was doing, she ran forward and grabbed hold of that waving hand. She felt quite brave as she did it, and proud of herself for reacting to a supernatural situation like a real witch, but then the hand grabbed back with unexpected strength and she wondered if bravery was such an admirable thing after all, or just a nicer word for *stupidity*. She wrenched and struggled, and then gave the tree a good hard kick. At that, the boughs shuddered, and Grace fell backward—

With a boy attached to her arm. He came tumbling out of the tree, and they landed in a sprawl on the soft grass.

"Oof," the boy said. It was a disappointingly unfairylike thing to say—Grace knew he was a fairy right away, because he couldn't possibly be anything else. His face was sharp and his eyes were violet, like the sky after sunset. He was barefoot and dressed in what looked like a tunic made of leaves, belted at the waist, and atop his head was a circlet of oak leaves like a crown, with a single green jewel at the front. From his shoulders rose the faintest hint of wings, like rain and spidersilk, only visible from the corner of her eye.

"You're welcome," Grace grumbled when the boy made no move to thank her. "You're very clumsy for a fairy."

The boy scowled. He looked about Grace's age, but he was skinnier, all knees and elbows. "Who says I'm a fairy?"

"*Aren't* you?"

He snorted. "*Fairy* is just a word you humans call us. We don't—" His face froze, and they both realized it at the same time: his foot was still stuck in the tree.

"Give me another pull," the fairy said urgently. "Hurry!"

"Hurry yourself!" Grace snapped. It was partly because of the boy's rudeness, but also because he'd elbowed her in the face as they fell. "I got most of you out. Surely you can take care of the rest. What are you doing stuck in a tree, anyway?"

She wandered over to the place where his foot was caught. Through the hole in the tree she caught a glimpse of a broad staircase of uneven roots and stones, dark and mossy, leading into the earth. But then the hole closed tight around the boy's foot.

"What do you think?" He scrabbled at the forest floor, trying to grab hold of a root. "Somebody tried to trap me."

"Did you deserve it?"

It seemed a reasonable question to Grace—after all, she didn't know if he was the gentle, wish-granting sort of fairy, or the Rumpelstiltskin kind who would try to snare her in some terrible bargain—but she knew instantly that she had made a mistake. The fairy's face darkened, and Grace was suddenly afraid. He *was* the bad kind of fairy, she realized, just as Grace was the bad kind of magic. She shivered down to her shoes, and it was only then that the reality sank in.

She was talking to a *fairy*.

"Listen, you silly girl," the fairy hissed. "If you don't help me, I'll put a curse on you. I'm good at coming up with curses."

"You won't," she whispered. A dreamlike terror had settled over her.

"Will too." He looked more like a wild animal than a person now, an angry one with its paw caught in a trap. "And I'll curse your parents, too."

At that, Grace froze. "I'm an orphan. My parents went missing when I was little."

Something in the boy's expression shifted before his face hardened again. "That doesn't matter. I'll find them, and they'll be sorry they ever had you."

Grace pictured her parents, stranded on a desert island drinking out of coconuts and roasting wild boar over a fire, sustained only by the thought of their dear daughter back home. How *dare* he threaten them! As if being lost at sea wasn't enough misfortune for a lifetime!

She took a step toward him, and at the same time, she stirred the leaves in the wood with her magic. The forest filled with a cacophony of creaks and groans and rustlings. The boy's eyes narrowed.

"I'll help you, all right," Grace said. In that moment, she hated him more than she'd ever hated anyone. "But I'll have none of your threats. I'm a witch, and a witch's favors come with a price."

She had no idea what she was talking about, but it sounded like something out of a story, which she took as a good sign. "You're not a witch," the fairy said scornfully, but Grace caught a flicker of doubt in his eyes.

She made the leaves swirl faster. The boy's eyes widened— after all, he didn't know it was the only magic Grace could do.

"All right!" he said. His other leg was caught now, too. "What do you want?"

Grace thought it over, all the fairy tales she'd ever read flitting through her mind like bright birds. She didn't know why she was bargaining with the fairy, but that was what people did in stories, wasn't it?

A slow smile spread across her face. Suddenly, she knew how she was going to impress the witch.

"You have to be my servant," she said.

The boy froze. Grace had surprised even herself—it was a terrible thing to ask of someone. But then she remembered Mrs. Silverwood's look, and her guilt faded. She was a witch—why shouldn't she act like one?

"Forever?" the boy croaked.

"Oh no!" Grace thought fast—things came in threes in stories, didn't they? Three wishes. Three days to undo a curse.

"For three years," she said finally, "you have to come when I call your name. And if I ask you for a favor, you have to grant it, if you can. The first thing I want you to do is go to Faerie and bring back the prettiest flowers you see." If flowers from another world couldn't convince the witch that Grace was a worthy apprentice, she didn't know what would.

The boy made an ugly face. "You dirty trickster. I never should have asked for your help. I'd rather let this tree swallow me whole than give you my name."

"Oh! So you *are* like Rumpelstiltskin," Grace said. In the stories, Rumpelstiltskin kept his name a secret, because names had magic in them, magic other people could use to control fairies. "That's what I'll call you, then—Rum for short. You don't have to give me your real name—just your promise."

The boy was in up to his chest now, and as he glared at

Grace, the tree yanked him in another inch.

"Fine!" he gasped. "Just get me out!"

Grace grabbed his hand and pulled with all her might. The fairy fell out of the tree with a creaking, snapping sound. Grace made sure he was free all the way this time, yanking his foot back when the tree leaned toward it. As soon as the boy was loose, the tree gave a sigh and settled back, and bark grew over the great gash in its trunk as if it had never been.

Grace let out a laugh of pure relief. "What *is* that? Is it an ordinary tree that somebody enchanted, or a tree that was already that way? I'll have to keep a closer eye on all trees from now on, to see if there are any fairy doors in the side of them. And who did that to you? What are you doing in the witch's woods? Is it because the woods are magic, too, like the witch?"

Suddenly she realized the fairy was still glaring at her. His legs were cut up where the tree had gripped them, and his eyes were full of such hatred that she took a step back.

"Three years," the fairy boy said. "You've cursed me for *three years*. What sort of cruel creature are you?"

"It's not a curse, it's—"

"Well, you made a mistake." A dark smile lit his face. "Humans always make mistakes. And now you've made an enemy of me. An *archenemy*."

Grace swallowed a lump of pure terror, but at the same time she felt a little thrill. She'd never had an enemy before. It was an important-sounding word, a word for heroes and quests. She liked the way it felt in her mouth, smooth and soft and dangerous all together. And *archenemy* was even better, the *ch* sound like the hiss of a deadly snake.

"You—you're my servant," she said. "You can't hurt me."

"Not yet," he agreed. "But you didn't say anything about what would happen when your three years are up."

The way he said it, three years was all Grace would ever have, not just in terms of their bargain. "You don't frighten me," she snapped. "I'm a witch. You're barely a fairy—you haven't even got proper wings."

The boy's face darkened again. "I might not have proper wings yet, but at least I'm not all covered in spots like a toad."

Grace let out a shriek and lunged at him. At the orphanage, some of the children had teased her about her freckles, which she hated more than anything in the world—having someone as strange as the fairy boy echo their taunts was more than she could bear. But he was gone before she could lay a hand on him, folding himself into the forest.

For that was what it looked like, a sort of *folding*—he stepped sideways and then sideways again, and the green forest shadows closed around him. And she was left staring at nothing, caught in a swirl of anger and fear, with a gift that was also a curse.

She stood in a daze, staring at the tree, which was now a perfectly ordinary tree—even the ring of daisies had vanished. Then something came soaring out of the forest shadows and hit her square in the face.

It was a bouquet—the loveliest she'd ever seen, made of

twilight-blue flowers that turned silver when she touched them, tied with a golden ribbon.

Grace rapped on the witch's door with a shaking hand. There came a clattering sound from within, and then the witch wrenched the door open, her face pink with rage. "I thought I told you—"

"I've come to bid you farewell," Grace announced. Her voice trembled, but she found that when she imagined herself as a tragic heroine again, doomed to live a lonely life of struggle and despair, she felt braver. "Though you have cast me out, I offer you a token of my respect as a fellow witch. I will overlook how you tried to bake me, and offer my heartfelt hope that we may one day meet again as friends, although it is true that I have no home nor shelter and may keep wandering until I fall down dead—"

"Where did you find those?" the witch interrupted. She was looking at the bouquet with a strange expression.

Grace swelled with hope. She had arranged the bouquet so that Rum's fairy flowers were right in the middle where the witch was sure to notice them. "Oh! In the forest, of course," she said in a mysterious voice.

"And you just *happened upon* them, did you? It takes most witches a century or more to recognize the Nine-Petaled Starholder."

"The nine what?" Grace felt a prickle of sweat at her back. The witch sounded angry rather than impressed—had Rum given her poisonous flowers, or something else offensive to witches?

The witch yanked the bouquet from Grace's hand. She plucked the buttercups from the bouquet and threw the rest of the flowers aside, even the blue-and-silver fairy flowers, as if they were nothing.

"The buttercups?" Grace blinked. "They—they were just by an old stump."

"These are no buttercups," the witch snarled, and suddenly Grace realized she was right—they had too many petals, for one thing, and now that she could see them properly outside the forest gloom, she noticed how they shimmered as if glazed with frost. "And I don't think you're what you appear to be, either. Am I supposed to believe that some untrained orphan girl would have the power to recognize the Starholder?"

"What?" Grace began. "I don't—"

The witch was suddenly looming over Grace again in her shadow shape, fangs glistening. "Who sent you?" she hissed. "Someone from the council? Was it Clario? Raphael? Or one of the Nameless Ones? I'll pluck out their eyes and turn their lying tongues into jelly if they think they can send spies to my door."

"N-nobody sent me," Grace said, lurching backward so fast that she fell over. "Please, I only wanted to make you a bouquet!"

The witch let out another hiss. Grace was certain the witch was either going to make good on her threat to drag her back to the orphanage by her hair, or else turn her into something dreadful, like a skunk cabbage. The terror must have shown in Grace's eyes, for the shadow suddenly shrank back down to an old lady. The witch stared at the not-buttercups, and then she stared at Grace, as all the while Grace lay in a messy sprawl that was very unlike a tragic heroine.

"Well, you ridiculous little witch," the witch said finally, "it seems we might come to an agreement after all."

6

WONDERFULLY HORRIBLE

Now the snow hides the ground, little birds leave the wood,
And fly to the cottage to beg for their food . . .
—John Clare, "The Robin"

The witch thumped a book onto the table inches from Grace's face.

Grace sneezed. The book was old and dusty, with a battered leather cover. Upon the spine was the Roman numeral *I* written in gold ink. It was small for a book and smelled of old cellars.

"My grimoire," the witch said. "That's a kind of spellbook. I will make you this offer only once, girl, so listen closely. You clearly have *some* magical talent, though I suspect your success with the Starholder was only dumb luck. I have never taken on an apprentice before, and have no interest in wasting my time with some half-witted child—I will only consider training you if you can prove to me that your gift is great. So! Here is my offer: If you can cast every spell within these pages, I will make you my apprentice and allow you to remain here. I will give you no help whatsoever in this task. You must work your way through these spells using your own brains, if you have any."

Grace's heart was galloping. It wasn't just the talk of spells and grimoires—it was the prospect of never leaving that eerie house in the woods with the stream coiling around it, sleeping in that beautiful bedroom with the every-flower quilt forevermore. But dread followed her excitement like a shadow.

"And—and if I can't cast every spell?" Her hands were already curling possessively around the grimoire.

The witch gave her a look that made the shadows flicker behind her eyes, just for a moment. "Then you shall give me your magic. All of it."

Grace's hand flew to her mouth. "Oh! But that—that's wonderful."

The witch looked furious. Grace was starting to realize the woman hated that Grace wasn't more afraid of her. "What?"

"Wonderfully horrible, I mean," Grace explained. "That's just what I imagined a bargain with a witch would be like. Of course I should have to pay some awful price if I fail. But what do you want with my magic if you have your own?"

Grace wasn't sure the witch would answer. She sat there with an ancient sort of look on her face that Grace didn't understand at all. "I am . . . not entirely well. It is nothing serious. But you see, another witch's magic can heal me. I cannot take it from you, as that goes against our laws, but if you choose, you can give it to me."

Dread stirred in Grace's stomach. She felt like she had when she met Rum, as if it had taken a few moments to wake up from her own imagination.

The witch wanted Grace to *give up her magic.*

"What—" Grace began. "What about Windweaver?"

The witch frowned. "Windwhat?"

"Windweaver. He's my best friend. He's a crow, and somehow I made him talk. But what happens if I lose my magic?"

"You will become an ordinary girl," the witch snapped. "Can ordinary girls talk to crows?"

A wave of cold went through Grace. She couldn't bear to lose Windweaver. She couldn't even bear to *think* about it.

"And I'll have to go back to the orphanage," she said dully.

"Of course you'll have to go back. What use would I have for an ordinary human girl?"

Grace was shivering. If she solved the witch's grimoire, she would gain everything. A home. A place to learn magic. But if she failed, she would lose everything.

"H-how many spells are in your grimoire?"

The witch smiled. "A hundred and a half."

"*A hund—*" Grace sank back into her chair, blinking rapidly. A great many questions swam in her head, but she asked the one that seemed most important: "Is that all the spells you can do? A hundred and a half? Surely there are more spells than that in the world."

The witch stared at her for a long time. "It seems you are not entirely hopeless after all. Most people would have asked about that half spell first. Only a true witch can see past the surface of words to what's really important."

"Well, I *am* a true witch," Grace said. Surely she'd proved that by now.

The witch looked disappointed, as if she'd been hoping for another reason to dislike Grace. "This was my first grimoire. I wrote down these spells as they came to me, when I was a girl only a few years older than yourself."

"And is there only one half spell?" Grace said, for she knew her math well enough. There could be ninety-eight full spells and five half ones, adding up to a hundred and a half.

"There is only one. I cast it once, a very long time ago, but I forgot to write down all the ingredients afterward."

"What does it do?"

"You'll find out." She smiled that awful smile again.

Grace sat back in her chair. A hundred spells! That would be quite enough to deal with, but add in the challenge of figuring out a spell that wasn't even complete?

She knew she shouldn't even consider it. She should just go back to the orphanage and not risk Windweaver and her magic.

"How much time would I have?" she asked.

The witch went to the window and pointed to one of the cherry trees that lined the stream. It looked to be the oldest of the lot, tall and gnarled and growing in lots of strange directions.

"My personal favorite," the witch said. There was a cruel note in her voice, as if she was enjoying a secret joke at someone else's expense. "You will have until that tree blooms again."

"When does that usually happen?"

"May," the witch said. "Maybe June. It depends on the weather."

Grace bit her lip. It was August, so that meant less than a year. It was either a lot of time or very little, depending on how hard the spells were to cast.

"I don't understand," Grace said. "I changed your poor cow's milk to ice cream without using a grimoire. And Windweaver—I made him talk. Why bother with a book of spells when we witches can simply will things into being?"

"If I was interested in hearing a list of all the things you don't understand, we'd be here all year."

Grace sighed. "And then there's the wind."

The witch stilled. "You can summon the wind?"

"Yes, of course." Grace looked at her. "Is that strange?"

The witch said nothing for a moment. "An idiotic question. Witches are the very definition of strange. But I can tell you that there are exactly four powers a witch does not need a grimoire for: calling upon the wind, summoning a familiar, clothing herself in shadow, and finding paths to other worlds." She frowned. "Most witches do not learn these skills until they are fully grown."

Grace barely heard this last part, as she was too busy marveling. "Finding paths to other worlds! How *fascinating*. Well, I don't wish to clothe myself in shadows, particularly—I don't imagine they're very warm. I suppose Windweaver is my familiar, then? I don't think I'll tell him. Birds are noble beasts and hate the idea of being owned by anybody. But what about the ice cream? Making ice cream isn't one of the four special witch powers—though it should be, I think. How did I do that?"

The witch didn't answer for a full minute. "I don't know," she said at last, grudgingly. Grace settled back, beside herself with glee. She was a mystery to the witch! That must mean her magic was special. And indeed, the mystery of the ice cream would remain a mystery for a long time.

Grace went back to the grimoire and flipped it open to one of the first spells, which was written in a spiky hand.

To her enormous relief, the spell seemed straightforward. At the top it read *For Mending What Is Broken*, which was a little vague, though quite innocent for a witch's spellbook. Grace would have expected *For Turning Your Enemies into Pudding One Limb at a Time* and so on. The spell itself was merely a list of ingredients, mostly plants and flowers that she recognized.

She flipped forward a few pages, and that was where she began to lose heart.

"'A pitcher of *midnight*'?" she read. "How am I supposed to get midnight into a pitcher, or anything else, for that matter?"

"How indeed?" the witch said.

Swallowing, Grace flipped to the next spell, then the next. Some of them were all right, apart from a few mysterious plants she'd never heard of. But others contained similarly nonsensical ingredients, like *3 left footprints of a deer* and *1 sneeze from a songbird (sparrow, for best effect)*. One of the spells deep in the grimoire had a short list of mostly ordinary plants, but these had to be *seasoned with thunder* and *soaked in the shadows of ravens*. The *pitcher of midnight* in spell forty-four had to be brewed with several other ingredients for *one day lasting twenty-five hours*.

Grace looked at the witch, and the witch looked back. Her face gave nothing away—strange, then, that Grace knew exactly how the witch felt. She supposed it was her own witch's intuition. If the witch had had a proper heart, it would have been racing with excitement. She wanted Grace to agree to her bargain, but only because she wanted her to fail. Because when Grace failed, the witch could drink up her magic like a glass of lemonade.

And who would Grace be if she didn't finish all the spells by "May, maybe June"? Would she still be herself, or would she be someone else—a girl who didn't talk of mermaids when she wasn't supposed to, and who didn't pull fairy boys out of trees or lie awake at night with poems flickering through her head?

On the other hand, what would become of her if she said no to the witch's bargain? Would she go back to the orphanage and pretend to fit herself into a world that would never fit her, until she forgot she was pretending at all?

She closed the grimoire and stood, holding herself very straight. "I will accept your offer, on one condition."

"Condition?" the witch repeated. "Condition! There will be no—"

But Grace raised her voice and plowed on. "If I lose, I will have to give up everything. Most terribly, I will have to give up my dearest friend. You should have to give up something if you lose—otherwise, it isn't fair."

"I will have to give up my sanity, if I'm forced to put up with you as an apprentice."

Grace ignored this. "If I cast every spell in the grimoire and become your apprentice, you must agree never to shove any more children into that oven."

The witch blinked. Grace thought she had surprised her, but it was hard to tell. "Fine," the witch said.

Grace started. "Really?"

"Why not?" she said with a smirk, and Grace realized that the witch wasn't being agreeable. She just didn't think Grace would succeed.

"And—and you also can't roast anybody while I'm here," Grace said, shuddering at the memory of being locked up with all those bones. "I can't stand the thought of another poor girl or boy going through what I did."

The witch's face soured at that. "*Fine.*"

Grace squared her shoulders. Now that she knew she would

be saving the lives of countless children if she succeeded, it was easier to feel like a heroine again.

Aloud, she said, "I accept this noble and pernicious challenge. I give you my oath, very solemnly, upon my honor as a witch, that I will do my best to cast these formidable spells before the flowering of the venerable cherry tree by the silver stream. If I fail, my magic shall be yours forthwith."

Grace felt a little better after her speech—noble, like a knight just before he plunges into an enchanted forest, knowing his cause is just and prepared to die for it. She held out her hand.

The witch, however, didn't look impressed—she had been rolling her eyes the whole time. She spat in her palm and clapped it against Grace's.

"Ew!" Grace exclaimed, honor forgotten, and then a shudder ran through her. She felt as if she had been plunged into the coldest of glacial lakes.

"We have a pact," the witch said.

"Was *that* what that was?"

"Yes. A pact between two witches is binding and cannot be altered or undone."

Grace opened her mouth again, more questions already beginning to tumble out, but the witch said, "I can see this is going to be a long year, and I have no more patience for you today. Begone."

Grace hesitated. "Where?"

"Anywhere, so long as it is out of my sight."

She turned and picked up a wooden spoon, then stirred the contents of the saucepan. Hesitantly, Grace gathered up the grimoire.

"That word," the witch called over her shoulder. "You got it wrong, I think."

Grace paused. "What?"

"*Pernicious.*" She went back to her stirring.

Later, when she got around to checking her dictionary, Grace found that the witch had been right. She had meant *propitious*, "a good omen." The entry for *pernicious* read "evil; wicked."

Grace decided to see this as a good sign. After all, she was a wicked witch, wasn't she? She might as well prove it.

7

SAREENA AND MISS PUDDLESTONE

Among the dwellings framed by birds
In field or forest with nice care,
Is none that with the little Wren's
In snugness may compare.
—William Wordsworth, "A Wren's Nest"

Naturally, the next thing Grace did was run into the woods.

She went upstairs, threw on her coat, and shoved the grimoire into her ragged carpetbag. She thought about reveling in the perfect little bedroom, but the problem with reveling is that you must be certain of the thing you're reveling in. Grace was still half terrified that the witch would change her mind, so she couldn't yet let herself fall in love with the strange white house tucked away in the strange, dark wood. She shoved away her fears about the terrible pact and the hundred-and-a-half spells looming over her like a blade—or at least, she tried to.

Once she was outside, the fear was easier to ignore, and

she forgot not to fall in love—for who wouldn't fall in love with that shining stream lined with romantic trees, that forest where every shadow seemed filled with birds and wildflowers? Now that she belonged there, it was a different place than it had been only an hour before.

She dove into the witch's woods like a fish diving into the sea. The woods were old Acadian forest, maples and spruces, birches and firs, leafy trees and evergreens all rustling together in a friendly murmur. The land dipped beyond the orchard, then rose again, forming a frame, and over all that spilled the deep, dark forest, carpeted with ferns and lilies.

Windweaver caught Grace's excitement. He darted over the bridge and into the trees, squawking his head off, while Grace followed close behind, laughing. She had never been able to run wild in the wood behind the orphanage. There, the day revolved around school, which took place in a room with the narrowest, highest windows imaginable, and chores. Every inch of the place had to be swept and scrubbed and dusted weekly, clothes had to be mended, socks and sweaters knitted, and hedges clipped so neat they barely looked like living things. Mrs. Spencer loved chores, and often said that the more chores you did, the more character you grew, and orphans needed all the character they could get to survive the harshness of the world.

"What a lovely, spooky forest this is!" Grace exclaimed when she stopped for breath. "How far does it go?"

She expected Windweaver to reply that it went on and on

forever, being a witch's forest and likely magic itself, but he just said, *Not far. There's a field with a cow in it coming up. And then there's another house.*

"Huh!" Grace hadn't known the witch had neighbors. You never heard about witches having neighbors in stories. She imagined that having neighbors would be quite inconvenient for a witch; what if they came around to borrow an egg when you were in the middle of a tricky spell?

Grace and Windweaver came to the field with the cow. It was a sleepy-looking cow, and gave her only a brief look before it went back to the business of chewing grass. She couldn't see the house, but beyond the cow's field there was a paddock for sheep, with a little muddy lane running between them.

An apple tree leaned over the fence, and she snatched one of the ripest fruits from its branches. It was still sour, but she was hungry enough not to care. She found a big maple to lean against and sat down with the grimoire, determined to start casting spells immediately. After all, she was a girl on a quest, and it was a grave and important quest indeed. If she succeeded, she would have everything she'd ever wanted. If she lost, she would lose everything, and even though her *everything* was less than most people's, still, it was precious.

Windweaver landed on the grass, pecking for worms. She wondered if he would stop talking when she lost her magic, or if she would just no longer be able to hear him—if she would forget him completely.

She shivered. She'd expected to feel bold—she was on a

quest, after all—but instead she felt cold and small and afraid that she had made a terrible mistake.

"Halt!" came a deep voice from the shadows. "Who goes there?"

Grace jumped. She couldn't tell where the voice had come from. "I'm—I'm not. Going anywhere, I mean."

"You are a thief," the voice hissed. "Tell me your name, or I shall put a curse on your head."

Grace's heart thudded. Was there another witch living in the woods? "I'm not a thief."

"I saw you steal one of my father's apples," the voice snapped. It was a girl's voice—Grace realized she had been trying to sound frightening before. The girl cleared her throat. "I am the guardian of the woods," she intoned.

"A-are you a fairy?"

"A fairy?" the girl repeated in an ordinary, scornful voice. "Ha! You sure are easy to fool."

She stepped out from behind a tree, and Grace knew right away that she wasn't a witch, nor was she a fairy. She was about Grace's age, with a long black braid tied with a pink ribbon tucked over her shoulder, light brown skin, and more freckles than Grace had ever seen on another person's face, enough for three people at least. Grace's heart lit up, seeing those freckles. The girl, though, looked as if she didn't feel any kinship with Grace at all, as a fellow freckle-bearer, and even wrinkled her nose when she got a better look at her.

"Who are you?" the girl said rudely. "You're not from

By-the-Sea." This, Grace would learn, was what the villagers called Brook-by-the-Sea, often saying it so fast it sounded like *Bidesea*. "I guess you're a bandit, is that it?"

"No," Grace said. "My name is Grace Greene."

The girl looked her up and down, taking in her dress—which, by that point, was one large stain of many colors—and the oven ashes in her hair.

The girl let out a laugh with a snort at the end of it. "What a mess!"

The snort made Grace like her instantly. She had always believed you could trust a person who snorts when they laugh, for those were the people who cared more about fun than they did about politeness. Unfortunately, her liking for the girl was immediately followed by a blaze of anger at her for sneering. Wouldn't anybody be a mess after fleeing the lonely life of an orphan, only to be shoved into an oven by a witch?

And so Grace pushed her—hard.

The girl stumbled, tripped over a rock, and landed on her back with an impressive *splat*, her feet sailing over her head.

She shoved herself up on one hand, staring at Grace with her mouth hanging open. Her pretty hair was covered in mud, including the ribbon, which was pink no longer. There was mud on her dress, mud on her arms, mud even on the tip of her chin.

"I'm sorry," Grace said, horrified by what she had done. "But—but you shouldn't laugh at strangers, particularly when you don't know what torments they've been through."

The girl kept staring. Then, to Grace's astonishment, she let out a peal of laughter, this time with two snorts at the end. She picked up a handful of mud and hurled it at Grace.

Unfortunately for Grace, the girl had good aim. The mud hit her square in the face, then slip-slopped down the front of her dress as she stood there, stunned.

Before Grace could recover, the girl was off running, laughing and screeching like a banshee. Grace scooped up a big wad of mud and followed. She could run very fast when she wanted to—sometimes she wondered if it was magic, for it felt as if the wind wrapped around her and swept her along like a leaf.

Grace grabbed the girl's arm, and she screeched again at how quickly Grace had appeared. She saw the mud in Grace's other hand and tripped her.

But Grace was still holding on to her, so they both fell over and tumbled down a little hill, landing in a heap at the bottom.

Grace couldn't help being impressed. Apart from a few grunts, the girl hadn't made any sound as they fell, even when she rolled over a big root, and she had even had the presence of mind to knee Grace in the stomach.

"Ugh," the girl said, looking down at herself. The mud had gotten squashed between them, and they were both covered in it.

Grace lay on her side, clutching her stomach. "I surrender," she gasped.

The girl squinted. "What?"

"You have vanquished me," Grace said. The ache in her stomach seemed to be getting worse. "If I perish, you must inform Windweaver that he is to bury me in willow fronds and roses, and say a poem over my corpse."

"You talk funny," the girl said.

Grace sighed. "I'm sorry. I'm just upset. You really jabbed me, you know."

The girl made a shrugging face. "What's a Windweaver?" She didn't bother waiting for an answer, though, but went on, "Anyway, I've got to get moving. Daddy'll be home soon, and if he sees me like this—" She gave a shudder.

"What?" Grace said. "Will he—will he beat you?"

"Worse," the girl said. "He'll cry. He despairs of me ever becoming a proper lady, you see. I don't have—what is it he says? 'Dignity of spirit.'" She snorted. "Anyway, he's my daddy, so I have to at least pretend that my spirit is dignified. Where is your home? Boy, you're a scrawny thing, aren't you? One kick in the stomach and you go pale as porridge. Come on. I'm Sareena Khalil, by the way."

She dragged Grace to her feet. Grace's stomach felt a little better when it was turned right side up.

"My home—" Grace stopped, realizing that it was the first time she had said those words. "My home is the white house in the forest. With the stream around it."

Sareena's jaw dropped. "You live with Miss Puddlestone?"

"Miss *who*?"

"Miss Evelyn Puddlestone." The girl blinked. "You live at Miss Puddlestone's house, but you don't know her name? Where are your parents, anyway?"

"Dead," Grace replied. "And I didn't know Miss Puddlestone was called Miss Puddlestone. I just thought of her as the witch."

Sareena nodded. "Lots of kids call her that."

"Then you all know she's a witch?" This surprised Grace only a little. After all, even the children at the orphanage, twenty miles away, had heard of the witch.

"Sure," Sareena said. "I mean, we don't know for certain, but that's what most of us think. I heard she ate a kid a while back. And sometimes boats wash up on Windy Beach after a storm, but nobody can ever find the sailors, so people say she eats them, too. What are you doing living with a witch?"

"I'm a witch, too." Grace stood up straight—not easy when one's stomach felt like a mashed potato.

Sareena looked her up and down. "No offense, but that seems unlikely."

Grace glared. "Why?"

"Well, for starters, you're as filthy as one of my daddy's pigs. If you're a witch, why don't you cast a spell on yourself to look beautiful? And why didn't you hex me when I walloped you in the stomach?"

"I don't know any hexes yet," Grace said, flustered by all of

Sareena's questions, which were annoyingly sensible. "I came here to learn them. The witch has adopted me. I'm going to be her apprentice."

"Hmm." Sareena cocked her head. "Well, maybe. You do have a funny look about you, like Miss Puddlestone does— that gleam in your eye. It's a little creepy, you know. But maybe you're just another kid Miss Puddlestone plans to eat. Maybe she wants to fatten you up first. Looks like you need it."

"*No*," Grace said. She didn't know why she wanted Sareena to believe her so badly—she would just end up terrified of Grace, like her old friends at the orphanage had. Grace had started off liking Sareena, for the freckles and the snort, then disliked her for her rudeness, and now, for some reason, was back to liking her again. She decided that anyone who could inspire such a great range of emotion was well worth knowing.

"The witch was *going* to eat me," she explained, "but then I proved to her that I was a witch, so she couldn't. It's against Witch Law to eat a fellow witch."

"That makes sense, I suppose," Sareena said. "Still, it seems funny that Miss Puddlestone would want an apprentice. She's always lived alone. Daddy says people like that enjoy the hermit life."

"I'll prove it to you," Grace said. "Listen to my heart. A witch's heart doesn't beat like a normal person's."

Sareena wrinkled her nose. "I'll pass."

"Come on!"

After a moment's consideration, Sareena leaned forward

until her left ear was an inch or two from Grace's chest.

"Oh!" she said, drawing back with a start. "I heard it! I mean, I *didn't* hear it. I mean—" She chewed her lip. "Your heart was beating normally for a while. And then it changed—all I heard was this sort of quiet roar, like the sea."

"The witch's heart sounds like that all the time," Grace said. "I think it's because witches grow more heartless as they age."

Sareena looked impressed, but doubt still flickered in her eyes.

Grace reached for the grimoire. "I'll cast a spell."

"All right," Sareena said, a grin spreading across her muddy face. "But not now—I have to get home before Daddy—he can't see me like this. Meet me here tomorrow at the same time."

They'd come to the edge of the forest, and there was the garden and the stream and the white house looming over it all. To Grace's surprise, the witch was out in the garden with a wide hat on like an ordinary old lady.

"You'd better run," Grace said, giving Sareena a nudge.

"It's all right," Sareena muttered. "She's never eaten any-body from the village—too risky, I wager. The grown-ups might get suspicious." She raised her voice. "Good afternoon, Miss Puddlestone!"

Sure enough, the witch smiled and waved back, looking every bit like a friendly grandmother. Sareena gave Grace one last skeptical look, then disappeared back into the forest.

"Good Lord," the witch said when Grace approached. "I've

never seen a more disheveled person."

Grace blinked. "I'm not much more disheveled than I was after you put me in your oven."

It was true. Grace had already been so covered in ash and grime that the second layer of mud was barely noticeable—and the witch hadn't seemed to care one bit about her appearance before. But she only scowled and dragged Grace inside.

8

FISH CAKES AND A NOTHINGNESS

Birds all the sunny day
Flutter and quarrel
Here in the arbour-like
Tent of the laurel.
—Robert Louis Stevenson, "Nest Eggs"

Eventually, Grace worked out that the witch *didn't* care about her appearance, and would have likely let her roam about unbathed until she'd collected a layer of grime so thick that she crackled when she moved. But now that one of her neighbors knew that the witch had adopted an orphan, it meant that everybody in Brook-by-the-Sea would know soon enough.

"Is this the only article of clothing you have?" the witch demanded as Grace sat in her beautiful claw-foot tub. She was examining the filthy dress with distaste. "It's more mud than cloth now. What an enormous heap of trouble you are! At least it's only for a year." This last sentence was muttered, though not quietly enough that Grace wouldn't hear it.

Grace leaned back in the tub, feeling as if nothing in the world could trouble her. She'd never experienced the luxury of a bubble bath before, even if the witch had only allowed the bubble mixture on account of her bad smell. Grace hadn't enjoyed being dunked in the stream first to remove the worst of the dirt, but one could put up with a great deal, she decided, if there was a bubble bath afterward.

"Do you have a familiar?" she asked the witch.

"I have no need for a familiar. I prefer my own company," the witch replied, not looking up from the towels she was folding. "Are you clean yet? Hurry up."

Grace blew on a handful of bubbles. "How did you come up with all those spells in the grimoire?" she said idly. "How do witches come up with spells generally?"

"If you become my apprentice, I'll tell you," the witch said with a smirk that clearly meant *Fat chance of* that.

Grace sighed. Then she had a thought—maybe she could get some information out of the witch that would help her with the spells in the grimoire. "Surely you didn't invent them all yourself, did you?"

"Of course I invented them all myself," the witch replied in a scathing tone.

Grace hid a smile. She had guessed right—she was more likely to get answers if she poked at the witch's pride. The witch was a lot like Windweaver in that way.

"It just seems like an awful lot of work," Grace continued, innocently blowing more bubbles.

"Not if you know what you're about," the witch snapped. She was so annoyed she knocked over the stack of towels and had to refold them.

"Yes, but what do you base your grimoires on? Other grimoires, surely."

"Every witch writes her own spells, her own grimoires," the witch said, somehow managing to fold angrily—not an easy feat. "You may cast another witch's spells—as you will do with mine, if you are not a complete ignoramus—but they will never turn out as well as your own would. Mind you, it takes most witches years of practice before they invent a single spell."

"But how can you tell, oh, I don't know, how many rose petals to use? How much rainwater? Or how to—"

"I simply *know*." The witch turned around and glared at Grace. "Magic does not have a single path. It is—it is like a vast wood with a thousand paths. Two witches may invent a spell that does the same thing, but they will take different paths to get there. A witch follows her own intuition and no one else's. We are solitary beings by nature."

"Marvelous," Grace breathed. "Then it's like each witch carries a little compass inside her, and she uses that to find her spells. To follow her path through the wood." It was such a delightful image that she closed her eyes for a moment to savor it. She imagined herself with a lantern in one hand and a compass in the other, making her way along a forest path, her jaw set bravely and her cloak billowing behind her—for she would be wearing a billowing cloak, naturally. Perhaps one in purple, with flashes of silver trim—

The witch made a disgusted sound. "It is *nothing* like that."

"What about that council?" Grace said. "Do they make rules about spells?"

"Have you not been listening? Spellwork has no rules. And the Halifax Council is none of your concern—useless busybodies, the lot of them. Every region of the world has a witch's council that watches over other witches, mostly to make sure we aren't attracting too much attention."

A hundred questions sprang to Grace's lips at that. "But what do they do if you *are* attracting attention? Something ghastly, I expect. How does one join a witch's council? Where do they—"

"Stop blathering and get to work on those feet," the witch snapped. "I won't have you mucking up my floors." And Grace understood then that the witch was only annoyed that she had revealed as much as she had.

After Grace was clean, the witch returned with her dress and underthings, which she must have washed by magic, for there wasn't a spot of grime on them. She looked tired and moved very slowly as she lay them on a chair. Grace didn't ask if she was well, though, for she knew the witch would only answer her kindness with insults.

The witch's house was a strange place, as one would expect a witch's house to be. Indeed, Grace thought, it would have been even stranger if the witch's house had been ordinary.

When Grace asked if the witch had built the place by magic, the witch gave her one of her most irritated looks and said, "What do you think? Can you imagine me with a hammer and nails?"

Which wasn't really an answer.

To a visitor, the cottage would likely appear ordinary at first—not that visitors to the witch's house were frequent, and those who did make it past the door were usually in for a short stay with a very disagreeable ending. The five steps at the front of the house led to a wide white porch with green trim, and it was hard for Grace to imagine a more welcoming place to lounge on a summer's day. The first floor of the house held the kitchen and parlor at the front, both cozy with creaky, solid floorboards and a variety of rugs.

In the parlor was a tall bookshelf that was mostly full of books of fairy tales in many different languages. The witch liked to pull them off the shelves and brag about all the fairy tales that were about her. Grace wasn't sure how much of this she should believe.

"But you weren't *really* the witch in 'Hansel and Gretel,'" she said doubtfully.

"In a way, I was," the witch said. "Oh, all right, I wasn't the first witch to build a candy cottage in the middle of a forest— the first one was terrible at getting the word out. Never let any of her captives escape, that was the trouble. But I was there when 'Hansel and Gretel' was written down, so who do you think those writers were inspired by?" She pointed the book at herself.

"Hmm," was all Grace said, because it seemed an unwise idea to argue with anybody who believed they were the witch from "Hansel and Gretel," whether they were or not. She noticed that as much as the witch claimed to despise Grace, she seemed to enjoy having someone around to brag to.

A narrow hallway ran from the parlor to the back door of the cottage. Along the hall was the bathroom, which held the impressive claw-foot tub—truly a mansion of a bathtub—and beside the bathroom was a mysterious cupboard. The witch told Grace that it had once been a portal to a forest in Romania.

"Of course, I'm too old for traveling now," she said, and for a moment she seemed to gaze at something Grace couldn't see.

"Where does the portal go now?" Grace asked.

"Nowhere. I couldn't decide what to replace it with, so for now it is simply a Nothingness."

Grace's eyes widened. "A Nothingness! Can I look?"

"Go right ahead," the witch said with a dark smile, and Grace never went near the cupboard again.

At the front of the hallway, beside the parlor, was the staircase. Upstairs were three bedrooms, including Grace's perfect little room, and above them, tucked into the triangular slope of the roof, was an attic that she was forbidden from visiting. The witch informed her that the attic contained the rarest of her spell ingredients, things she had collected from the far corners of the world, and she knew that Grace would just mess everything up. Grace was tempted many times to go up there anyway, reasoning that the witch would surely encourage her to do so if the attic was dangerous, as she had with the Nothingness in the hall cupboard. But then Grace thought that perhaps this was the witch's plan: to make her so curious that she would go climbing up into another Nothingness and disappear—or perhaps the actual Nothingness was up in the attic and not the hall cupboard, and it was all a game of reverse psychology. So she avoided the attic as well, though it did bother her—literally. One of those mysterious ingredients liked to tap on the floor of the attic just above her bedroom and wake her at strange hours.

Grace spent her first few days at the witch's house in her little bedroom, reading the grimoire in a haze of dread and nervous excitement. She had decided to tackle the easiest spells first, which seemed to be the ones near the beginning. These were mostly sensible—as sensible as magic spells could be—with ingredients that one could find in a garden.

She was beginning to feel hopeful. She did not read the half spell, though, which was at the very back of the grimoire, nor the spells with the longest lists of ingredients. Perhaps once she had a firm understanding of the basics of magic, she thought, she would be able to face the trickier spells without feeling like she would be sick.

Fortunately, the witch wasn't a bad cook—on the first night, she served ham and greens, and on the second, fish cakes with mashed potatoes and an apple cobbler for dessert, and if the potatoes were chewy and the fish had bones, well, what did one expect from a witch? Spider stew and worm cake, that's what.

The witch ate nothing at supper or any other time that Grace saw. She hovered at the back of the kitchen, still stirring that saucepan of hers, occasionally coughing into her handkerchief.

"Perhaps you'd feel better if you ate," Grace ventured. "Nothing soothes the spirit like a hot meal after a day of adventuring—or I suppose, in your case, witchcraft."

"You need not concern yourself with either my health or my spirit, you impossible, airheaded child," the witch said.

"Impossible," Grace said with a sigh. "Is there anything better than that?"

The witch groaned. Grace was disappointed, as she had hoped the witch would ask her to explain, but she went on anyway. "It's wonderful, though, to be impossible, isn't it? Mrs. Spencer always said that magic is impossible. You know what I think about sometimes? How nobody sees the world the same way as anyone else. Some people look at a beautiful day and see it as a little bit more green than other people do. Some people see the way the sunlight moves along the ripples in a stream as if it's dancing, while others just see the shadows along the bank and think about all the things that might be hiding in them. I think *impossible* is like that—it's different for everybody. Maybe for Mrs. Spencer, magic is impossible, and always will be. But that doesn't mean it isn't real, or that other people can't see it. And I'd rather be impossible to someone like Mrs. Spencer, wouldn't you?"

"I haven't the slightest idea what you're talking about," the witch said. "For God's sake, eat your food and be silent. Children are supposed to be seen and not heard."

"How would you know what children are supposed to be?" Grace said. "All you do is bake them."

"Only thing they're good for," the witch said nastily, but Grace wasn't bothered by her cruelty anymore, now that she knew the witch couldn't harm her. She had never expected the witch to treat her kindly, though she *had* hoped for a little sympathy and fellow feeling along with the wickedness. Well, she was used to going without that, she thought with a silent sigh.

She went up to her room, intending to get down to business that very night—after all, she had vowed not to rest until she had cast every spell—but unfortunately, her body was not at all interested in vows and straight away she fell asleep, and stayed asleep until noon the next day.

9

THE MOURNFUL CLOUD

I dreamt I caught a little owl
And the bird was blue—
But you may hunt for ever
And not find such a one.
—Christina Rossetti, "I Dreamt I Caught a Little
Owl"

The rest of the week followed the same pattern. After assuring herself each night that she would get up early to work on the grimoire, Grace awoke to find the morning half gone and a cold bowl of oatmeal and a cold cup of tea awaiting her in the kitchen. She had often slept poorly in the orphanage, for it had seemed there was always one girl having nightmares or coughing all night, keeping everyone else awake, and now it seemed she was making up for it, as she had never known such peaceful slumbers as she had under the witch's roof. She didn't mind missing breakfast, for she had found the strawberry patch in the witch's garden, poorly tended but full of ripe berries. She would eat until her fingers turned pink, then collapse in the warm shade of a cherry tree to page through the grimoire. From there she could gaze over the green beauty of the witch's orchard and the eerie beauty of the cottage tucked beside it, and shiver with delight that she *lived* there. She was home at last.

After thinking things over, she decided that she wouldn't cast any spells right away—instead, she would gather all the ingredients she needed for the easier spells, then cast those all at once. Many of them called for the same ingredients, and she reasoned that this sort of mass production would make the task go more quickly.

She *certainly* wasn't putting off casting the spells because she was worried she wouldn't be able to, that perhaps she wasn't magic enough. No, of course not.

Some of the most common ingredients included ivy, lavender, spider's eggs, and the feathers of various birds, which Windweaver helped her collect, scouring old nests and perching branches. The leaves and whatnot she gathered into jars, though she asked the witch if there was any substitution for the spider's eggs, for she didn't like the idea of murdering hundreds of innocent spiders for the sake of a spell "For Clarifying" (whatever that was).

"Substitution?" The witch stared at Grace as if she'd sprouted another head. She was stirring that saucepan again. In fact, she seemed to spend most of her days stirring it, although there were plenty of times that she simply disappeared. Grace had no idea where she went; perhaps she simply became invisible, or drifted off to another dimension. Grace tried many times to get a look inside the saucepan, but whenever she got close, the witch clamped the lid on.

"Well, yes," Grace said. "Like how you can substitute raisins for currants when making scones. At the orphanage, the girls used to take turns making scones, though mine would always come out lumpy. Once I tried—"

"Magic has nothing to do with scones, you nitwit," the witch said.

The witch wouldn't answer any more of Grace's questions about magic or the spells in the grimoire. Grace supposed it would have been cheating if she had, for their pact was for Grace to cast all the spells on her own. Still, she'd never imagined magic being such lonely work. She decided to go outside and spend some time with Buckley, the witch's cow.

Poor Buckley. Before Grace came along, the old cow had been enjoying the sort of quiet, ordinary life that cows like best. The witch couldn't work out how to stop her from giving ice cream instead of milk, so every morning the cow had to put up with the witch muttering and cursing at her, and the disconcerting sound of her milk landing in the bucket with a wet *plop*. The milk came out of the udder just like ordinary milk, but as soon as it hit the bucket, it was solid ice cream. Buckley would sniff the bucket's contents and let out a troubled *mrooo*. Grace felt guilty and made a point of taking Buckley out into the sunshine and bringing the cow her favorite grasses whenever possible.

She tried not to think about how quickly August was slipping by—ordinarily, she looked forward to fall, particularly October, the king of months. But now she resented every passing day, for each one brought her that bit closer to the witch's deadline, while taunting her that she hadn't cast a single spell yet. Every drifting yellow leaf was like a grain of sand falling through an hourglass.

Then one day about two weeks after Grace had come to the cottage, the witch informed her that they were going into town.

"What for?" Grace said.

"You are an utter disaster," the witch replied, which Grace thought a nonsensical answer. Wouldn't the witch prefer for her to remain a disaster here, Grace thought, where she would not cause a scene?

"You have only that one mangy dress," the witch said. "We cannot carry on like that, particularly with all the filth you drag back to my house. You must have new things. Perhaps you will care enough about them to not go rolling around in mud."

"New clothes?" Grace gaped at her. "*New* clothes? Oh, but I've never had new clothes in all my life! This is simply the most wonderful thing that's ever happened to me. Not that I've experienced many wonderful things, given that mine has been a life of tragedy."

The witch rubbed between her eyes. "You are the most melodramatic little thing I've ever encountered."

Grace frowned. "I don't know about that. I think there are some people who have more reason to be dramatic than others. I don't think such people should be called melodramatic. Very few people have spent their lives in a lonely orphanage after their parents were tragically lost at sea, then had a wicked witch try to cook them alive."

"Keep harping on that and I may try again."

Grace put her hands to her face, lost in her fantasies of new clothes. "At the orphanage, all we had were awful hand-me-downs that were too large or too small, never just right, and they were all the same shade of gray beige, the exact color I think ghosts must be. I used to imagine—"

"I don't care what you imagine," the witch said. "On this or any other subject. Close your mouth before I think better of this."

Grace closed her mouth immediately.

"We shall bring this along," the witch said grimly, lifting a full bucket of ice cream into the cart. "Perhaps the grocer will be able to take it off my hands."

The witch's horse, Marigold, was not like Buckley. He was the witch's creature through and through, a huge grayish beast with a mane of drifting shadow and eyes like small green flames. He tried to bite Grace whenever she came near, and today was no exception.

"Ouch!" she said, and showed the witch her arm, which had a row of teeth marks on it. The witch gave Marigold a pat on the head.

"Shall I call you Miss Puddlestone when we are in the shops?" Grace said as they clattered down the lane. The velvety feel of the summer breeze brushing Grace's cheeks had made her forget all about being silent.

"No, you shall not."

"But everyone else—"

"Witches call each other by their true names, or none at all," the witch replied.

"Then what is your true name?"

"I have none."

"Oh!" Grace drew in a breath. "Then you are one of the Nameless Ones, are you? You mentioned them before. What does it mean, to be Nameless? For you must have had a name when you were born. Did you give it up in exchange for more magic? Was it stolen from you by another witch?"

"None of your business."

Grace sighed and sank back against the carriage seat. The lane had big maple trees marching alongside it, knitting their starry leaves together. The dirt road was reddish, like all the earth on the Island, as if it were flushed with pride at its own prettiness, and on either side stretched a wonderland of pastures and groves threaded with cheerful brooks.

Grace gave a sigh of pure happiness. "I have never known a place so beautiful as Brook-by-the-Sea," she said. "Of course, I've known fewer places than most people—mostly just the orphanage. You'd think a place called Rose & Ivy would be more than just four brick walls with a brick path leading up to it, wouldn't you? There were no roses, nor ivies, nor any flowers at all."

The witch frowned at her. Again Grace had the sense that she was disappointed Grace was not more frightened of her. But Grace supposed that most witches wanted to be scary, even if she herself did not.

At that moment she noticed an odd little cloud clinging to one of the maples. It was odd because it was all alone against the blue sky, and very low for a cloud. As Grace watched, it spilled a great tumult of raindrops along the lane.

"Isn't that strange?" she said.

The witch glanced over her shoulder. "Pay no attention to him."

"What?" Grace said. Surely the witch had misspoken. She muttered something under her breath that sounded like *melodramatic*, but for once, she didn't seem to be talking about Grace.

Grace looked back. The cloud had disappeared.

"I have decided that you require an education," the witch said. "In September, you shall join the other children at the school in Brook-by-the-Sea."

Grace whirled around, eccentric clouds forgotten. "*What?*"

"If I don't send my adopted daughter to school, it will look very strange." The witch said *adopted daughter* in the way most people say *I have stepped on a slug*.

"Why do you care if I go to school?"

"I do not. But the villagers know about you now, or they

will soon enough, once my neighbors spread the news around." She said *neighbors* the same way she had said *adopted daughter.* "If I don't send you to school, they will think I'm not looking out for your welfare."

"Well, you aren't," Grace pointed out.

The witch gave her a jagged look. "I don't wish for my neighbors to start poking about in my affairs. Asking questions. Witches do not raise questions. Witches blend in."

"They do?" This was news to Grace. "What about all the stories? All your fairy tales?"

"Do you know how many more stories there would be about witches, child, if we weren't as careful as we are? Stories are a tricky business, you know, when you're inside them. We don't want grown-ups to start believing in us again."

Grace gave a sigh. She couldn't help a pang of disappointment, though it came as no surprise that the witch was only pretending to care about her. "Oh, but how marvelous! I've never been to a proper school before. Do you think they'll teach poetry? Windweaver would be ever so pleased if I could learn more about poetry, particularly the poetry of far-distant lands—I'm sure the poets living in, say, the jungles of the South Pacific have many interesting things to say about birds. We had school at the orphanage, but poetry was never part of it. We only learned our letters, and did times tables over and over . . . "

Grace told the witch all about school at the orphanage and was pleased when the witch did not interrupt or snap at her to be silent. Then she realized this was because the witch wasn't paying any attention to her at all but was instead sitting there with a frown on her face gazing at nothing. Occasionally she looked over her shoulder. It seemed to Grace that the roar of the witch's heart was even louder now, like a storm at sea with lots of ships crashing about in it.

They went over a narrow bridge and arrived in the lovely village square, which was lined with several shops and had a green space with trees in the middle. A man tipped his hat at the witch as they passed by in the carriage, and she nodded back, though rather stiffly. She adjusted the buttoning on her cardigan, which was gray with small white daisies on it. Now that they were in the village square, Marigold looked like an ordinary horse with ordinary brown eyes and a mane made of hair, not shadow.

"Miss Puddlestone!" a voice called. A thin, tidy-looking woman with her gray curls tucked beneath a practical sunhat marched toward them. The witch leaned away, as if that would spare her from an onslaught of friendliness.

"What a remarkable thing!" the woman said. "I've not seen you in town for months. Had old Peter Knox deliver your supplies the last few times, did you? And the last seventeen occasions I've called upon you at teatime, you've been mysteriously absent. Peter tells me you've grown quite fond of walking—interesting, isn't it, for I've made a point of stopping by only during the worst weather. And this must be the girl."

While the witch gritted her teeth, the woman turned her

hard blue gaze upon Grace. Grace was familiar enough with the witch by now to know she was not particularly fond of talkative people, but of course, grown-ups couldn't tell other grown-ups to close their mouths and begone, much as they might wish to sometimes.

The witch said, "Mrs. Charity Crumley, this is Grace Greene, who is here from the orphanage in Charlottetown."

"You are full of surprises, Miss Puddlestone," Mrs. Crumley said, an approving note in her voice. "Taking in a poor, friendless orphan—and one with an ill look about her, too. The pretty girls always have the easiest time of it, which I find deplorable. An orphan is an orphan, but all the folks I know who've taken in a foster child have gone for lots of curls and rosy cheeks and the like. You'll do just fine, won't you, girl? The plain ones are the hardest workers, mark my words."

Grace's mouth fell open. Anger flashed through her, hot and sharp. Wishing only to get away from the horrible Mrs. Crumley, she lurched to her feet, and her shoe knocked against the ice-cream bucket. A wicked inspiration filled her—a result of her witchly nature, she supposed—and she kicked the bucket out of the carriage. It struck the ground at Mrs. Crumley's feet with a great *splot*, and the melting ice cream exploded outward—all over the old woman's dress. Mrs. Crumley froze in shock.

"What have you done?" the witch hissed.

For a moment, Grace froze too, for Mrs. Crumley's gaze was fixed upon her. Now it would happen—now Grace would see the old woman's worst memory, and Mrs. Crumley would know there was something wrong about her. But Mrs. Crumley seemed to be made of the same stuff as Mrs. Spencer, who had never seen anything bad when she looked at Grace. Perhaps neither of them had any guilty memories like Mrs. Silverwood had, though Mrs. Spencer certainly had plenty of memories of *other* people's mistakes. There was no horror in Mrs. Crumley's eyes, just plenty of indignation.

Filled with a mixture of shame and anger, and not knowing what else to do, Grace leaped from the cart and ran.

She ran around the back of the blacksmith's shop and leaned against the woodpile, trying to steady her breathing.

"What are you doing back here?" a voice demanded. Grace whirled, and there was Sareena, looking fresh as a crocus in a mauve dress with her hair tied in a mauve ribbon. It seemed impossible that this was the same person who had thrown mud at Grace's face and wrestled her in the forest.

"I've made another archenemy," Grace said sadly. "One almost as fearsome as my first. I loiter here in cowardice, afraid to accept my dolorous fate."

"I don't know what half those words mean," Sareena said. "Do you want to get a soda?"

Grace did not, and instead told her the whole story of the incident with Mrs. Crumley. When Grace was finished, Sareena said, "Where did the ice cream come from?"

"A magic spell gone wrong."

"Wrong? What could be wrong about ice cream?" She

paused. "Was it just the one bucket?"

"Oh, there will be more in the morning." Grace groaned. "Another thing I got wrong! What if the witch decides that I'm simply too much trouble and breaks our pact? What then? I'm right back where I began, forced to choose between a barren life at the orphanage and certain starvation."

"Hmm," Sareena said. "Do you mean first thing in the morning? Or closer to tea?"

Grace sank to the ground and buried her face in her hands.

Sareena sighed. "Look," she said, "Miss Puddlestone hates everybody, including Mrs. Crumley, though Mrs. Crumley fancies that they're friends, for she's an old lonely gossip and needs to be friends with everyone. Miss Puddlestone wouldn't care if you threw manure on her."

"Really?" Grace said. She looked up at Sareena hopefully. "What happened to you before? You promised that you would meet me in the forest to see one of my spells."

"I went to the forest, but you were late," Sareena said. "So I left."

"Oh. Sorry."

"That's all right."

They chattered together as they walked. Grace learned that they were the same age, and that Sareena's father had a large farm mostly made up of dairy cows. He was from Lebanon, while her mother's family was French Canadian. Sareena went to Quebec every year and had twice gone all the way to Saskatchewan to visit relatives. Grace, who had never left Prince

Edward Island, found Sareena's travels fascinating.

"Really?" Sareena said, when Grace told her this. "But Saskatchewan isn't so interesting. I mean, it is *very* interesting, but I'm not sure it's as interesting as being a witch."

Grace didn't argue, for she was suddenly even more afraid that Sareena would grow bored of talking to her.

"What are you doing here, anyway?" Sareena said. "Miss Puddlestone doesn't usually come into the village."

"She's buying me new school clothes," Grace said, unable to suppress a shudder. For of course the witch would not be buying her any new clothes now, after what she had done.

A smile broke across Sareena's face. "How lovely! Then I'll have a friend at school this year. An interesting friend, I mean. I'm friends with Priscilla, but she's so annoying it's almost like not having friends at all."

Grace stared at her. She had always thought one had to wait awhile before becoming friends with someone. But if there was one thing Grace would learn about Sareena, it was that she hated to wait for anybody or anything.

"Come on," Sareena said, not waiting for Grace to reply. "I'll help you choose a bonnet. I suppose you want a wide brim, to hide those eyes of yours. They're a bit funny-looking, you know, though I'm not sure exactly why."

"Wait," Grace said as Sareena dragged her toward the hat shop. She had to plant her feet and grab on to a tree to stop her. "You shouldn't say things you'll regret."

"Regret?" Sareena furrowed her brow.

"Most people regret being friends with me," Grace said, allowing sorrow to creep into her voice. Sorrow was always creeping into the voices of tragic heroines in stories. "For the companionship of a witch is not for the faint of heart."

Sareena stared at her. "Are you saying you've never had a friend before?"

When she said it like that, Grace stopped seeing herself as a tragic heroine, and instead as just plain tragic. "Never."

"That people are too afraid of you and your funny eyes to be your friend?"

"That's not entirely what I'm saying," Grace said, wishing Sareena wouldn't keep harping on about her eyes. Grace already spent enough time worrying about her freckles, and there were quite a lot of them to worry about without adding other features to the list.

Sareena's face shone, and she grabbed Grace's hand. "Do you want to know something? I was the first girl in school to get into a fight with a boy. I was the first one to climb the oak tree in the gully—no matter what that cow Mabel Fitzpatrick says. She barely made it halfway!"

This was all interesting, but Grace had no idea how to respond. "Oh?"

"I'm always the first at everything," Sareena continued in a fervent voice. "I'll be your first friend, Grace Greene. And we shall be the best friends that ever were, until we both are dead."

Grace burst into tears.

"Ugh," Sareena said, pulling a handkerchief from her pocket. "This is going to be harder than I thought."

Grace blew her nose. "You don't know what you're saying. I'm really—I'm quite scary."

"Yes, I'm shaking in my shoes," Sareena said. "Blow again, will you? You're still drippy. Come on, let's go try on all of Mrs. Swanson's hats and not buy any of them."

And that was all Sareena would say on the matter. Grace tried to make her see reason, though truthfully, she didn't try very hard. The way Sareena had promised to be her friend forever had filled her with such hope that she could hardly think. Grace had never had any sort of friend—a forever friend was unimaginable. She began to cry all over again in the hat shop.

"Good grief," Sareena said, removing the lacy bonnet she'd tied under Grace's chin. "It's true that pink isn't your color, but there's no need to get hysterical about it."

Grace followed her around the shop in a daze. She would have tried on every hat in the world for Sareena, even if they were the color of toads.

"There you are, my love." A tall woman who looked like a stretched-out version of Sareena, except with blue eyes and pale skin, strode up to them. "It's time to head home. You don't need any more hats."

"Mama, this is Grace," Sareena said. "She has no friends at all, except me. The first and only."

"Oh dear. I'm sure Grace has friends, darling, and if she hasn't, it's not something for you to boast about." Mrs. Khalil looked Grace up and down. "It's very nice to meet you, Grace. Sareena tells me you've come to live with Miss Puddlestone. So it seems we'll be neighbors—"

That was when it happened. Grace looked at Mrs. Khalil, and suddenly Grace was seeing her when she was young, the same age as some of the older girls at the orphanage.

She was climbing out her bedroom window late at night and running through fields to the beach, where several of her friends were waiting. They swam in their dresses, whooping and laughing at the cold, then dared each other to climb the slippery rocks that lined the shore. In the darkness, Mrs. Khalil didn't see her best friend fall. But when she reached the top, still breathless with laughter, she saw a figure sprawled on the beach below, perfectly still with her pale hair fanned out around her.

Mrs. Khalil jerked back as if Grace had shoved her, staring at her with that dreadful look of shock that Grace knew so well.

"I'm sorry," Grace whispered, but she had no idea if Mrs. Khalil heard her. Then, suddenly, the witch was there, glowering. She gave Mrs. Khalil a frosty smile, and before Grace knew it, she was being hustled out of the shop.

Grace didn't remember much about what happened after that. The witch brought her to the dressmaker, a small man who took her measurements and clucked that she was scrawny for her age, which for once did not infuriate her. Grace was far too full of despair to have room for anger.

She had finally found a friend—a best friend, in fact—only for her to be snatched away. That was her fate as an eternally unlucky orphan. Mrs. Khalil would forbid Sareena from ever visiting, and Grace would remain as friendless as always.

The witch barely paused for breath during the ride home, muttering away and occasionally shouting. She seemed to be talking to herself half the time, which made her sound mad, though in an expected, witchlike way.

"And then she demanded that I have her around for *tea*," the witch ranted. "And this time, I couldn't refuse, for she forced me to agree to a *date*, and appearances must be maintained— and this is all your fault, you brainless, impossible girl. I will not ask what you were thinking, as I know there is nothing more than air and nonsense floating about in that useless head of yours . . . How Patrick would laugh if he heard of this. Well, he won't hear of it, for I shan't tell him. I shall stick to ignoring him, the way he carries on . . . "

Grace didn't know who Patrick was, and she didn't care to ask. She could think of nothing but her own misery. The leaves fluttered and the yellow ones dropped to the ground, *pit-pat, pit-pat*, more grains of sand falling through the hourglass, and there was another thing to darken her mood.

As she drifted off to sleep in her perfect little bedroom that night, Grace became aware that there was a lot of cloud outside her window—a sudden change in weather. She had the impression that the cloud was gazing mournfully through the window at her. This, she knew, was impossible, for how could a cloud gaze at anyone, let alone gaze mournfully? And yet somehow this cloud managed it.

And then she was asleep.

10

THE BACKWARD HICCUP SPELL

The wrinkled sea beneath him crawls;
He watches from his mountain walls,
And like a thunderbolt he falls.
—Alfred, Lord Tennyson, "The Eagle"

Grace woke early the next morning, full of grim purpose. She had decided it was silly to be sad about Sareena—they would not have stayed friends for long, anyway. Eventually Sareena would have grown frightened of her, like all the others. Grace had to forget about friendship and focus on the grimoire.

Grace pulled on one of her five new dresses, and it was impossible not to feel her mood lift. How she loved those dresses! They were all very plain, made from sturdy cotton without a single flounce, but one was pale blue with tiny unknowable flowers, and another had the slightest hint of pink in it, almost too slight to see, like the color of apple blossoms. Grace had asked the witch several times if she could see it, until the witch had stopped answering altogether and simply gritted her teeth murderously. Grace thought the bit of pinkness was put there on purpose, for the sleeves also had a swish to them. Again, it was the slightest of swishes imaginable, and the witch said the seamstress had simply measured wrong, but Grace thought the dress was designed to have a bit of secret romance in it for someone just like her—the witch would never have bought the dress if she'd thought there was anything interesting about it.

Grace resolved to put her fears aside and cast her first spell that day. After all, if she *wasn't* magic enough to use a witch's grimoire, it was best to find out before she fell any more in love with the cottage.

She had her eye on spell number three in the grimoire, the "For Hiccups" spell. She didn't have the hiccups, but they were easy enough to come by.

The spell read:

3. FOR HICCUPS
1 pinecone
2 stones, skipped (5 or more)
1 handful dandelion roots
1 cup teaberries
12 rose petals, west
½ teaspoon dewdrops
Dash of smoke

Dig a hole beneath a yew tree (the older the better).

Bury ingredients. Water with rain to set.

Clap three times and may it be, by sun and stars.

Grace had puzzled over "12 rose petals, west." After thinking it through, she had decided that it must mean twelve rose petals plucked from the westward side of the rosebush.

The real difficulty was the "2 stones, skipped (5 or more)." Grace had never skipped a stone in her life. And did "5 or more" mean she had to throw each skipping stone five times, or skip them each five skips?

She must have been by the stream for nearly an hour, flinging stones this way and that in increasing desperation, when Sareena strode out of the forest.

"What are you doing?" she said. "We came to see if you wanted to play. Well, we mainly came to see if there was any of your magic ice cream."

Grace was so astonished that she leaped on Sareena at once, hugging her as tears ran down her face. "I never thought witches would be so leaky," Sareena said.

"You shouldn't be here," Grace said, wiping her face. "Surely your mother has forbidden it. What if she punishes you? What if she locks you in your room for a year and a day?"

"That sounds like something *your* mother would do," Sareena said. "And she hasn't forbidden anything, though I don't think she likes you."

A twig snapped in the woods, and Grace turned. A little girl stood gazing at them. She had a long dark braid and a halo of frizz around her face, and she was wearing a yellow dress with what looked like a green blanket wrapped around her shoulders. Very strangely, as soon as the girl saw Grace looking at her, she leaped toward a tree and threw her arms around it.

"That's my shadow," Sareena said. "My sister, Daisy. I call her Daisy Bean."

"Why?"

"I don't know." Sareena thought for a moment. "Because she's little, I guess."

"Hello, Daisy Bean," Grace said.

"Shh," Sareena muttered. "She thinks she's invisible."

The little girl pressed herself more tightly against the tree trunk.

"Oh!" Grace pretended to scan the forest. "I thought I saw your sister, Sareena, but she vanished. Like smoke!"

Daisy Bean's shoulders began to shake.

"Good," Sareena said quietly. "It's a bit annoying, but if she thinks she's hiding, she leaves me alone." She raised her voice to a normal level. "Is that your grimoire?"

Grace handed it to her and explained her predicament.

"'For Hiccups,'" Sareena read. "Really? I wouldn't have expected a spell like that in a witch's grimoire. Hiccups can't be very big magic, can they?"

"I know just what you mean," Grace said, and she told Sareena all about the spells she had been daydreaming about, including the one that called tame bears out of the woods so that witches could ride them.

Sareena nodded. "Yes, that's more like it," she said. "Oh well. At least this isn't anything dangerous."

Sareena read the spell, blew out her breath, and picked up one of the stones. She bent her wrist just so and let the stone fly over the stream: *skip-skip-skip-skip-skip-skip-PLUNK.*

"Six skips!" Grace cried. She had never seen anything so impressive.

"That's nothing." Sareena picked up another stone. *Skip-skip-skip-skip-skip-skip-skippity-PLUNK.*

"The last one was a bit weak," Sareena said. "We'll call it six and a half. How many skipping stones do you need for the spell?"

"Two. But I think I have to skip them myself, which is the trouble."

Sareena folded her arms and looked serious. "Show me."

Grace lifted a pebble, but before she had gotten off even one throw, Sareena was full of criticisms of her technique. Grace's stone selection was poor, her wrist position was all wrong, and why did she keep making that face, as if she was smelling a bad smell?

"What does this mean?" Sareena said, squinting at the grimoire. "You need at least five skips per throw, or you need to throw each stone five times, with any number of skips?"

"I don't know," Grace said.

"Well, you'd best do both, to be on the safe side," Sareena said, and Grace could not argue with such practical advice.

With Sareena's help, Grace was soon an expert stone-skipper. Getting to the point where she could achieve five straight throws of five or more skips was a little trickier, as her hands were always sweating fiercely by throw number four, but at last she managed it. They waded out into the stream and retrieved the stones, giggling at the startled dragonflies whirring about their heads, their wings flashing like silver coins. Then Grace led Sareena and Daisy Bean to the root cellar, where the witch had taken to storing poor Buckley's ice cream each morning. They had a merry feast, devouring the half-melted dessert with their bare hands.

Daisy Bean whispered something in her sister's ear. Sareena nodded. "I'll tell her."

"What?" Grace said.

"She says that this is the best day she's ever had," Sareena said. "She's only four, so the competition isn't stiff, of course, but I think she likes you."

Daisy Bean went pink and pulled the blanket over her head, returning to her invisible state of being.

After that, they went into the woods to finish the spell. Grace had already found a terribly old yew tree to bury the ingredients beneath, knobby and half-dead on one side. She knelt among the needles and began to dig while Sareena leafed through the grimoire.

"Listen to this!" she exclaimed. "You're supposed to cast spell number forty-four 'on a day that lasts twenty-five hours.' That's impossible."

Grace shook her head grimly. She had been trying very hard not to think about spell number forty-four. "Impossible or not, I have to do it."

"What happens if you don't? If you can't finish them all before—when did you say?"

"May, maybe June." Grace wiped her sweaty forehead with her sleeve. "Then I have to give the witch my magic."

Sareena rolled her eyes, as if expecting Grace to say that she was joking. When she didn't, Sareena's eyes widened.

"Seriously?" she breathed. "Gosh, if I had magic, I wouldn't give it up for anything."

"Bet you would," Grace said, picturing the bare walls of Rose & Ivy. "Bet you'd give it up for your home."

"Do you mean the farm?" Sareena said. "Or Mum and Daddy and Daisy? Or Brook-by-the-Sea?"

"For all of it," Grace said.

They were quiet for a moment.

"Anyway, I thought you weren't convinced I was a witch," Grace said.

Sareena shrugged. "This is fun either way." She set the grimoire aside. "I'll help you with the other spells, too."

The way she said it, as if it were something that was simply true and not to be argued with, like the color of grass, made the tears come to Grace's eyes again. But she swallowed them, remembering Sareena's complaint about leaky witches.

"We should go in order, I think," Sareena said. "If it's true that the spells get harder as you go on. We'll go back and do spells one and two next, then carry on with spell four. We'll be sure not to forget any that way."

Grace nodded, admiring her new friend's good sense.

The hole was deep enough now. Grace put the ingredients in it—the dandelion roots, the dew, the rose petals, the skipping stones. For the smoke, Grace lit a match, blew it out, and dropped it in with the rest. Daisy Bean sneezed as the smoke drifted in her direction.

Grace buried everything and soaked the ground with rainwater she had gathered in a jar. Taking a deep breath, she clapped her hands three times.

Absolutely nothing happened.

"Oh no," Grace whispered, certain her worst fear was confirmed.

Sareena's nose was buried in the grimoire. "I think you're supposed to say, 'May it be, by sun and stars,'" she said.

"Really?"

"I think so. Most of the spells end like that. Probably you're supposed to say it out loud."

Grace drew a deep breath. "May it be, by sun and stars!"

She lowered her hands. A bird chirped. Daisy Bean adjusted her blanket.

"What's this spell for again?" Sareena flipped the page over. "Oh, right. 'For—'"

"Good grief!" Grace clapped her hand to her forehead. "I completely forgot! I was supposed to give myself the hiccups first. You can't cast a hiccup-curing spell if you haven't got the hiccups. What a waste!"

"Maybe we can try again," Sareena said. "Getting the hic-cups is easy. Too bad we ate all the ice cream. Maybe the witch has a cake. Chocolate cake and a nice big glass of milk always do it for me—"

HIC.

It was a sound so loud, so terrible, that every bird in the grove took flight. Feathers flew in all directions and the trees shook, releasing a shower of leaves. Sareena shrieked and clapped her hands over her ears.

At first, Grace couldn't tell where it had come from. Then she realized Daisy Bean had fallen onto her back and was lying there looking owl-eyed. Then—

HIC.

This time, the force of her own hiccup made Daisy Bean do a backward somersault. Pinecones thudded to the forest floor. Puddles trembled and squirrels fled for their lives. Daisy Bean pushed herself up on her elbow—she didn't look hurt, but she held her stomach as if the wind had been knocked out of her.

HIC. HIC.

"It's getting worse!" Sareena shouted. "Hold your breath, Daisy Bean—"

HIC.

Sareena grabbed for her sister. Just in time, too, for Daisy Bean had drawn herself to her feet and the hiccup sent her flying backward, as if she'd been hit by a wave. She fell into

Sareena and the two of them landed in a heap in a pile of leaves.

"The witch!" Grace hollered over the ringing in her ears. "Hurry!"

And they set off running back to the house.

The witch was not amused.

It took her all of one minute to cure Daisy Bean's hiccups. Grace had expected her to use a potion, something thick and smelly and very witchlike, but she only gave Daisy Bean a spoonful of sugar and made her stand on her head.

Unfortunately, in that one minute, Daisy Bean's hiccups had shattered the windows in the parlor and the kitchen, sent the spices wobbling off the shelves, broken all the eggs in the larder, and knocked over the grandfather clock.

"Do you have any sense at all, you beastly child?" the witch demanded, after sending Sareena and Daisy Bean home. Daisy Bean, fortunately, was none the worse for wear, and actually seemed to have enjoyed being able to shatter windows by hiccupping at them.

"It still counts," Grace said. Now that the hiccup emergency was over, she felt weak with relief. "I cast the spell, I just—got it backward, that's all. The hiccup-curing spell became a—a hiccup-granting spell."

"'That's all,' she says. 'That's all.'" The witch loomed up in her shadow shape, clicking her fangs together, and Grace leaped backward with a strangled shriek.

"I didn't—" She choked. "I mean, I'm—"

"*Look at my brother's painting,*" the witch hissed, pointing.

Grace looked. The painting was hanging lopsided, but worse than that, there was a big dent down the middle, as if a bull had charged it. It was a rather ugly painting of a meadow with a lot of sloppy flowers, and Grace wondered why the witch had hung it in the first place. She didn't seem interested in decorations generally.

"I'm sorry!" Grace cried.

The witch shrank back to her human form and gazed down at Grace, trembling on the floor. "I suppose I should be happy," she said after a moment. "If you can foul up such a basic spell so badly, perhaps next time you'll turn yourself inside out, and then I'll be rid of you."

"I won't," Grace said, still trembling. "I'll—I'll do better. I swear."

"We'll see." The witch gave her a nasty smile. "Only ninety-nine and a half to go. And you've not even begun the higher magics. Oh, that will be interesting indeed."

11

"FOR FIRE" AND "FOR TICKLES"

The Nightingale begins its song ...
In nature there is nothing melancholy.
—Samuel Taylor Coleridge, "The Nightingale"

As August melted into September, Sareena and Grace ran wild through the woods and the witch's garden, gathering as many spell ingredients as they could find.

Grace cast spells number one and two in the grimoire. Fortunately, both went better than the "For Hiccups" spell. Though in the case of spell two, this was only true in the sense that it wasn't possible to do worse than the "For Hiccups" spell.

Spell number one, "For Fire," had been a worrisome one. Given her luck, Grace had been afraid she would set fire to the whole forest.

1. FOR FIRE
1 stick
1 handful fireweed, dried and crushed

1 teaspoon charcoal from a lightning-struck tree
Spoonful of summer honey
½ cup wild strawberries

Mix the charcoal with the fireweed, strawberries, and a little
honey to make a paste.
Coat the stick and cast one breath upon it.
May it be, by sun and stars.

To be safe, they decided to cast the spell on a tiny island in the middle of the stream. The island was a sandbank only a yard or two in length covered with a scattering of river stones and a forlorn little cherry tree.

But, miraculously, the spell came off. When Grace blew on the tip of the stick, it lit like a struck match. The flame had an odd bluish hue, but what did that matter? The witch glared at Grace when Grace called her out to inspect it, then retreated to the house without a word, so she knew that she had succeeded. Her heart sang, and the sun seemed to shine brighter. She was full of confidence at having finally, at long last, done something right in the magic department.

Looking back, Grace knew this was where she went wrong.

Right before the "For Hiccups" spell was spell number two, "For Tickles." Sareena and Grace ventured out to the Magician's Keep—which, following Grace's triumph with spell one, was what they had decided to call the island in the stream—at dawn on a drizzly day.

2. FOR TICKLES

1 snakeskin
1 handful cobwebs
¼ cup prickles
5 holly leaves
3 cinnamon fern fronds
1 teaspoon pepper (freshly ground)
3–5 feathers, assorted
1 cup sand

Bottle ingredients with rainwater; let brew overnight in a warm place.
When the world is gray, pour in a circle upon freshly turned earth.
Whistle once and may it be, by sun and stars.

"Where did you find the snakeskin?" Sareena asked, chafing her arms. The damp had put a chill in the late summer air.

"I didn't," Grace said. "Windweaver did. He likes to eat snakes. Do you think the world is gray enough today?"

"I expect so." Indeed, it would be hard to imagine a grayer day, with the sun just brightening the horizon and everything drippy and wan. Still, there was that lovely petrichor smell in the air, Grace's favorite of all smells, as the earth greedily drank in the rain.

They began turning the earth, raking the little pile of dirty sand and stones that made up the Keep.

"There's only one problem," Grace said. "Well, two problems, actually. The witch keeps a clean house—for a witch—so I could only find half a handful of cobwebs."

"Perhaps it will only cure half of our ticklishness," Sareena said. "What's the other problem?"

"I can't whistle."

"Oh." Sareena thought for a moment. "Well, how about if I do it?"

Grace bit her lip.

"It doesn't say you have to do everything yourself," Sareena said. "And I already helped you pick the thorns, didn't I?"

Grace couldn't argue with that, although she felt there *was* a difference, even if she couldn't have said what it was. In any case, Sareena was already handing her the bottle, so they moved through the rest of the spell. When it was time for the whistle, Sareena gave a single piercing trill.

"May it be, by sun and stars," Grace said, waving her hands. The spell didn't say anything about waving her hands, but what sort of witch would just stand there with her arms at her sides?

Suddenly, Sareena began to giggle and twitch.

"What—?" Grace began. Then she began to giggle, too.

The tickling started under her chin, then moved to her sides and feet. The strangest thing was that Grace could almost *see* something tickling her—there was a ripple in the air, particularly in the region of her feet.

"How long—will it—last?" Sareena asked between gasps of laughter.

"I don't know," Grace replied, and though she was laughing, too, her neck prickled with dread. Surely the tickling would stop. Wouldn't it?

Sareena screamed. It was a peculiar sound, given that it was mixed with giggles. Were they to be tickled to death?

Then Grace screamed, too. The ripples in the air had grown solid, horribly. Now they were *fingers*—actual fingers—floating through the air, fluttering like monstrous butterflies. As Grace watched, three of them broke off from the pack and made tracks for Sareena's exposed chin, which they ruthlessly began to tickle.

Grace batted away a half dozen fingers, which had formed a nightmarish sort of hand that was now attacking her left side. "RUN!" she shrieked.

They ran. Splashing through the knee-deep stream, up over the bank, across the field, and through the garden. Grace looked over her shoulder once, and oh, it was the ghastliest thing. She couldn't imagine anything worse than being chased across a field by a horde of disembodied fingers, all wiggling and waving. It was a sight that Grace would not wish upon her archenemy, as awful as Rum was.

Then they were crashing through the door of the witch's cottage, filling it with a cacophony of shrieks and laughter, which brought the witch running down the stairs in her nightgown, her hands pressed to her ears.

She looked neither startled nor frightened by the wiggling swarm, and instead fixed Grace with one of her glowers. The

113

fingers seemed to have gained an evil intelligence—half had attached themselves to Grace's feet like barnacles and were attempting to trip her, the better to expose her soft pink soles. She knew that if she fell upon her back, it was curtains for her, and so she half hopped, half lurched around in a very silly way, trying to crush the fingers with her heels.

Perhaps the witch wasn't ticklish, for the fingers left her alone. She picked up a log from the pile beside the fireplace, opened the door, and began neatly swatting the fingers outside one by one. *Thwack. Thwack. Thwack.* It was a most unpleasant sound, exactly what you would expect it to sound like, really.

Once all the fingers were outside and strewn upon the lawn, seemingly stunned, the witch slammed the door.

"Are they—will they—?" Grace was collapsed against the armchair by this point, her sides aching as if they were on fire. Sareena lay in a sprawl on her back in the middle of the floor, still twitching with giggles.

"They'll fade soon enough," the witch said. "Tickles can't exist without a human host."

Grace straightened up. "I did it—another spell—"

"Yes, and another example of your incompetence," the witch said. She stepped over Sareena and went into the kitchen.

Grace trailed after her. "But—"

"You did something wrong," she said. "Each spell must be cast precisely as described. If you did that, you wouldn't have a catastrophe on your hands each time."

Grace sucked in her breath. The witch had given her

advice! Like a real teacher would, as if Grace were already her apprentice!

"I thought you weren't allowed to help me with the spells," Grace said. "That was part of our pact, wasn't it?"

"Pointing out that you might want to actually *read* the grimoire isn't help, you ninny," the witch said. She turned her back on Grace and looked inside that saucepan of hers. By now Grace was nearly mad with curiosity about the saucepan. What sort of spell needed weeks to brew? Would it stop time? Cure a hundred different diseases? No, more likely it would cause them.

"Would you like me to help you with that?" Grace said, for the witch's advice had made her brave. Surely they were entering a new era of their relationship, where the witch would begin to see Grace as a powerful witch in her own right, or at least an assistant who might be useful to have around—

"Get out before I throw you out, you ridiculous calamity," the witch said.

12

THE SCULLION

A linnet in a gilded cage—
  A linnet on a bough—
In frosty winter one might doubt
  Which bird is luckier now.

But let the trees burst out in leaf,
  And nests be on the bough,
Which linnet is the luckier bird,
  Oh who could doubt it now?
—Christina Rossetti, "A Linnet in a Gilded Cage"

By-the-Sea School was a tidy little wooden building, spotlessly clean and still smelling of its summer coat of white paint. By the pocket watch the witch had given Grace, it took precisely twenty-two minutes to walk there from the witch's house if she took the shortcut through the Khalil farm. A stately oak leaned over the school, and behind it flowed a little brook, its waters wonderfully chill after a long walk in the drowsy heat. Brook-by-the-Sea was in the thick of what the residents called Second Summer, and even the mornings left a sheen of sweat upon Grace's brow.

Grace was horribly nervous, even with Sareena by her side. She already knew the other children would hate her, though, so she wasn't sure why she was worrying about it.

She said goodbye to Windweaver at the gate. He had been trailing them through the trees, and flew off in a bit of a sulk. Windweaver often went off on his own—Grace assumed he went hunting, though Windweaver liked being mysterious and usually didn't tell her—but he didn't like being separated from Grace for an entire day.

When she and Sareena stepped inside, they found that the schoolroom was already full of children, the younger ones seated at their desks while the older ones hovered by the windows or leaned casually against the walls. There were twenty students, ranging in age from six to sixteen. Every single one stared at Grace as she entered. Her heart wasn't roaring wickedly like the sea at all, but thundering away as an ordinary girl's would.

"Sareena!" A girl bounded forward and wrapped Sareena in a hug. She was beautiful—plump and round-faced with gleaming hair the color of wheat. In her wake trailed several other girls like shadows, all of them pretty but not quite as pretty as her.

"It's so lovely to see you again," the girl gushed. "It's been simply *ages*. The last time my mother and I called upon you,

117

your mother said you were out."

"Yes, I was playing with Grace," Sareena said, taking Grace's arm. "Grace is my best friend, Priscilla. She lives next door."

"She lives with the witch?" Priscilla said it so loudly that several other children turned to stare. Grace noticed with interest that she spoke with a slight accent. Sareena had told Grace that Priscilla's parents were French—from France originally—but Priscilla had been born in a small French-speaking town in New Brunswick.

"She sure does," Sareena said mysteriously. "And you know what else? I've been inside the witch's house."

Priscilla looked Grace up and down. Grace saw a familiar shadow pass over the girl's face, a slight furrow as she took in the witchlike aura that only other children could sense.

"Nice to meet you," Grace said, a bit too loudly. She was always nervous around popular girls, probably because she had always wished to be popular herself.

Priscilla backed up a little, frowning, and Sareena swept Grace away.

"That was close," she whispered as she led Grace to the back of the schoolroom.

"I thought you said you were friends with Priscilla," Grace whispered back.

"I am. That doesn't mean I like her," Sareena said. "We used to play together when we were little—her parents' farm is across the lane from mine—but then she stopped wanting to play outside. Plus, she only cares about being popular. She collects friends like dolls." She grabbed Grace's hand. "She'll try to steal you away from me. We can't let that happen."

This was so ridiculous that Grace snorted. "She's terrified of me! You saw."

"That won't stop her for long," Sareena said grimly. Grace glanced over her shoulder. Priscilla was surrounded by a knot of girls, but she was indeed watching Grace thoughtfully.

"Who's the new kid?" A tall girl with dark hair and pale skin stuck her foot out, blocking Grace's way.

Sareena frowned. "This is Grace, Poppy. You'd better let her past. You don't want to make Grace angry, trust me."

Poppy snorted. Though Grace thought Poppy was only a year or two older than herself, the girl was as tall as a grown-up, a gangly collection of sharp angles, with dark brows that shadowed her eyes. The other children, Grace noticed, gave her a wide berth. Grace soon saw why, for she stuck her foot out again and tripped one of the littlest students as he passed.

"Is that supposed to scare me?" Poppy smirked. "Your friend is so scrawny she'd fall over if I sneezed on her. And those freckles! Are you two starting a club?"

Grace reddened with anger. If there was anything that got her worked up, it was a jab about her freckles.

"Poppy's a bully," Sareena said. "Ignore her, Grace. Everybody else does."

Poppy blew out her breath. "I guess you know all about being ignored, don't you?"

Grace expected Sareena to have a smart retort ready, but

she just glared, her face going red. Grace noticed that nobody else said hello to Sareena—some of the students even smirked in her direction.

"Mud all over her skirt," one of the girls whispered as Grace and Sareena went by.

"Probably climbing trees again," her friend replied scornfully, as if there was nothing worse.

Sareena held her head high and flounced past. Grace didn't think there was much mud on Sareena's skirt—only a little around the hem.

In a selfish way, Grace liked that Sareena was an outcast among the other children. Surely that would make her less likely to abandon Grace—something Grace still expected to happen one day, with a heavy sort of dread. Grace grabbed Sareena's hand and squeezed it.

Poppy followed them to the back of the room. At first Grace feared another attack on her freckles, but Poppy immediately sat down and began firing spitballs at the younger children through a paper straw.

Grace sat at her desk, feeling a little better. She had survived the moment she had worried about the most—walking into the schoolroom and facing the stares of the other children. She picked up the slate on her desk and began to copy out the cursive letters the teacher had written on the board for the day's lesson. Unfortunately, her nerves made her press too hard. *Snap* went the chalk.

Sareena looked in the shelf below their desks and shook her

head. "There's never any extras in the back desks." She tapped the shoulder of the boy sitting in front of her. "*Psst!* Do you have an extra chalk?"

The boy turned around. He had dark hair with a crown of autumn leaves woven into it and violet eyes like twilight.

It was the fairy boy, Rum.

Grace nearly fell out of her chair. "What are *you* doing here?"

Rum put his elbow on the back of his chair and leaned his head against his hand, his eyes full of mischief. You could barely see his fairy wings; Grace caught flashes of them out of the corner of her eye. His coloring had shifted slightly, as if with the changing season—now there was a golden flush in his skin, and his clothes were the color of tired, late-summer grass. The odd crown of leaves was yellowing at the edges, though the green of the jewel was as bright as ever.

"Me?" he said. "I've always been here."

Grace's mouth fell open in astonishment. "Can you see him?" she hissed at Sareena.

She blinked. "You mean old Rum? Of course I can see him."

"'Old Rum'?" Grace stared at Sareena, yet nothing in her face suggested she saw anything other than an ordinary schoolmate, despite the crown of leaves, impossible violet eyes, and all the rest of it.

Grace whirled back to face the fairy. "Did you *enchant* her?"

"Maybe I did," Rum said with a smirk. "Maybe I didn't." He

was dressed like any of the other boys, in dark slacks and a crisp button-down shirt with a vest over it. Rum's clothes, though, looked like they had been made of spidersilk and sedge grass, yet nobody else seemed to notice that either.

"You did!" Grace turned back to Sareena. "He's enchanted you. He's not a boy—he's a wicked fairy I found in a tree last month."

"Really?" Sareena frowned. "But he was here last year. He pulled my hair once."

Grace glared at Rum. "Where does he live? What's his last name? If he's from the village, you'd know all that."

"He lives—" Sareena's eyes went glassy for a moment. "Sorry. What was the question?"

"He's changed your memories. Fairies can do that."

Grace said it in a voice of despair—she was certain Sareena wouldn't believe her. But to Grace's astonishment, Sareena squeezed her hand.

"All right," she said. "We'll keep an eye on him."

Grace gave a sigh of relief. Sareena crossed her arms and glared at Rum, and Grace did the same. Rum glared right back. Grace supposed fairies didn't like it any more than witches did when their enchantments went awry.

"What do you want?" Grace demanded.

"Well." He suddenly looked nervous, though he tried to cover it with more glaring. "If you must know, I wanted to apologize."

Grace would not have been more surprised if he'd burst into flames. "Apologize!"

"I thought about it, and I shouldn't have been so rude to you. After all, you *did* save my life. I should have offered you a favor without you having to ask—that's fairy custom. Especially in your case, given how pathetic you are."

Grace gaped at him.

"I don't mean that in a bad way," he said quickly. "Only—you're like me. I'm an orphan, too. At first I just saw you as a horrible, spotty witch who wanted to order me about. I mean, you *are* that. But you're also alone in the world." He gave Grace such a solemn stare that he almost looked like a different person. "So—I'm sorry."

Grace had been angry. Now her fury was a wave crashing about inside her, searching for a way out. Perhaps Rum meant well in his heart, but he'd called her "spotty" again, and unloved, and the worst part was that it was all true.

Grace would never forgive him.

Rum seemed to sense some of this from her expression. "Grace—"

At that moment, Poppy fired off an enormous spitball with deadly accuracy. It struck a small boy who couldn't have been older than six, and he burst into tears. Grace whirled on her.

"Does that make you happy, to hurt someone half your size?" she snapped. "Were you raised by wolves, or are your parents as spiteful as you? There is nothing more cowardly than attacking the weak—it only shows how weak *you* are on the inside. Just leave him alone, you—you scullion!"

Grace didn't actually know what *scullion* meant. She'd come across it in a book of William Shakespeare's poetry, and she couldn't understand even half of William Shakespeare. But *scullion* was such a delicious word, harsh and slippery at the same time, the sort of word meant to be spat at an enemy in a moment of dramatic rage. For months, it had floated at the back of her head, waiting for an opportunity to burst free.

The children sitting at the neighboring desks gasped and giggled, especially those still picking bits of wet paper from their hair. Poppy's face darkened, and Grace realized she'd gone too far. The problem with knowing a lot of words, Grace thought, was that it was hard to resist the temptation to throw them at people.

Maybe if the other children hadn't heard her, nothing more would have come of it. But they had, and now they were laughing at Poppy.

"I'll punch you in the nose for that," Poppy said, her face flaming.

Rum let out a low hiss that would have been very peculiar coming from an ordinary boy, but nobody seemed to notice that, either.

"You will *not*," Sareena said. "Miss Gordon will expel you this time, Poppy. Look, she's coming."

Indeed, not a second later, Miss Gordon strode into the schoolroom. She was young—not much older than some of the eldest students, though she still seemed very grown-up to Grace, particularly with the stern expression on her pale face and the plain black ribbon in her hair, which did not look as if it had been brushed. Everything about her, including her brown muslin dress without a single flounce in the skirt, said, *I live a life of the mind, and the mind does not care what the body looks like.*

"I'll get you later," Poppy hissed. "I know where you live, you spotty little goblin."

The frightening part of this statement—the threat, that is—went right out of Grace's head, and all she felt was fury. For the very worst insults are those with a grain of truth in them—Grace was small and skinny, with delicate features that some people called elfin, which made *goblin* horribly appropriate.

Grace stood up in full view of Miss Gordon and brought her slate down on Poppy's head, snapping it in two.

13

"FOR GHOSTS"

Driven in by Autumn's sharpening air
From half-stripped woods and pastures bare,
Brisk Robin seeks a kindlier home . . .
—William Wordsworth, "The Redbreast"

Unsurprisingly, this sent the whole class into an uproar, with some children cheering and applauding and a few letting out shrieks, as if worried that Grace might attack them next. None of this set Grace off on the right foot with Miss Gordon. Grace spent the rest of the day sitting alone in a corner, and after school she had to write lines for an hour.

"How was it?" Sareena said as Grace stepped outside, for she was the dearest friend Grace could have ever hoped for and had waited for Grace by the brook.

Grace shook her head grimly. She had avoided looking at Miss Gordon, so at least the teacher did not think Grace a monster, but she certainly thought Grace was a very naughty child. In addition to forcing her to write *I am a young lady, not*

a bull in a ring two hundred times, she'd given Grace a note to take home to the witch. Grace knew the witch wouldn't care one whit that she'd broken a slate over Poppy's head—probably she wouldn't care if Grace turned Poppy into a flea—but she would care if it inconvenienced her.

"Well, it was the most memorable first day we've ever had at school," Sareena said. "Even the older kids said so."

"They all hate me, don't they?"

"I'm not sure," Sareena said. "They hate Poppy, so they like that you stood up to her. But they're also a bit afraid of you—because you're the witch's daughter, of course, and because you're funny looking."

Grace sighed. "Where did Rum go?"

"Who?" Sareena asked, and Grace had to spend the next quarter hour telling her about Rum all over again, for it seemed that his enchantment, which made the other children think he was one of them, also made them forget about him when he wasn't around. Oh, he really was the worst.

Grace expected the next school day to be much like the first—rotten, in other words—and in many ways, it was. The other children kept their distance from her, though golden-haired Priscilla was brave enough to say hello (which earned her a scowl from Sareena). Poppy did not speak to Grace, nor did she shoot spitballs at anybody. Grace almost thought their feud forgotten, but then there came a moment when Poppy's eyes met hers across the room, and the other girl gave Grace such a look of hatred that Grace felt her stomach shrivel. Grace very much hoped that if Poppy did punch her, it wouldn't be in the nose, as her nose was the only feature she liked.

After school, Miss Gordon called Grace aside. She started to sweat, certain she was in for another lecture. But Miss Gordon only handed Grace a book.

Grace took it nervously—no doubt it was a book about manners or something equally dreadful. But when she read the cover, she gasped.

"Poetry!" she cried.

"I thought you could get some use out of that one," Miss Gordon said. Miss Gordon was not from the Island, but America, which Grace found terribly fascinating, and spoke with a drawling accent that was somehow both calming and intimidating.

"I hope you like it as much as you like Shakespeare," the teacher added. Grace had told her how she'd come by *scullion*, having decided to be honorable in the face of her disgrace.

"Oh, I adore poetry," Grace said. "Though I don't really care for Shakespeare. He's a bit of a show-off, isn't he? All those big long speeches and his 'betwixt' this and his 'wherefore art' that. A person could go cross-eyed with confusion reading poetry like that. No, me and Wind—I mean, *I* prefer plain, hearty poetry, the kind you can really sink your teeth into."

Miss Gordon's mouth did something odd at that. It was sort of a twitch, as if she were suppressing a sneeze.

As she made her way home, Grace couldn't help marveling.

She had another book of poems! *Poetry of the Far East*, the title read, and though she did not know where the Far East might be, nor what Close East it lay beyond, she was immediately filled with a desire to see such a mysterious-sounding land. She couldn't wait to show Windweaver.

Grace cast another spell that day. It was an easy one.

4. FOR GHOSTS

1 frond of bracken fern
1 handful bitter nightshade
1 cup charcoal from a lightning-struck tree
1 ghost flower
Animal skull (snake, for best effect)

Mix the ingredients together and set alight with white flame.
May it be, by sun and stars.

Grace was full of nervous excitement. She had always wished to speak to a ghost, to find out what the Next World was like. But underneath that was something more important—the question of whether her parents were there. Perhaps the spell would summon them.

She felt a stab of guilt. Shouldn't she be hoping that the spell *wouldn't* summon them? For that would mean they could still be alive somewhere—off having adventures, as she had suggested to Windweaver. Surely it was more evidence of her wicked nature if she was hoping her parents were ghosts.

But if they're still alive, a small voice inside her thought, *that means they left you behind.*

Sareena had found a science book that said magnesium could make a white flame, so once they had the ingredients burning, they threw on a handful of her mother's Epsom salts. Unfortunately, after Grace's "May it be, by sun and stars," absolutely no ghosts appeared.

"Did I do something wrong?" Grace asked the witch when she called her out to the Magician's Keep to inspect her spell-work.

The witch poked at the ashes and made a sharp sound with her nostrils. "No more than usual."

"But it didn't work," Grace murmured. She picked up the photograph of her parents, the only one she had, which she had set by the fire. They stood in the shadow of a birch tree, blurry and smiling. Her father was tall, and her mother had a wild mane of hair; that was about all you could be sure of. Grace didn't look at the photo often, for the same reason she didn't think about her parents often—it hurt. Because her parents were only an idea, a word in a dictionary, not real people she carried around in her memory.

"I thought they would come," she said, so quietly that Sareena didn't hear. When she looked up, she found that the witch was watching her. The witch quickly looked away.

"Is the spell for summoning ghosts, or banishing them?" Sareena asked.

The witch made that sound with her nostrils again. "What a silly question. Like many spells, it has more than one use, and can be unpredictable. Magic is not some tame creature that you can put into a harness—magic is wild. I have used this spell both to summon ghosts and to banish them. I have used it to summon other things, too, things that are not quite ghosts." She paused. "When one casts a spell, one must put their own intention into it. Magic listens to our intentions."

She peered into the ashes. "The spell worked. Most likely, no ghosts came because there are no ghosts nearby."

The witch gave one last glower and stomped back to the house. It was only after she had gone inside that Grace realized the witch hadn't insulted her.

"Oh well," Sareena said. "It's a boring spell, but at least you did it right. That's another one down."

Grace nodded and silently tucked the photograph back into her pocket. Her parents hadn't appeared because they weren't dead. That must be it. They were on a tropical island, like she'd always thought, training red-and-green parrots to carry messages across the sea. One day a message would reach Grace, a message that smelled of tropical flowers, and when she unrolled it, a handful of sand and crushed coral would spill out. She drew a shaky breath and pictured the island as hard as she could until it drove away the darker thoughts.

Sareena tapped the grimoire, startling Grace out of her daydream. "This is a problem."

"You mean the harder spells?"

"I mean all of them. Have you thought about this mathematically?"

"I don't think about anything mathematically if I can help it."

Sareena blew out her breath. "You've cast four spells so far. You've been here about six weeks. Do you know what that means?" Naturally, she went on without waiting for an answer. "At the rate you're going, you'll finish between thirty and forty spells before that cherry tree blooms again. And that's assuming all the spells are as easy as the ones you've already cast. That's less than half of the spells in the grimoire, and that isn't even taking into consideration the unfinished spell."

Grace's stomach gave a nervous gurgle, and suddenly she wished she and Sareena hadn't devoured another pail of Buckley's ice cream between them.

"Well," she began hesitantly, "we've gathered quite a few ingredients for the next ten spells. So it should be faster from now on—"

"We haven't gathered everything," Sareena said. "Not even close." She began ticking things off on her fingers. "We're almost out of rainwater again. We still haven't found a good source of cobwebs, and white orchids are hard to find on this part of the Island. We need a whole handful of those. And we haven't even started gathering blackberries—three of the spells call for them."

Grace gazed at the ancient cherry tree. Its leaves were beginning to golden. Some of the flowers still held on, but they were brown and shriveled, though somehow this didn't make the tree any less beautiful. It looked like autumn itself, the brown bringing out the richness of the green leaves with their September gilding.

"I'll just—I'll just have to work faster," Grace said.

Sareena tapped her fingers on her knee. She did this whenever she was worried, Grace had noticed. "Me and Daisy Bean will help, of course."

Grace nodded. Her stomach gave another gurgle, and she didn't want to talk about the terrible mathematics of the grimoire anymore. She couldn't lose her magic. She couldn't lose dear Windweaver. Surely, once she got used to doing magic, everything would go more quickly.

Wouldn't it?

"Well," she said with a heartiness she didn't feel, "let's clean this up. We'll start fresh tomorrow with spell number five."

14

NOT QUITE A GHOST

In the clear green water—the shimmering moon.
In the moonlight—white herons flying.
—Li T'ai-Po, "Autumn River Song: On the Broad
Reach"

After Sareena went home, Grace curled up against one of the cherry trees with her new poetry book. She knew that she should have been working on her spells, but Sareena's words had put a kernel of fear in her stomach, hard and sharp.

What if she couldn't finish all the spells in time? What did it feel like to lose your magic? Would the witch draw it out of her like blood? Would it hurt?

The one thing that could make her forget her fear, if only for a moment, was poetry, and so into poetry she went.

Windweaver settled on her shoulder. He didn't like strangers, so he often kept his distance when Sareena was around. Grace plucked him from his perch and wrapped her arms around him.

Windweaver gave a croak, looking very undignified on his back with mussed feathers. He tugged himself free. *What was that for?*

"Oh, nothing," she lied. "I just miss you when I'm at school, that's all."

I miss you too. It's silly that you have to go to school. Crows don't bother with school, and look at how smart we are. He gave the book a curious nibble. *New poems?*

"Keep your beak to yourself," Grace said. "Yes, these are new poems. Marvelous poems."

Windweaver made a skeptical noise, which Grace knew was his way of telling her to read one. She read:

The end of autumn, and some rooks
Are perched upon a withered branch.

Windweaver waited. *That's it?* he said.

"Yes. Doesn't it paint such a lovely little picture in your mind? The book says this kind of poem is called a haiku. Even the word *haiku* is lovely—it sits on your tongue like a piece of chocolate, doesn't it?"

Windweaver made a skeptical noise again. But after a little silence he said, *Well? Are there any more about birds?*

Grace flipped through the book. All poets were obsessed with birds, and it didn't take her long to find something she thought Windweaver would approve of.

"Here," she said. "This is by someone called Kikkawa

Gomei. The book says he's from Japan. Oh, wouldn't it be wonderful to go to Japan? Just imagine sailing all the way across the Pacific—those big waves tossing you about like a bee in a rosebush on a windy day. And I bet there would be dolphins—"

What does the poem say? Windweaver huffed.

"All right, all right." Grace began to read:

Of course the nightingale stays not
Upon a tree bereft of flowers.

Grace found another poem with birds in it, and then another, and when she was finished, they both sat quietly for a long moment. It seemed almost wrong to say that the poems were lovely, or to say anything at all.

Those poets know birds, Windweaver said, which from him was the highest of compliments.

"I think you're right," Grace said, "though I don't know if I understand it all. What's 'bereft'?"

It's only right that you're confused, Windweaver said. *Birds aren't for humans to understand.*

"Do *you* know what all the words mean?"

Windweaver gave a low rumble in his throat. *I'm a bird! Nothing about birds is a mystery to me.* But before Grace could ask him anything else, he said quickly, *Read another one.*

They sat there for an hour, or maybe longer—time always went a little funny, Grace found, when you were reading poetry. She knew she would have to return to the cottage soon.

The witch always served dinner promptly at seven o'clock whether Grace was there or not. If she was late, it would be a cold piece of shepherd's pie that awaited her, or a bowl of soup with the fat congealing upon the surface.

But Sareena's warnings were still fresh in her mind—and creating more gurgles in her stomach—so she decided to look for moonweed. Moonweed was the main ingredient in spell number six and at least three others, and it had given Grace no end of trouble.

For one thing, "moonweed" was not a flower that appeared in any book, and when Grace asked Mrs. Montague in the flower shop, she said there was no such thing. When Grace asked the witch if there was any in her garden, she laughed and said that it grew where it pleased, and when Grace asked where that might be, she said, "Everywhere and nowhere." Good grief!

Clearly, moonweed was a magical flower. There were several other plants mentioned in the grimoire that Grace suspected to be magical, given that they, too, did not appear in any books. Perhaps only witches could see them.

"Keep your eyes open," Grace instructed Windweaver as they dove into the forest's golden shadow.

Open for what? You don't even know what moonweed looks like.

"No, but I'm sure it will have an aura of magic about it," Grace said in a wise and witchlike tone of voice.

Windweaver gave a derisive *crah.*

"It was a full moon last night," Grace said. "I bet it's called moonweed because it grows after a full moon."

What makes you say that?

"I don't know. Just a feeling."

They went to a clearing in the woods that Sareena said became a pond in the winter but was now a marshy meadow. Grace poked around in the long grasses, sometimes humming to herself, sometimes chanting little bits of poetry that were stuck in her head, like the seeds that get stuck in your teeth after eating sun-warmed blackberries.

What would a moonweed look like? Grace wondered as she muttered snatches of poems about the moon. She felt as if she were casting a spell, but then poems often gave her that feeling.

She wondered if she should summon Rum. After all, he *had* agreed to be her servant for three whole years. Maybe he would know what moonweed was—after all, who would be more likely to know about magical plants than a fairy? But then she thought about what he had said about her freckles and how unloved she was, and the surge of anger made her crush a pinecone in her fist. She would *never* summon him.

She brushed aside a clump of ivy, and there, hidden half in shadow, was a patch of moonweed.

Though she'd never seen moonweed before, she knew it right away. The flowers were white—the precise shade of the moon, there was no mistaking it. The petals were crescent-shaped.

If that's not a moonweed, I don't know what is, Windweaver said.

Grace gazed at the forest floor in astonishment—she hadn't

expected to be right. She couldn't wait to show the witch.

The sky darkened as she plucked the flowers, being careful to take only what she needed. Then she felt the telltale *tap-tap* of rain on her face.

She looked up, confused. There hadn't been a single cloud in the sky a moment ago. Now the nearest treetops were clothed in a thick mist.

Grace stifled a cry. It was that cloud again! The one she'd seen from the witch's carriage, and outside her window—she could tell by the size and strangeness of it. It hovered directly above her, turning slowly. She had that strange feeling again, as if the cloud were watching her.

She thought of what the witch had said about the ghost spell—that it could also summon *things that are not quite ghosts.* "Not quite a ghost" seemed like a good way of describing a cloud that stared at you. Had her spell worked after all?

I don't like this, Windweaver said.

"Me neither," Grace replied. "Let's go."

They dashed back through the woods, but the cloud followed. It was raining in earnest now, big wet drops that exploded against the earth. The cloud stirred up the breeze, and poor Windweaver was tossed about, nearly colliding with an oak tree.

"Stop that," Grace shouted at the cloud. They had reached the witch's garden, and Grace whirled around, placing her hands on her hips. Windweaver landed on her shoulder and burrowed into her hair, shaking.

The cloud didn't seem to like being yelled at. It poured even harder, but Grace didn't care.

"Now, you listen to me," she yelled. "I don't know what you are, but you have no business scaring my friends. Keep that up and I'll—"

She stopped. How did one threaten a cloud? What were clouds afraid of? This particular one was a raincloud, and maybe there was something in that.

"I'll blast you all the way to the Arctic," Grace finished triumphantly. "And all your rain will freeze up and you'll have nothing to do but drift around shivering and snowing all over everything. Is that what you want?"

The cloud gave a shudder. It stopped raining and grew so thin that the sun shone right through it. Then the cloud skittered over the trees and was gone.

"I saw that cloud again," Grace told the witch as she sat down at the table. The chicken and onions were stone cold.

"Mmm," the witch said. In a completely unsurprising development, she was stirring that saucepan of hers and ignoring the food on the table. Grace supposed that when witches reached a great and venerable age, they no longer needed to eat ordinary food.

Grace poked at the chicken. She was soaking wet, and there was a *drip-drip-drip* sound beneath her chair.

"It's all right," Grace said. "I scared it real good. I threatened to banish it to the Arctic. Too bad there's no 'For Bothersome

Clouds' spell in the grimoire—"

The witch set down the wooden spoon and turned slowly to face her. "You did *what*?"

Grace gulped. "Well, it was pouring all over me. And poor Windweaver—"

"Do not speak to that cloud again." The witch spoke each word as if it had a period after it. "You will ignore him completely. He is no concern of yours."

"'He'?" Grace repeated. "It's a cloud."

"Once it was a boy." The witch was looking at Grace, but her attention seemed far away. "A very tiresome worrywart of a boy who kept poking his nose into my business."

Grace stared at her in confusion. The witch pursed her lips, then left the room. When she came back, she was holding another grimoire, bigger than the one she had given Grace.

She opened it to a spell near the beginning, which read: *For Nosy Brothers.*

"Oh," Grace breathed. "You—you turned your brother into a *cloud*?"

"I didn't know what I was turning him into," the witch snapped. "I only knew that I wanted him to leave me alone. Patrick was always following me around with that mopey look on his face, warning me that I was going down a dark path, that I should give up magic. It was like being followed by a gloomy raincloud. I only meant to send him away temporarily and scare him a little, but I—well, I couldn't work out how to reverse the spell."

"Poor Patrick," Grace murmured.

"Poor Patrick!" the witch cried. "When we were children, they were burning witches alive. And he wanted me to stop using magic? It was all I had to defend myself! And the only way I could give those horrible men what they deserved." She was stirring rapidly now, spattering droplets of dark liquid from the saucepan that hissed when they hit the stove.

Grace thought this over. She didn't know exactly when people had been in the habit of burning witches alive, but she was pretty sure it was at least two hundred years ago. That meant the witch must be very old, older than Grace had imagined.

"It sounds like your brother was just trying to protect you," Grace said carefully. "I imagine he didn't want you to be burned alive."

"Oh, he was trying to protect me, all right." The witch turned, wiping her hands on her apron and smiling. "But not from those men—from myself. Ha! As if I needed it. I knew exactly what I was doing. This is a dark world, child, full of monsters. But unlike my poor, silly brother, I have never been afraid of the dark. When those men came for me, I was ready. I took their hearts and their bones and put them into my spells. I even took a few fingernails."

Grace was quaking. Shadows swirled at the witch's back, and her eyes were full of them. "F-fingernails?"

"Quite useful, fingernails," the witch said. "For the more advanced spells, of course. You don't need to worry about those now—most likely you never will. Come now, child—why do you look at me like that? Surely you would agree that those men got what they deserved."

"Yes," Grace managed. She was horribly aware of her fingernails in a way she'd never been before. She thought about all the hangnails she'd ever had, and about how having your fingernails stolen must hurt a hundred times worse than the worst hangnail, and then she felt nauseous and wished she hadn't thought any of that. "I expect they did, if they were burning people alive. But there's other stories about you, where you don't hurt just bad men. You tried to bake *me*, after all! And the kids at the orphanage said you like eating children."

"I don't *eat* them. I merely use them for my spells."

"I suppose you think that's better," Grace said with disgust.

"Not particularly," the witch said. "I think it's accurate."

"Well, anyway, you won't be able to do that anymore, if I solve your grimoire." Grace lifted her chin. She realized she had been focusing on what she would lose if she failed—not about the good she would do if she succeeded. How many children would be spared from the witch? Her spirts lifted, and she felt like a heroine again.

"Actually," the witch said, "it's been a while since I've taken a child for one of my spells. When a child goes missing, at least these days, people notice. But there was a time—" She stopped. "Do you know the story of the Flower Children?"

Grace nodded slowly. "The Flower Children" was a story

as famous as "Hansel and Gretel." It was in every book of fairy tales she had ever read.

The story was about sisters who lived beside a wood—a spooky one, naturally. The youngest sister would be playing in the trees, where she would find a meadow of beautiful flowers. She would pick them, of course, and weave them into her hair. Then, in the night, she would sleepwalk into the woods, where the witch would get her. You never saw the witch, or what she did to the girl, though sometimes, if the book had illustrations, you would see a pair of hands reaching out of the darkness. The second sister would make the same mistake—for children in fairy tales were often silly like that, and she too would disappear. The third and eldest sister would set off into the forest to rescue the other two, following a path of flowers. In some tellings, the path led to an enormous rosebush in which her sisters were entangled, and which she set fire to. The sisters slipped free as the witch burned, for she was connected to the rosebush through her magic.

But in the oldest book of fairy tales in the orphanage library, which had a worn leather cover, the witch got the third sister in the end. In that version, the youngest sisters were greedy, but the eldest was even worse—she was rude and arrogant and wild, and those girls were always punished in fairy stories. She tried to kill the witch *and* steal her magic flowers. For that, she was turned into a lily, and that was when she learned that all the flowers in the witch's forest held the souls of stolen children.

"Are you saying the story is about *you?*" Grace said. "You stole those children away?"

She expected the witch to laugh, or possibly brag some more. But the witch only tucked the shadows back into herself and turned away, as if she'd grown tired of scaring Grace. She pressed her arm against her mouth as another coughing fit rattled through her.

"All stories grow and twist over time," the witch said. "It's true that I've always kept a lovely garden. You might want to keep away from the lilies, though."

She set the spoon aside and went up the stairs. "Give that pot a stir before you turn in."

Grace stammered out a *yes ma'am*, her mind too full of the story to be astonished by the witch's request—for she had never even let Grace near the saucepan before—and the witch disappeared upstairs.

15

THE PINECONE WAR

Open here I flung the shutter, when, with many a flirt and flutter,
In there stepped a stately Raven of the saintly days of yore;
Not the least obeisance made he; not a minute stopped or stayed he;
But, with mien of lord or lady, perched above my chamber door . . .
—Edgar Allan Poe, "The Raven"

As soon as she heard the groan of the witch's bed, Grace dashed outside, where twilight slowly drew the darkness across the sky like a quilt. She found the lilies, but they looked like ordinary lilies, so she went back inside and stirred the saucepan. She wondered if the witch had just been trying to scare her.

The saucepan was filled with a dark liquid that slid strangely off the spoon, leaving no trace behind. The witch had left a grimoire on the counter beside the stove, open to the spell she was casting.

For Sleep, the spell read.

Grace wondered who the witch wanted to put to sleep. She

hoped it wasn't her. Perhaps the witch had decided to send Grace to dreamland until May, and when Grace awoke the witch would say, *Ha! Now hand over your magic.*

Still, Grace thought, it was nice to know, at long last, what sort of spell the witch was working on. The grimoire was very unhelpful, though, for it had hardly any instructions. *Simmer ingredients in a pot, stirring as often as possible*, it read.

Grace's eyes drifted over the ingredients. She stirred the saucepan, humming to herself, and added a few more rose petals from a bowl beside the stove. They were "snow roses," apparently, and the instructions said to add the petals "regularly."

She breathed in the steam that floated off the potion. It smelled nice—sweet and sort of creamy. But something was off. It didn't smell like a sleep spell to Grace—it was too *pleasant*, somehow. Sleep could be pleasant, but it could also be fitful or haunted with nightmares.

She thought about it for a while, then scooped up the snow roses and set them in a pot over the fire. The edges began to crisp slightly, and she breathed in the smell. Yes, that was better. She gave the pot a shake, as if she were making popcorn.

Windweaver tapped on the window, and Grace went over to open it. He soared through, feathers disheveled, and buried himself in her hair.

"Oh dear, what's wrong?" Grace said, petting his head. "Was it the cloud again? His name is Patrick, and apparently—"

No, he said sullenly. *It's* them.

There came a squawking sound from outside, and a black shape darted past the window. Grace gave an angry huff. "Are they bullying you again?"

He made no reply, but he didn't need to. Poor Windweaver was bullied by other crows wherever he went. They sensed that he was different and ganged up to torment him—even though he was kind to them and brought them food and shiny trinkets to make peace.

"I've had it up to *here* with bullies," Grace said. "First that dreadful Poppy and now this. I won't have it."

She strode outside. The crows were loitering in the apple tree beside the cottage, making a great racket. Grace stomped her foot to get their attention.

"Clear out!" she yelled at them. "That's right, I mean *you*. You're not welcome here. This is Windweaver's home, and if you can't be nice to him, you can leave!"

The crows paused for a moment, as if taken aback. Then they took up their jabbering again. One of the bigger ones alighted in the neighboring fir tree and plucked a pinecone. He took flight and dropped it on Grace's head.

"Why, you stinker!" The pinecone hadn't hurt, of course, but now she was hopping mad. "Get out of here! I can hex you, you know!"

The crow gave a derisive *squawk*. The others picked up on the game and plucked pinecones of their own, though not everyone got the point and most simply dropped them on the grass below the tree.

"That's how you want it, is it?" Grace picked up a handful of pinecones and threw them at the crows. "Go away! Get!"

I think we should go back inside, Windweaver said from his burrow in her hair.

"I'm not letting them have their way," Grace snapped. And because she had to yell *something* at the crows to scare them off, why not yell something interesting?

"Ungainly fowl!" she cried. "Ghastly, gaunt, and ominous birds of yore—"

Another pinecone bounced off her head. She threw it right back and kept on yelling Edgar Allan Poe at them. She did love "The Raven." Windweaver hated the poem, calling it offensive to ravens and all other birds of that family. And perhaps the crows in the treetops saw things in the same light, for they started to make an ungodly ruckus, squawking and *crah*-ing and rattling the boughs.

"Take—thy form—from off—my door!" Grace shouted between throws. Windweaver let out a groan.

"How does the next part go? Oh yes. Get thee back into the tempest!" she hollered.

Crah! returned the crows defiantly, dropping another pinecone on her head.

Now, by this point, Grace was thoroughly enjoying herself. A little breeze had come up, which made her skirt billow, and it was twilight, that haunted time of day that was the perfect time to shout furious poetry at people—or, in this case, birds. Indeed, she was so captivated by the effect she was having on herself (for she didn't seem to be having much effect on the crows, alas) that she didn't notice the smoke wafting out of the open door behind her. Only when she heard the witch come thundering down the stairs, and then a string of curses, did she turn.

"The roses!" she yelped.

The roses indeed. The kitchen was filled with smoke and a sour burnt-flowers smell. The witch snatched the pot off the fire and threw it into the sink, then ran her hand under cold water.

"I'm so sorry," Grace babbled. "I didn't mean—I only thought if I—"

"Be silent."

The words cut through her like a knife. The witch gave her a look of such venom that it rooted her to the spot.

"Do you know how rare snow roses are?" The witch's voice was so quiet that Grace had to strain to hear it. "How difficult to come by? Only the most skillful witches can see them. They grow only in the winter, and as you have burned the entirety of my supply, my spell is ruined. I will not know a restful night from now until December."

The realization sank in slowly. "Then—then that spell was for *you*?"

The witch opened her mouth to reply, but all that came out was more coughing. It was worse than before, a terrible, wet sound that rattled in her chest.

Of course it's for her, Grace thought numbly. How had she not guessed it before? The witch's cough would keep anybody awake.

"I'm sorry," she whispered.

The witch turned away from the saucepan, closing her eyes briefly. Then she went unsteadily up the stairs. She had always looked like a grandmother—when she wasn't a monstrous shadow, of course. But now she simply looked old.

"I will deal with you in the morning," she said over her shoulder, and then she was gone.

Naturally, Grace was in a state after that.

What would the witch do with her in the morning? Throw her out? Shove her in the oven again? There were so many unpleasant possibilities.

She paced the kitchen for a while, then opened a window to let the smoke out. The twilight floated in, wonderfully cool. Slowly, she felt her heart return to its ordinary pace.

She scooped up a handful of the snow rose petals that the witch had tossed in the sink. They smelled dreadful, and were so burnt that they crumbled to a fine powder at the lightest touch.

The witch had left the potion on the stove. Grace gave it a stir, thinking. If it was worthless now, it wouldn't matter what she did with it.

She smelled the rose petals again. Something told her that

a teaspoon would do, so she ground up the petals and dropped them in.

Immediately, the potion changed from a murky brown to pure black, black as a starless night. Grace gasped. She seized the wooden spoon, hoping that somehow, stirring would fix this new mess, but the liquid stayed that strange black color.

Oh well. It wasn't as if you could ruin something twice. She set aside the spoon with a sigh, then motioned to Windweaver, who had been watching from the top of one of the cabinets, and he alighted on her shoulder. Wearily, she put herself to bed.

16

DREAM MAGIC

The sun rose while I slept. I had not yet risen
When I heard an early oriole above the roof of my house.
Suddenly it was like the Royal Park at dawn,
With birds calling from the branches of the ten-thousand-year trees.
—Po Chü-i, "Hearing the Early Oriole"

Grace rose very early the next morning, a Saturday, and crept around her bedroom like a mouse as she dressed. She planned to be well out of the witch's way when she awoke. Grace knew she couldn't avoid the witch forever, but perhaps if she gave her time to cool down, she wouldn't—well, eat her.

Or curse her.

Or turn her into a cloud.

There really were *far* too many possibilities.

Grace went very carefully down the stairs, avoiding all the creaky spots she could remember. Then, holding her skirts up to her knees to prevent rustling, she heron-stepped her way into the darkened kitchen on tiptoes—where she presented a

153

very silly picture to the witch, who was already seated at the table.

"G-good morning," Grace squeaked. "Um. I thought I would—ah, help you with breakfast."

She had intended nothing of the sort and had, in fact, been planning to slip off to the woods to work on the grimoire. The witch gave Grace an exasperated look that filled her with hope. There was no murder in that look, which was a definite improvement over yesterday.

"You will tell me precisely what you did to my spell," the witch said.

"Your—" Grace's gaze drifted to the saucepan on the stove, which was still bubbling away. "I—I'm sorry. I thought that, as it was already ruined, it wouldn't matter if I—"

"You put more rose petals in," the witch said. "Why? And for that matter, what led you to burn them in the first place, you little catastrophe?"

Grace tried to gather her scattered thoughts into some sort of defense. In the end, she gave up and just answered honestly. "The spell was missing something before."

The witch gave her a long look. "And what is this?" She tapped the satchel Grace had left on the table, which was full of the moonweed she had picked the day before.

"Um—moonweed?" Grace said. Her nervousness, as usual, led her to babble. "At least, I think it's moonweed. Doesn't it look like just the sort of flower that might fall from the moon? Not that flowers grow on the moon, of course, for I've seen it through an old spyglass donated to the orphanage, and it seems quite a bony, barren place, unless of course the flowers there are accustomed to such conditions. I read once that desert flowers—"

"Stop talking," the witch said. "Where did you find it? How long did you search?"

Grace stumbled over the story, trying very hard not to babble, though the witch, who sat drumming her sharp fingernails against the table, didn't make it easy. Grace didn't think she would ever look at fingernails the same way again.

"You found moonweed on your first attempt," the witch muttered, as if to herself. "And you sensed a missing component in a second-order spell."

Grace didn't know what any of that meant, but she was too nervous to ask. The witch watched her with an unreadable expression. "How old are you?"

Grace realized it was the first time the witch had asked her age. "Twelve."

"Hmmph." This was delivered in a moody tone, though Grace couldn't guess the mood in question. "Well. Get out of my sight, child."

Hardly believing her good luck, Grace hurried to do as the witch said. She paused to scoop up two of the scones cooling on a rack. The witch had never in Grace's history of living at the cottage awoken early to bake. Grace froze with one hand on the door as the witch spoke again.

"I slept well last night." *Drum, drum, drum* went those

fingernails. "Better, in fact, than I have in years."

Grace sucked in her breath. So the sleep spell *had* worked—she had fixed it! Did this mean she was better at magic than the witch? Surely not, since she was barely muddling through the witch's simplest grimoire, but clearly she was better at *some* spells. She hadn't made a mess of things after all—what a relief!

Grace knew she would not be able to hold back her grin for long, and she also knew that it would only make things worse if the witch thought she was gloating, so she simply took herself out of the witch's sight.

That was the start of a very strange time in the witch's house.

A few days later, Grace tromped inside for dinner. She was in a good mood, as she and Sareena had successfully cast two more spells at the Keep. She showed the results to the witch for approval: red roses she had turned an oily ebony (spell number nine, "For Black Roses") and two pebbles stuck fast together, as if by cement (spell number ten, "For Making One from Two"). That was ten whole spells they'd finished now! It was a big dent in the grimoire, though Sareena kept warning her that they still had to work faster. September was nearly over, and even if they managed to cast ten more spells every month, they wouldn't finish by May *or* June.

The witch nodded and turned back to serving dinner—roast beef and corn cakes, and a raisin pudding for dessert (with ice cream, naturally). It was a more elaborate meal than usual, and Grace's mouth watered at the smell.

The witch set Grace's plate down abruptly and said, "Children are very expensive to keep. We have a pact, yes, but I don't see why that should excuse you from housework. Of course, the chores I have in mind are magical ones, and since it seems that you are not completely useless in that area, you will assist me when I need an extra pair of hands."

The witch glared, seeming to expect Grace to argue. But Grace thought it a fair request. There was only one thing that worried her.

"But then how will I have time for our pact?" she said. If the witch kept Grace busy with her own spells, Grace couldn't work on the grimoire. Her good mood suddenly faded. Last night she'd dreamed about her magic draining away, leaving her as empty as a rain barrel with a hole in the bottom.

"You needn't look at me like that. I will not require your help very often," the witch said grudgingly. "You may say no if you find it is delaying your progress with the grimoire."

Grace nodded, relieved. "All right. Is there a spell you are working on now?"

The witch blinked, as if surprised Grace had given in without more protests. She had been looking healthier lately. She still had that terrible cough, but it had eased a little, and she moved more lightly than before.

"Yes," she said, looking away. "The foundation of the cottage is beginning to crumble, and the roof has a leak. You will help with the repairs."

"Oh, I'd be happy to help with *that*," Grace said. "I was

worried you'd say you wanted me to help you summon a plague of wasps or turn one of your enemies inside out. But I would do anything for the cottage—absolutely anything. It's home, after all." She began sawing at her roast beef. "You know, I think that might be my favorite word. *Home*. It's so round and soft and comfortable to say, isn't it? I've hardly ever had reason to use it in my life, given that I've never had a home before. Sometimes I wonder how many beautiful words there are in the world that I shall miss out on because my life has been different from other people's."

Frowning slightly, the witch turned away, and Grace tucked into her food. As she ate, she chattered about her progress with the spells, and about school, where she was learning cursive letters—what a bitter disappointment, when she had hoped to be learning about foreign lands and strange and wonderful science, to instead have to content herself with learning how to stick letters together, which seemed useful only for making things harder to read. She also told the witch all about her feud with Poppy, who had yet to strike back after the scullion incident but who still spent at least half of each school day glaring at her menacingly. Grace had become convinced that Poppy was glaring specifically at her nose, though Sareena said it was just Grace's imagination.

The witch stirred away at the saucepan. She had been much less prickly since the sleep spell, though Grace often had the sense that she was being ignored. Her suspicion was confirmed when she asked if the witch had any spells for scaring crows and the witch turned around and said, "I want you to gather three dreams."

Grace forgot to chew. "Gather—what?" she said around a mouthful of pudding and ice cream.

"That repair spell for the foundation requires nine dreams," the witch said. "I have only a half dozen in the pantry. You will gather the rest."

Grace swallowed. She was beginning to understand, but she didn't want to. "Magic uses *dreams*?"

The witch scowled. "Are you that inattentive, child? The grimoire I gave you contains a dozen spells that call for dreams."

Grace looked away. She still hadn't read half the spells in the grimoire—beyond spell number twenty-five or so, they became extremely confusing, with contradictory if not impossible instructions, like dreaded spell forty-four, which called for the ridiculous "pitcher of midnight."

Her stomach instantly twisted in knots at the thought of that spell.

"But that—isn't that black magic?" Grace said. "Stealing dreams, I mean."

"There is no such thing as black magic," the witch said. "There is only magic. I suppose that a witch may content herself with spells that call for flowers and cobwebs and the like. Small spells, simple spells—first-order spells, they're called. Spells to stop hiccups or turn roses black. But the big spells, the second-order spells . . . those require sacrifice."

"Someone else's sacrifice, you mean," Grace blurted, thinking not just of dreams but of bones and fingernails and the like. She bit her lip, but the witch didn't look angry.

"Yes," she said. "Magic is part of nature, and nature—well, it is not always kind. But in this case, what's the harm in taking a dream or two? How often do you remember your dreams, child?"

Grace could see her point, though her unease didn't go away. "How do you even go about gathering dreams, anyway?"

"It's the easiest thing in the world," the witch said. "You simply go to sleep. Oh, and one more thing. I would prefer you to gather children's dreams—those have the best effect." And with that, she turned back to her saucepan.

17

A NOSE IS IN DANGER

The gander and the gray, gray goose,
She drove them all together;
Her cheeks were rose, her gold hair loose,
All in the wild gray weather.
—Edith Nesbit, "The Goose-Girl"

Grace spent the next morning helping the witch with the roof repair spell. It was an awkward one; she had to climb up the apple tree next to the cottage with a pot and a brush and paint funny symbols on the roof. The paint was a strange, claylike potion that smelled of death and looked like mashed insects. Windweaver took one sniff and launched himself up into the treetops, where he could keep a distant eye on Grace but stay out of range of the fumes. She hoped the spell wouldn't take long, not just because of the smell, but also because she had an idea for spell number eleven in the grimoire that she was dying to discuss with Sareena. And now, of course, they would also have to figure out a way to steal dreams, in addition to filling a pitcher with midnight and all the rest of it.

Her head was beginning to ache.

"Is it working?" the witch called from the ground.

Grace stuck her head off the side of the roof. "What is this stuff? It stinks!"

"It doesn't matter what it smells like, you fool."

Grace slopped more of the potion onto the roof, trying hard not to splash. "I think potions should always smell nice. See, the roof doesn't like it."

There was a great *whoosh*, and suddenly the witch was standing beside her, having dissolved into a tower of shadow and lunged onto the roof. Grace shrieked and almost fell off.

"Stop dillydallying and get to work," the witch snarled, shadows fluttering around her like ribbons. "That leak needs to be patched up. I have a number of souvenirs from my travels in the attic, and I don't want them getting wet."

Grace was shaking all over. In that moment, she almost wanted to leap off the roof just to get away from the witch. "I'm not dillydallying. I don't think the roof likes the potion."

She motioned at the mossy roof and the symbols she had painted. They weren't sticking very well—several had already dissolved. To Grace's eye, the roof *did* look irritated—the sag in the middle had grown worse since she started.

The witch pressed a hand to her eyes. "The *roof* has no opinion. Of all the harebrained, irrational—"

"It's a witch's cottage, though," Grace said. "Why would it

be rational?"

Though she was half convinced she was inches away from being blasted to bits, Grace climbed back down the apple tree and took the witch's potion into the garden. She mixed in a generous helping of lavender buds, and then she went into the witch's pantry for rose water. When she was finished, the potion smelled—well, not exactly pleasant; more like something unpleasant was being hidden, like a rug covering a stain. But anything was better than what the potion had smelled like before.

She went back up to the roof. The witch had been following her the whole time, muttering about how Grace had surely ruined her potion. Grace heard the word *oven* several times, an empty threat but still extremely unpleasant. But then she began painting the symbols again, tracing over the old ones she had done, and they stuck much better now. The witch grew quieter and quieter.

Eventually, she disappeared again. When she reappeared, she said, "The leak has stopped. Thank you."

These two words seemed to take such effort for the witch to get out that Grace wondered if she had ever thanked anybody in her life. They went back into the cottage and the witch baked chocolate crinkles. Grace happily munched her way through a dozen. The witch, while an indifferent cook, was an excellent baker.

"What was that potion made from, anyway?" Grace said, dunking a crinkle in her tea.

"Oh, this and that," the witch said. Now that her precious souvenirs were safe, she seemed almost merry. "Ground-up flies, for one. Mud from a stagnant pond. Thistledown. Teeth. Tears shed during a full moon by a one-eyed woman with—"

"*Teeth?*" Grace repeated, choking on a crinkle. "Human teeth?"

"Naturally. Many second-order spells call for teeth. They're quite powerful."

Grace pushed her plate away. "Do—do witches get them from graveyards?"

"You certainly *can*," the witch said. "It's much more work that way, though." She turned and gave Grace something that was almost a smile. "If you manage to complete my grimoire and become my apprentice, you'll learn just how useful teeth are."

This had a confusing effect upon Grace. On the one hand, she was delighted that the witch had actually spoken about Grace becoming her apprentice, the first time she'd ever done so. On the other hand—teeth.

"The foundation still needs fixing, so don't forget about my dreams," the witch said as Grace's stomach twisted. The witch plunked another plate of cookies on the table and added heartily, "Eat up!"

"Dreams?" Sareena repeated. "Is she serious?"

"Unfortunately," Grace said.

They were in the barn the following weekend, milking poor Buckley. The cow had not gotten over her embarrassment at having her milk turned to ice cream, and often tried to kick over the bucket. Sareena and Grace had to move quickly to grab it the moment they saw her hoof twitch.

"Just say you can't do it," Sareena said. "It wasn't part of your pact, so she can't throw you out or anything."

Grace heaved a sigh. "It's not that simple. The witch *likes* me now. I don't want to disappoint her."

Sareena snorted. "Really, Grace. She's far too wicked to like anyone."

"Well, maybe. But she dislikes me less than she dislikes other people, and isn't that something?"

It was true. Now that the witch had decided Grace was a proper witch who, if she was able to keep her magic, would one day be murdering people in various ghastly ways, she seemed to have warmed to her. Grace knew she should admit that she had no intention of murdering anyone or stealing teeth for spells, but she was too happy that the witch had stopped hating her to raise the subject.

Sareena scooped some ice cream into a bowl and went to give it to Daisy Bean, who was being invisible behind a bale of hay.

"Wherever did Daisy Bean go?" Sareena said loudly. "Oh dear, she must have wandered off again."

Muffled giggles from the bale of hay. Sareena gave a dramatic sigh, then left the bowl on the floor. A small and stealthy hand reached out and dragged it out of sight.

Sareena went back to Buckley and dipped her spoon into

the bucket. "Have you managed to steal any dreams at all?"

"Of course not!" Last night, Grace had fallen asleep as she usually did, reading poetry with Windweaver. He had requested a very long poem called "The Rime of the Ancient Mariner" by a troubled Englishman called Coleridge. Windweaver didn't often ask for "The Rime of the Ancient Mariner" because the bird in that poem—a huge albatross— got shot by a sailor for no reason at all. Though Windweaver did enjoy hearing how awfully the sailor was punished for it afterward. The other sailors made him wear the dead bird around his neck like a horrible scarf, and that wasn't even the worst of it.

Grace had awoken in the morning without any dreams, either in her pockets or trapped in the empty jar she had set hopefully beside her bed. (Did dreams keep in jars? She had no idea.)

"The witch didn't tell me what to do," she said plaintively.

"She did. She told you to go to sleep."

"That's useless." Grace moodily squirted more ice cream into the bucket. "That's like saying 'go to the kitchen' when someone asks you how to bake a cake. They'd end up staring at the oven, scratching their head. There's got to be more to it than that."

"Maybe not," Sareena said thoughtfully. "After all, you didn't need anybody to tell you how to find moonweed. Or how to fix that sleep spell. You just *knew*. I think magic must come naturally to witches. It's like how I learned to swim last summer. Nobody told me how, I just worked it out."

Grace sighed. "But magic isn't always guesswork. Look at all those instructions in the grimoire."

"And who wrote that grimoire?" Sareena said. "Who figured out that you need three pieces of ivy for the 'For Black Roses' spell? The witch did. Once you're the witch's apprentice, you'll learn how to invent your own spells."

"*If* I become the witch's apprentice," Grace said darkly. Her favorite month, October, had arrived at last, and the world was awash in orange and gold and things that crunched underfoot. But as lovely as it all was, it was also terrifying, for it meant that Grace was another month closer to the witch's deadline. Every time she saw leaves falling, she thought of that hourglass again.

"Oh, look," Sareena said suddenly. "It's Rum, from school."

Grace whirled. Rum was leaning against the door of the shed, looking very fancy in his spidersilk fairy tunic and a cloak woven from autumn leaves, which matched the red and yellow of his crown. He wasn't even *trying* to look like an ordinary boy, the way he did at school.

"Are you in a play?" Sareena asked.

Grace groaned, and then she explained to Sareena—for the hundredth time—about Rum being a fairy and how they had a bargain. Oh, she was tired of repeating herself.

"What do you want?" Grace snapped at Rum. "I didn't summon you."

"I can do what I like." Grace raised her eyebrows, and he

went red. "Not that I *like* you. I was bored, that's all."

"You're always turning up out of nowhere," Grace said. "Are you *following* me?"

For some reason, he went even redder. "As if I don't have better things to do!"

Grace rolled her eyes and went back to her milking. "Well, where did you go? You haven't been in school all week."

"Haven't I?" He shrugged. "I didn't notice. Time moves differently in Faerie."

"Hmmph," Grace said. "Well, since you're here, you can help me and Sareena figure out this nonsense about spells that—"

"Oh no." He held up his hands with their long fairy fingers. "I don't want anything to do with witch magic."

"Relax," Grace said. "I'm not putting a spell on you. But as you're a magical creature, you must be able to give magical advice. That's logical, isn't it?"

Sareena nodded. Rum said suspiciously, "I s'pose so."

"Well then. How would you go about stealing a dream from somebody?"

"I wouldn't," he said scornfully. "What a waste of time! What on earth would I do with some silly human dream?"

"Well, use it in a spell, of course—"

Rum just laughed, and when Grace tried asking more questions, he laughed at those, too. In truth, Grace was quite interested in the differences between witch magic and fairy magic, but Rum was very mysterious about it, and the one time she'd asked the witch, the witch had replied that the differences didn't matter, for she made it her business to avoid fairies, who were nothing but mischief and trouble wrapped up in bones and skin, and if Grace had any brains at all, she'd do the same.

Grace shook her head. She truly was surrounded by the most unhelpful people.

"Try again tonight, Grace," Sareena said in a soothing voice. "Maybe you'll work it out."

Grace forced a wan smile of agreement. The witch hadn't specified what she'd do to Grace if she didn't bring her any dreams—which, when you thought about it, was worse than actually knowing.

"In the meantime," Sareena went on, "we should gather the ingredients for spells twelve to fifteen. Rum can help."

Rum stood up straight, looking self-important. "Of course. As long as I can be far away when you cast your next spell."

Grace scowled at him. He was still trying to get her to forgive him, Grace knew, but she wasn't having it. Still, she couldn't deny that she and Sareena needed as much help as they could get. They were still behind schedule.

"Fine," she said. Then she told Rum the list of ingredients they were looking for. To cast spells twelve to fifteen, they would need:

- 17 dandelion heads
- 17 handfuls of dandelion seeds
- 2 bushels of wild apples

- 45 flowers from a plant called "common witch's helper"
- 3 cups of pink lady's slipper
- 12 cups of wild pigeon berries
- 70 inkcap mushrooms
- 23 pinecones (10 white pine, 5 red pine, 1 from something called a "dwarf honey pine," 7 unspecified)
- 3 buckets of rainwater
- 3 hairs from a squirrel's tail
- 1 set of rat's teeth
- 15 cobwebs
- 1 pint of milk from a goat born under a full moon

"That's a lot for one day," Rum said.

"We need it all," Sareena said, a stern note in her voice, "if Grace is to get through that grimoire by May."

Rum picked up the baskets Sareena had set by the door next to several sacks and jars. "I can pick the apples. There's an abandoned orchard a mile or two from here."

"You can't use magic to help you," Grace warned him. She had a strong suspicion that the witch would know if there was fairy magic mixed up in one of the spells, and that she wouldn't be happy about it.

He grimaced. Grace guessed that fairies weren't much used to manual labor.

"The goat's milk will be the trickiest bit," Sareena said.

"What's it for?" Rum asked.

"Spell thirteen," Sareena said. "'For Lightning.' My father

has three goats, but we don't know if any were born under a full moon."

Rum shrugged. "I can tell you that."

Sareena's eyes widened. "You can?"

"Sure. That sort of thing's dead obvious." Rum shook his head as he flicked through the grimoire. "Why would anybody *want* lightning, anyway?"

"Well," Grace began, then stopped. Secretly she had imagined herself standing dramatically on a hilltop at night, cloak billowing, while lightning flashed all around her. She had to admit, though, that this wasn't a very practical use.

"To kill somebody, I suppose," Sareena said. She slashed her hand down. "Split them right in half."

"Lots of ways to kill people that don't involve setting the forest on fire," Rum said. So *that* was what he was worried about.

"We're not setting the forest on fire," Grace said. At least, she was fairly certain they weren't. "Come on, let's get to work."

Sareena nodded. "Let's Rum and I visit the goats first. Then we'll walk over to the apple orchard. You and Daisy Bean can look for plants in the forest."

Grace was grateful for Sareena's efficiency, though she couldn't help feeling that Rum had been right—it *was* a lot to get done in one day. And yet Sareena was right, too—they had to hurry.

Grace's stomach began its worried gurgling yet again. More and more, she had been wondering if *hurrying* would be enough. After all, no amount of hurrying would allow her to walk to Australia in a day. The plain cold truth of the matter was that a hundred and a half spells was a lot to finish by May-maybe-June. Was it even possible?

Sareena paused at the door of the barn. "Gosh, I sure hope Daisy Bean turns up," she said loudly. "And I hope she doesn't follow Grace into the woods—Grace is on witch business. It's very secret and not something a little girl should see."

"Definitely not," Grace agreed. "It's too bad, though, that Daisy Bean isn't here. She's the best at finding pinecones."

Sareena gave her a grin, then she and Rum headed off toward the Khalil farm.

Grace took the rest of Buckley's ice cream to the cellar, then headed into the forest, trailed by a small green shadow. Whenever she glanced over her shoulder, the shadow would curl into a ball, drawing the blanket around itself, and might have passed for a mossy rock but for the hair sticking out at the top. Occasionally, this very helpful shadow would stop below an evergreen and scoop fallen pinecones into a sack.

Grace set her sights on the "common witch's helper." This was clearly another type of magical plant, but unlike moon-weed, it was hard to imagine what it might look like.

She called Windweaver, who—as usual when she had company over—had been lurking in the nearby trees, and asked him to go looking for the rat's teeth and squirrel hairs. Dandelions were always easy to come by, of course, and within an hour Grace had gathered all she needed.

"Witch's helper," she muttered. "Witch's helper."

She tried to guess what it might look like. She thought it would probably be covered in prickles. And she had a strong sense that any plant called "witch's helper" would grow in the darkness. After all, didn't the witch hide herself away in her cottage, only going into town when absolutely necessary? Her feet took her deeper into the forest, to a birch grove she'd always considered a spooky, haunted sort of place, those trees the color of bone all whispering to one another.

Keeping her eyes on the ground, she went even deeper, to where there were no natural paths at all, only a dense tangle of underbrush.

There!

She saw it out of the corner of her eye first. It was a surprisingly ordinary little plant, with tiny white flowers tucked among a mass of twiggy stems and teardrop-shaped leaves. As with the moonweed, Grace knew instantly that it was witch's helper, as if the plant had told her.

She could see no thorns, but when she picked one of the flowers, she gasped. Tiny drops of blood formed on her fingertips. The plant had hidden thorns, pointed downward, which only pricked when you pulled at it.

Grace touched one of the white flowers. To her astonishment, it drifted free and hovered in the air, glowing faintly like a will-o'-the-wisp. She brushed her hand over a cluster of the flowers, and they rose into the air like bees. They bobbed gently, as if waiting for instructions.

Witch's helper indeed!

She pulled out a pocketknife and began cutting the stems. She was so intent on her task that she didn't notice the sound of leaves rustling behind her, nor the snap of a twig.

She had forty-five flowers, but she decided to count again, just to be sure. As she did, the little orbs flickered. They nudged her cheek and lifted strands of her hair, trying to pull her head back. She waved them away, annoyed.

Snap.

Grace froze. The orbs kept on snatching at her hair—they seemed to be *pointing*. Slowly, she turned.

A pair of strong arms wrapped around her waist and tackled her to the ground. Grace screamed as she tumbled over bushes and branches and mud and prickly weeds. Her attacker let out a grunt as their head hit a stump, and Grace realized the voice was familiar.

It was Poppy.

Grace shrieked, shoving her away. Poppy responded with a punch that Grace only just dodged, and her fist glanced off a tree. She let out a curse.

Grace scrambled to her feet, desperate to run away. But she was all banged up from tumbling through the forest, and the trees were spinning.

The older girl dragged herself to her feet. She was clutching her hand and glaring at Grace as if it was her fault she'd punched the tree. "I told you I'd smack you in the nose, Spots. Well, now I'm going to do worse."

And just as that horribly mysterious threat was sinking in, a pinecone came whizzing out of the forest with deadly accuracy, hitting Poppy square in the face.

For a moment, Grace thought fuzzily that the crows had forgiven her and come to her aid like a knight in a story, but then she saw a familiar green shape dart out of the underbrush.

Daisy Bean drew back her arm and threw another pinecone. *THWACK!* it went against Poppy's head.

"Get out of here, runt," Poppy said. She marched over and shoved Daisy Bean so hard that Daisy Bean rolled end over end and one of her shoes went flying. Daisy Bean pushed herself up on her hands, too stunned to cry, a streak of mud on her round cheek.

"You—you *bully!*" Grace cried. The sight of Daisy Bean, less than half Poppy's size, sprawled across the grass kindled her temper. A swirl of wind wrapped around her, lifting the leaves from the forest floor in a beautiful bright whirlwind. Poppy stood frozen and wary, eyes darting from Grace to the leaves. Daisy Bean quite sensibly drew her blanket around herself and crawled behind a tree.

"What's going on?" Poppy demanded. "Is that—is that magic?"

The other kids at school were still whispering about Grace being a witch, but Grace could see that Poppy, like many of them, hadn't really believed it.

Well, she'd believe it now.

Grace spread her arms. "I am an all-powerful sorceress,"

she proclaimed in a loud and melancholy voice. "And all sorceresses hate bullies." Not true, for the witch was quite the bully, but it sounded right. "You must depart my forest forthwith and never return, or I shall—"

BOOM!

Her threats were interrupted by a crash of thunder. Astonished, she craned her neck to look at the sky, but then she realized the thunder was something she should be taking credit for. She lifted her arms again and glared at Poppy, whose eyes were buggy.

"That's right!" Grace cried as another peal of thunder rang out. What a convenient storm! "Leave now, or I shall—I shall bring that tree down upon your head!"

Poppy had been backing up until she collided with a tree. She let out a shriek and started away from it.

Then the sky opened, and it began to pour—*really* pour. It was as if a thousand rain barrels had been emptied over the birch grove.

Only the birch grove, Grace realized. Just a few yards away, there was pure sunlight.

Poppy began to shriek. The rain was so fierce that the shriek came out a bit—burbly.

"Patrick!" Grace hollered at the sky in desperation, though she was half laughing. "That's enough!"

"Grace!" Sareena's voice called. "Daisy Bean! Where are you?"

"Over here!" Grace shouted back.

Sareena and Rum came sprinting through the birches, their feet going *smuck-smuck* over the now muddy ground. They each carried a basket full of apples over their backs.

"What on earth are you doing?" Sareena cried, holding her hands above her face.

"It's not me!" Grace waved her arms at the sky. "Patrick! Cut it out!"

Fortunately, Patrick seemed to hear this time, or maybe he was just running out of rain. He gave one last rumble of thunder, and the downpour slowed to a few fat drops.

Grace turned to Poppy. She had stopped screaming and stood against the tree with her mouth hanging open, her hair flattened to her head and a cascade of water running down her nose.

"Thanks," Grace said to the cloud wonderingly.

Patrick gave a low rumble of thunder.

"Daisy Bean!" Sareena raced to her sister's side. Fortunately, the little girl had hidden beneath a log and was only slightly damp.

"Did she hurt you?" Rum demanded.

Grace nodded. "She pushed Daisy Bean, too."

Rum's face darkened. He walked toward Poppy, and as he did, the ivy carpeting the forest floor began to rustle and slither like snakes. It curled around Poppy's ankles, then her knees. Then the ivy gave a sharp tug and Poppy fell into the pool of leaves.

She let out a muffled shriek, her hands flailing desperately, like someone drowning. Grace ran forward—for the first time, she was afraid of Rum. "Rum, stop!"

He glared. The ivy fell back a bit, and Grace was able to pull Poppy through the whispering leaves. She was shaking and taking great gasps of air. To calm her down, Grace gave her one of the apples. Poppy stared at it as if she'd never seen an apple before.

"Well done," Grace said to Rum. "You've scared her witless."

Rum snorted. "How much wit did she have to begin with?"

"Shall I tie her up?" Sareena asked. Then, not waiting for an answer, as usual, she began plucking ivy from the forest floor to tie Poppy up with.

"No," Grace said.

"She was going to beat you up bad, Grace," Sareena said. "That's why she came here."

"I know," Grace said. Part of her was happy about what had happened to Poppy, and would have been even happier to let Rum drown her in ivy again. But that part of her was the bullying part, and she would rather climb back into the witch's oven than become a bully. "But she's changed her mind about that. Particularly where my nose is concerned. Haven't you, Poppy?"

Poppy nodded frantically. "You're—" She stopped, took a shaky breath. "You're not going to curse me?"

"No."

Poppy looked amazed. Well, of course she did. Grace had

seen how Poppy picked on the little kids at By-the-Sea School. In Poppy's head, if you were stronger, that gave you the right to stomp all over everybody else.

"Go home," she told Poppy. "And don't *ever* hurt me or my friends again," she added with a glare.

Poppy nodded once more, her eyes still wide, and they left her there in the mud.

18

TO BOTTLE THE WIND

Wrens and robins in the hedge,
Wrens and robins here and there;
Building, perching, pecking, fluttering,
Everywhere!
—Christina Rossetti, "Wrens and Robins in the
Hedge"

To Grace's annoyance, Poppy didn't go home. She trailed after them through the forest, eavesdropping on their conversation. It was difficult to ignore her, for she was clumsy and heavy-footed and made a dreadful noise in the underbrush.

"What are we going to do with her?" Sareena muttered.

"I could cover her in ivy again," Rum said.

"No," Grace said. "Just leave her be. She'll lose interest eventually."

But she was wrong about this, too. And when Sareena finally found a patch of inkcap mushrooms flourishing in a little marshy area, Poppy helped pick them. Despite her general clumsiness, Poppy's hands were graceful and quick.

For the next few days, Poppy followed Grace and Sareena home after school. They grimly ignored her, and even tried giving her the slip sometimes. But Poppy always caught up to them. One day, Grace noticed Daisy Bean showing her how to gather acorns.

"This is getting ridiculous," Sareena said.

Grace sighed. "Maybe we should put her to work. She's obviously keen to help."

"No way! She's *horrid*. Just this morning, she pushed poor Gavin Carpenter into a bucket."

Grace waved the grimoire. "We're still behind, remember? We need all the help we can get."

Sareena blew out a breath, but she couldn't very well argue with something she'd been warning Grace about for weeks. That afternoon, while Grace and Sareena cast spell number twenty at the Keep, Grace sent Poppy into the forest to harvest birch bark. It was one of the more tedious jobs, but Poppy didn't give a word of complaint, and returned with a full basket.

"What is it?" Sareena said in a suspicious voice as they trooped back to the cottage. She and Grace were both shivering in their damp coats and eager to dry off by the fire.

Grace blinked. "What?"

"You're quiet," she said. "It's always a bad sign when you're quiet."

"I was just thinking," Grace said. "Poppy's given me an idea."

"Poppy?"

"Yes. She was a big help today. And Rum found us those apples. And then there's Daisy Bean—she can find almost anything in the woods."

Sareena still looked suspicious. "And?"

"And," Grace said, as a smile spread across her face, "I think I know how we can get through the grimoire faster."

"Oh no," Sareena said. "Please tell me you're joking, Grace. *Her?*"

Priscilla folded her arms. "Good morning to you too, Sareena. I hope your family is well."

Sareena rolled her eyes. Grace couldn't blame her—Priscilla talked as if she was a duchess making conversation over a cup of tea.

It was the following Saturday, the first of November, a cold and clear morning after days of rain. All the harvest had been gathered in Brook-by-the-Sea, and many of the trees were barren or clinging to the last of their autumn finery. Sareena, Daisy Bean, Poppy, Priscilla, and Grace were standing under the old cherry tree, the dreaded cherry tree, the cherry tree of doom, frowning at each other.

"We talked about this," Grace reminded Sareena. "So far we've only cracked twenty-two spells. That's still only about ten a month. We need to work more quickly if we're to finish by May. And we can, if we have extra hands. I think we can trust Priscilla—that's why I told her everything."

Priscilla beamed at Grace.

"You can't trust her at all!" Sareena said. "She'll run off and tell all our secrets to her dozens of friends. Do you want everyone knowing you're a witch?"

Grace bit her lip. Truthfully, the main reason she had brought Priscilla into the group was because she was the only other person at school who had ever spoken to her. It wasn't a very good reason to trust someone, Grace knew, but given the desperate circumstances—her looming failure with the grimoire and the loss of her magic—she had decided to risk it. Also, she had often noticed at the orphanage that popular girls seemed to like having lots of secrets to keep, and maybe Priscilla was no different.

"I won't tell anybody," Priscilla said earnestly, tucking a wheat-gold lock behind her ears. She had a purple ribbon in her hair and was wearing a dress with a lot of white lace that filled Grace with envy whenever she looked at it. "Not even Veronique or Rosemary or Helena or Mabel or Elizabeth S. or Elizabeth E. And they're my best friends!"

Sareena gave Grace a meaningful look.

Priscilla went on, in a hurt tone. "I don't know why you don't trust me, Sareena. I never did a thing to you. Not one thing."

"You were my best friend, and then you weren't," Sareena snapped. "How about that?"

Priscilla's face went red. "I never cut you out, and you know it. You're the one who—"

"Are we going to stand around listening to you two argue all day?" Poppy said.

"All right, all right," Grace said, waving the grimoire. It had the desired effect—Sareena, Priscilla, Poppy, and Daisy Bean all shut their mouths and stared at it. The grimoire was plain, but there was something about its plainness that said *I am not for the likes of you.*

"Is that really a spellbook?" Priscilla said in an awed hush.

Grace didn't reply, merely gave her a mysterious look, and they all got a little quieter. Nobody argued when she read out a list of mushrooms she needed. Priscilla, Poppy, and Daisy Bean scattered with baskets under their arms, with Grace and Sareena following more slowly.

"What really happened with you and Priscilla?" Grace said. "*Did* she cut you out?"

Sareena sighed. "We-ell—not exactly. But she got *popular.* We used to play together all the time when we were little. But when school started, she made all these other friends. They were always laughing together and sharing secrets. And she wouldn't play with me anymore, just the two of us—we always had to play with these other girls, too, and I hated it."

Grace frowned. "Why?"

"Because!" Sareena said. "You shouldn't *share* best friends. When I have a best friend, I want her all to myself."

Grace grabbed her hand and squeezed it. How desperately she hoped that Sareena would never become scared of her! "Me too."

A smile broke across Sareena's face, and she squeezed Grace's hand back.

It only took a few hours to gather the mushrooms, and afterward Grace invited the other girls in for tea. She was half afraid that Poppy would do something dreadful, but she kept her bullying side in check around Grace, and only pinched Daisy Bean once. As for Sareena and Priscilla, they were coldly polite to each other. The witch had baked lemon scones, and they also had a delicious batch of *poutines à trou*, an Acadian apple pastry that Priscilla's parents had sent over with her.

"These scones are delightful, Grace," Priscilla said. "Please give my compliments to the witch. And ice cream! I *live* for ice cream."

Sareena rolled her eyes. She passed a bowl to Daisy Bean, who was under the table.

"You can take a bucket home with you, if you'd like," Grace offered. "We have lots."

Priscilla grinned at her, and suddenly Grace understood why she was so popular. That smile was like being hit by a ray of sunshine.

"I can fetch more wild roses," said Poppy, who was the first to finish eating. "I'm not tired."

"Don't you need to head home, Poppy?" Grace said. She lived the farthest out of town, nearly an hour's walk.

Poppy shrugged, looking away. The rest of them waited, even Sareena, but she didn't say anything more. Grace had seen Poppy's parents in the village a few times. They had hard faces and always seemed to be complaining about something, whether it was children running about or an improperly parked wagon. Poppy didn't talk about her family much—Grace knew she had three older brothers and that her father was English and her mother had been born on the Island, but that was it.

"Well, I'd best be getting home myself," Priscilla said, dabbing her fingers daintily on a napkin. "I shall need time to wash up before supper."

This time, Sareena and Grace both rolled their eyes. Priscilla had managed to stay remarkably clean, avoiding the muddy patches in the forest as if they were full of poison ivy. Still, she'd picked mushrooms without complaint, even when they left her hands and cuffs dirty, which was more than Grace had expected of her.

"I thought you didn't like playing outside," Sareena said.

"Oh, I don't." Priscilla's eyes shone. "I'd much rather sit by the fire and read. But this is different. This is like being in a fairy tale, like the Brothers Grimm or *The Thousand and One Nights*."

Grace's eyes widened. "You've read *The Thousand and One Nights*?"

"Oh yes!" Priscilla said, and suddenly they were both yammering away about their favorite tales.

"I have a bookshelf in my bedroom that goes up to the *ceiling*," Priscilla said, pointing at the ceiling in case they didn't appreciate the wondrousness of this. "And you know what else? It's full."

Grace let out a gasp of delight. "Can I see it?"

"Oh yes." Priscilla's eyes gleamed. "And you can borrow anything you like. Even my favorites—I only loan those to my dearest friends, you know."

Priscilla began listing all her favorite books—it was quite a long list—with Grace getting excited and interrupting every time Priscilla mentioned one that she had read, too. Grace decided that Priscilla was nowhere near as bad as Sareena had warned.

Grace realized that Sareena was frowning, and she remembered what Sareena had said about Priscilla stealing her away. Grace quickly told them that the witch expected her to help with supper, and would be angry if she dawdled. Priscilla and Poppy left quickly after hearing that. It was a good thing, too, for Poppy's mother was coming up the lane to look for her. She grabbed her daughter by the arm and hauled her away, yelling about how late it was and all the chores Poppy had left undone. Priscilla trailed behind them, looking shocked and sympathetic.

Sareena gave Grace a hug on her way out. She took Daisy Bean's hand and they stepped into the gathering twilight.

Grace watched the two of them cross the garden until they were swallowed by the dark woods, and a little shiver of foreboding ran down her spine. She told herself it was just the draught, and closed the door.

The witch came down the stairs shortly after. She generally shut herself away in her room whenever other children were over.

"What a noise!" she said. "I'm not sure I like your little friends poking about my house."

"They don't poke about," Grace said. "They're too afraid of you."

She harrumphed, and Grace felt a giddy *whoosh* of happiness fill her, for the witch was right—Grace had *friends* now. Not just one friend, which would have given her enough happiness to last a lifetime, but *friends*. Such a lovely variety of letters that word had, with a silent little *i* in the middle like a secret.

"These days you're always off with your friends," the witch said, which brought about another little *whoosh*. "I rarely have to put up with your silly chatter anymore."

Was it Grace's imagination, or was there a trace of unhappiness in her voice? Surely not. The witch complained constantly about how much noise Grace made and how annoying she was.

"Do you mind?" Grace said. "About my friends knowing you're a witch. Knowing for certain, I mean."

"Why on earth would I mind?" the witch said irritably.

"Well, they may tell their parents. And when they grow up—"

"When they grow up?" The witch looked amused. "You silly child. Tell me, what do the grown-ups in Brook-by-the-Sea think of me?"

Grace frowned. "They think you're an old woman living by herself. Some of them think you're strange."

"And?"

Grace thought about it. "And—that's it."

"That's it. Exactly. And yet all of them were children once—many of them children in this very village. Some believed that I was a witch back then. They believed it to the core."

Grace thought about how good children were at spotting witches. "Oh! Did you cast a spell on them to make them forget?"

"They didn't forget. They simply grew up and dismissed it as childish fancy. That's always the way of things. You don't need to cast spells on grown-ups to make them forget about magic. They don't *want* to believe. Magic is something they can't control, and grown-ups are terrified of things they can't control. More terrified than they are of witches."

Grace drew in a sharp breath. "Does that mean—will Sareena forget? When she's grown, will she forget about me, and about the grimoire and the spells? Everything?"

"Of course not. As I said, it isn't about *forgetting.* She'll simply turn the memories over, rearrange them. The witch in the woods becomes a lonely old woman, the spells the product of a wild imagination—do you see? It's a powerful magic, fear."

"I won't let her forget," Grace said. "Surely not *all* grown-ups forget about magic."

She said it desperately. A lonely life stretched out before her, just as lonely as her old one, in a way—a life that she wouldn't be able to share with other people because they wouldn't believe any of it.

The witch gave her a look that Grace couldn't read. "No, not all," she agreed.

Grace let out a sigh of relief. "Sareena will never forget," she said firmly.

She kept quiet for a while as the witch cooked, but as usual, she soon forgot herself and began telling the witch all about school and the horrors of geometry, a nemesis worse than cursive letters. Then she went on for a while about Rum and his latest nonsense. He was bringing Grace *flowers* now, to get her to forgive him for insulting her—nearly every morning at school he put a fresh bouquet on her desk. From there she told the witch about Miss Gordon giving her another marvelous book of poetry, this one full of Canadian poets who wrote about things she knew, like sweeping dark forests and the chill of a February night, or how it felt to glide over a frozen lake in your boots. And though she'd always liked reading about faraway places, wasn't it also nice, she asked, to have somebody make you see all the beautiful things right under your nose?

As usual, the witch wasn't listening. She said, "You still haven't brought me any dreams. I asked you *weeks* ago."

"Ah," Grace said. "About that. I don't understand—"

"I want you to fetch them tonight," the witch said. "No more dithering. We need to fix the foundation before winter sets in, else that crack will freeze up and get bigger. I will be very . . . disappointed if the crack gets bigger."

The shadows at her back began to swirl. Grace swallowed hard and stammered something that wasn't really words.

The witch set a plate in front of her—codfish cakes with

fried dulse. "Eat up. I'm going for a walk before I turn in."

Something about the way she said it made Grace ask, "Are you going to visit Patrick? He was hanging about this afternoon. I think he likes watching us."

"Yes, I—I noticed," the witch said. "I doubt he'll see me."

There was an odd sort of longing in the witch's voice, as she gazed out the window into the twilight. "Why not?" Grace asked.

"He's a terrible grudge-holder," the witch said. "You see, I promised to find a way to turn him back into a man. And, well, I haven't."

Grace thought this was a reasonable thing to hold a grudge about. "Oh."

The witch blinked and glared, as if Grace had somehow tricked all this out of her. "Get me those dreams, you hare-brained child."

She drew a shawl around herself and slipped out the door.

Almost as soon as the witch was gone, Windweaver tapped on the window. Grace pushed it open, and he fluttered in. The witch had banned Windweaver from every room except Grace's, saying that he was sure to leave little bird surprises everywhere, an idea that civilized Windweaver found highly insulting.

Grace thought for a while about poor Patrick, trapped up there in the sky by his own sister, with nothing to do with his life but rain on people. She hadn't thought the witch cared about him, as she usually acted as if he was dead. But the tiny tremor in her voice had made Grace wonder how true that was.

She did the washing up, gave the witch's sleep potion another stir and a few more rose petals, then went upstairs to her bedroom with Windweaver on her shoulder.

She gave a happy sigh as she stepped inside. There was the every-flower quilt, the cedar chest of drawers. She slipped off her shoes and buried her feet in the soft wool rug, convinced that any problem would seem less grave if considered in her perfect little bedroom.

The thought of losing her magic was terrible. But far worse was the thought of losing her home. She prayed that she was right, and that things would indeed go more quickly now that she had more helpers.

Windweaver and Grace read a few Canadian poems, though her mind was too full to concentrate. She needed to get her hands on those dreams—not just for the witch, but for the grimoire's spells. Windweaver's warm, soft weight on her shoulder wasn't the same comfort it usually was. In moments like that, she couldn't help thinking about how close she was to losing him. A grim determination settled inside her.

"I think I should try to sleep now," she said.

All right. Windweaver hopped over to his nest, a pile of socks between her pillow and the wall. He had stolen several from the witch, and the rest from who knew where. Windweaver loved socks. *Good luck.*

Grace's heart was thudding. "Thanks."

She lay down and tried to think very hard about sleep, and dreams. What were dreams, anyway? They had no substance, no shape. So how could a person gather them up? It was impossible.

She took a deep breath and closed her eyes.

19

THE LAND OF SLEEP

Sing to us, cedars; the twilight is creeping
With shadowy garments, the wilderness through;
All day we have carolled, and now would be sleeping,
So echo the anthems we warbled to you . . .
—E. Pauline Johnson (Tekahionwake), "The Birds'
Lullaby"

When Grace opened her eyes again, everything was foggy. It was as if the world had been turned into a pencil drawing with a lot of smudges in it.

She gave a cry of surprise and fell out of bed. When she looked up, she screamed, for there was her body, lying on the bed, snoring away.

She had fallen out of her *body*.

She stood up. Her body mumbled something and rolled over. Grace was afraid for a moment, but then her fear faded. Like the world, she felt a little foggy.

194

"*Psst*," she said. "Windweaver, wake up."

Windweaver lifted his head, blinking. *Oh*, he said. *You're in the Land of Sleep.*

"The Land of Sleep?" Grace squeaked. "What's that?"

It's another world. He sounded irritated. *Where people dream.*

"Why didn't you tell me about this?"

I don't tell you lots of things, Windweaver said. *All crows know about other worlds. We pay attention, unlike humans. Now hush, I'm trying to sleep.*

Grace's mouth hung open. How he could be so nonchalant about other worlds and Grace falling out of her body was beyond her. But that was crows for you, she supposed.

She poked her body, and it grumbled in its sleep. She had a sudden horrified fear that her body's eyes would open and stare at her, but then that calming fog settled over her again.

Well, she had dreams to gather, didn't she? She might as well get started.

She walked through the wall of her bedroom and into the witch's room. She was quite calm about it, for the fog had her firm in its grip. Anyone would have thought she walked through walls all the time.

The witch's room was full of souvenirs from her travels, mostly in the form of oddly shaped vases and colorful rugs. On the mantelpiece was a skull with a crown perched on it in a mocking sort of way, and there was also a sword mounted on the wall that was clearly cursed, for every few seconds it would drip blood onto the floor and whisper, "*So this is how it ends.*" Grace decided that she would not be visiting the witch's room again.

Her gaze was caught by a photo propped up on the witch's desk, which was otherwise empty. It was turned so that the witch would be able to see it when she sat there. The photo was very old, made from a sheet of copper and tarnished round the edges. A man gazed boldly out from it—he had thinning hair and an impressive mustache and wore a dashing neckerchief. Scrawled in ink at the top of the photo were the words, *From Freddy, with love.*

With love? Grace thought, astonished. Who would give anything to the witch—let alone their photograph—with love? She wondered if the witch had taken the photograph from one of her victims. But if she had, why did she keep it on her desk like that?

Grace bent closer to examine the photograph. Tucked into one corner was a sprig of pressed flowers—they looked like cherry blossoms. How strange!

She looked over her shoulder at the witch, as if she might explain the mystery. But of course, the witch was asleep. She seemed to have drifted off holding another one of Patrick's paintings—the small type of painting called a *miniature*. Grace recognized the thoroughly ugly style.

Well, Grace wasn't going to steal any of the witch's dreams, that was for sure. She didn't *want* any of the witch's dreams— they were probably full of people being burned alive or having their fingernails baked into a cake.

She turned and walked through the witch's wall back into her own bedroom. When she went through the opposite wall, she found herself in Sareena's bedroom. Sareena was scribbling in a notebook, her curtain pushed open so that the moonlight fell on the page.

Grace moved closer and found that Sareena was writing notes about one of the spells they had been working on. She paused to tap her pencil against her mouth, then she scribbled something else.

Grace's eyes filled with tears, and she wanted to leap on Sareena with a hug. But unlike Windweaver, Sareena didn't seem to be able to see her, and Grace doubted she would appreciate being hugged by a person with no body. Grace wasn't going to take any of her dreams, anyhow, not from her precious Sareena.

Grace stepped through Sareena's wall and found herself in yet another bedroom. She supposed that all the bedrooms on earth must be connected in the Land of Sleep, and that if she walked far enough, she would end up in Egypt or Japan. She continued to feel very calm about the whole thing.

It was Priscilla's bedroom. She was asleep with her arms at her sides, her golden hair fanned out on the pillow and a book lying open on her face. She took a moment to marvel at Priscilla's bookshelf, which was indeed as tall as the ceiling.

Priscilla gave an unladylike snort and the book fell onto the floor, waking her with a start. Smiling, Grace turned around and walked back through the same wall into Sareena's room, then out through the wall on the other side. Right away, she recognized the little boy asleep before her. His name was Henry, and he was one of Poppy's favorite targets. In his hair, Grace thought she could make out fragments of spitball that he hadn't quite combed out. His room was dark, apart from a strange, faint glow that hovered above him.

She tiptoed up to Henry's bed. The glow came from a dozen or so tiny orbs, bobbing like dandelion down caught on a breeze. As she watched, one of the orbs floated down to the boy and slipped inside his mouth when he breathed in.

"Dreams," she murmured. She didn't know *how* she knew this, but she did, just as she had known the moonweed and the witch's helper.

Cautiously, she unscrewed the lid of the jar she had brought with her. Then she dragged it over the dreams like a net. Several darted out of the way in time, but she managed to trap two.

She peered into the jar. The dreams hovered there, glowing like fireflies. Grace smiled. This wasn't hard at all!

She decided to let Henry keep the rest of his dreams—she could get more from other children. But just as she was turning to step through Henry's wall, something caught her eye.

It was the dreams. There had been thirteen glowing ones before. Now there were eleven glowing ones and two that were black as night.

Grace frowned. The dark dreams were the same size as the

others, but they had an unpleasant, twitchy way of moving. As she watched, Henry breathed one in.

He whimpered in his sleep.

Grace backed away nervously. Perhaps she simply hadn't noticed those particular dreams before. They *were* difficult to see—like holes in the air.

She gathered the remaining dreams quickly. She needed a round ten—three for the witch, and seven for her own spells. Some of the children she visited had a few black dreams floating above them when she arrived. After she had taken the dreams she needed, the black ones multiplied.

She passed through the bedrooms of several grown-ups, all of them snoring away. The grown-ups had fewer dreams than the children, and many of them were grayish, neither light nor dark.

When Grace had enough dreams, she retraced her steps. The bedrooms were logically organized; the bedrooms in Sareena's house were closest to Grace's, because Sareena's house was closest to the witch's house. Next to those bedrooms were the bedrooms in Henry's and Poppy's houses, who were Sareena's nearest neighbors on the other side of the Khalils' large farm. Grace supposed that if she had walked through the north wall of her bedroom, she would come to the bedrooms of the witch's neighbor to the north, a farmer who lived on the other side of the forest.

She breathed a sigh of relief as she stepped back into her bedroom. She set the jar—now full of dreams—on her nightstand.

Her body was snoring away. Windweaver was still nestled beside it in his sock pile, fast asleep—how disappointing. Grace didn't think *she* would be able to sleep with an empty body beside her. Really, Windweaver should have been terribly awed by it all.

Grace shook her head. There was still the tricky business of getting back into her body. Should she jump into it, or close her eyes and sort of . . . *drift?* In the end, she sat down on her body's stomach and lay flat, drawing her body around her like a cloak.

The next thing she knew, she awoke with a noisy snort, her eyes flying open.

Keep it down. Windweaver was glaring at her, his head feathers sticking up. *Some of us would rather sleep than go traipsing around in other worlds, you know.*

At breakfast, Grace set the jar of dreams down on the kitchen table and beamed at the witch.

The witch glanced up from the sink, where she was rinsing a bucket of rose hips from the garden. "Finally," she said, and kept on rinsing.

Grace was disappointed, but not much—she'd largely given up hope of ever receiving a compliment from the witch.

Over a breakfast of eggs, toast, and fried tomatoes—the witch no longer served cold oatmeal, thankfully—Grace told her all about her adventure in the Land of Sleep. She was hoping that the witch would be a *little* impressed by how easily Grace had found her way around, but alas, the witch seemed even less interested than Windweaver.

"Well, what did you expect, you ridiculous girl?" she said when Grace told her about the strange, twitchy dreams that had appeared over the sleepers. "Magic always has a price."

Grace froze. "A price? Then *I* made those dreams appear?"

"Of course you did. And they weren't dreams. They were nightmares."

"Then all those kids—" Grace's hand flew to her mouth, and she stared at the witch in horror. "Those nightmares appeared because I took their dreams?"

"Of course. Something had to fill the gaps you left behind. Sleep is like a tapestry. You can't just snip out a square without putting something in its place, or the whole thing will unravel."

"But why—"

"It's the way it is," the witch said. "Did you truly believe that magic has no consequences? That you could have all that power for free?"

Grace was shivering. "I'll use my own dreams from now on. That way—"

The witch gave a humorless laugh. "No, you won't. A witch's dreams won't work. We are . . . different. We don't have the same substance that mortals do. That's what allows us to move between worlds. We are like shadows hiding in the cracks of the mortal world, slipping in and out of their stories."

Grace didn't understand half of this, but something made her lean away from the witch. Maybe it was because, for a brief moment, she saw a reflection of herself. Was this what Grace would be like when she was old? Would Grace be a creature made of shadows and teeth, who stole children's dreams and left them with nightmares, and never gave it a second thought?

The witch wasn't paying any attention to Grace. She adjusted her cardigan—green today, with pink flowers. "Eat up, child. I want that foundation fixed by sundown."

20

A KITCHEN WANDERS OFF

I see the great blue heron
Rising among the reeds
And floating down the wind,
Like a gliding sail . . .
—Bliss Carman, "The Blue Heron"

"Do you think the witch has ever cast this spell on herself?" Sareena asked.

Grace gave a quiet snort. "The witch in a good mood? Can you imagine?"

They were sitting in their usual places at the back of the schoolroom, passing the grimoire back and forth. Miss Gordon thought they were reading quietly from their primer, like the other students. Fortunately, the winter rain drumming against the wooden shingles of the schoolroom covered up their whispers.

They had reached the most fearsome spell of all.

44. FOR GOOD CHEER

1 bunch lavender

1 teaspoon thistle milk

2 lemons, rind only

1 black robin's egg, shell only

1 square of honeycomb

1 pitcher of midnight

5 pinecones

Cover ingredients with rainwater and simmer for one day
lasting twenty-five hours.
May it be, by sun and stars.

Grace had probably read the spell a hundred times, hoping an idea would come to her. Now the ingredients barely looked like words.

"What did I miss?" Rum said, appearing out of thin air in the empty chair in front of them. Grace let out a strangled cry.

"What's wrong?" Sareena whispered.

Grace glared at Rum. "I just wish he wouldn't do that."

"Do what?"

"Appear out of nowhere like that."

"Appear out of nowhere like what?"

"Like a fairy!"

"Who's a fairy?"

Grace buried her head in her hands.

 204

Rum smirked and picked up his primer. "What chapter are we on?"

"Oh, why do you even bother?" Grace snapped. "You missed half the school day again."

He balanced his chair on its back legs with his usual fairy grace. "I try to be on time, but it's tricky. Time moves more slowly here than it does in Faerie. Well, sometimes. Other times, it's faster."

She was going to throw the grimoire at him if he gave her any more fairy nonsense. Rum seemed incapable of understanding that Grace was on an enormously dangerous and important quest. You'd think a magical being would understand quests, but Grace had found—much to her disappointment—that creatures from stories don't always behave the way that stories said they should. For instance, if they did, an enchanted crow like Windweaver would be mysterious and elegant at all times—he certainly wouldn't pick his beak with his talons or leave half-digested worms on the bed.

"Why do you even come to school, anyway?" she said. "Do fairies need to know their times tables?"

"I don't have to tell you everything," Rum said, glaring at her. But he was blushing too, so of course Grace guessed the real reason—he still hoped she would forgive him.

"*Psst.*" Priscilla, sitting in the desk on the other side of Grace, leaned over and handed her a note. It read, *I had a lovely time yesterday. I am ever so glad that I made your ackwaintance. Your friend, Prissy.*

Grace looked up and found Priscilla beaming at her with her rosy cheeks and her dimples. She couldn't help but beam back, even though Priscilla made it sound as if they had spent yesterday embroidering cushions rather than conducting dangerous witchcraft. Sareena read the note and made a gagging sound.

Grace noticed one of Priscilla's friends glaring at her. They did this a lot whenever Priscilla sat with Grace and Sareena at the back of the classroom.

Grace had wondered if Priscilla's friendship with her might make Priscilla less popular, but it seemed the opposite was true. Grace guessed that being friends with a suspected witch made Priscilla seem kind, as well as brave—which Grace supposed she was, all things considered. Though Grace sometimes had the sense that Priscilla's kindness was a little show-offy. She had made it clear to everyone at By-the-Sea School that she and Grace were dear friends now, but became very mysterious whenever the other students demanded to know what they did at the witch's house. Everyone was terribly curious. The long and short of it was that Priscilla was now even more the center of attention than she had been before Grace showed up.

After school, Sareena and Grace walked home as quickly as they could, arms linked to keep themselves warm. Christmas was only a few weeks away, and the world felt gray and stark. Night was already gathering along the horizon, and the trees chattered as the wind carried the cold damp in from the sea.

"I simply love this time of year," Grace told Sareena. "I've always felt that summer and spring get all the glory—and summer and spring are lovely, of course—but there is something to appreciate in every season. Just look at this! Everything is mist and darkness and roaring wind—and even if it isn't snowing, you know that it could, and that one morning soon we will wake up to a different world. It's just the sort of time when one might imagine ghosts wandering the fields, lonesome and wailing for revenge."

Sareena shivered. "Do you suppose *all* ghosts go around wailing for revenge? Perhaps they only do that in stories, and actual ghosts spend their time traveling the world and spying on interesting people. That's what *I* would do, if I were a ghost."

"Who would you spy on in Brook-by-the-Sea?"

"Mr. Pentwhistle," Sareena said immediately. Mr. Pentwhistle was the village baker. "I would see how he makes those nine-layer cakes, and what he puts into the raspberry tarts to make them melt in your mouth. My mother thinks it's goose fat."

"I don't believe I'm strong enough to haunt a bakery," Grace said. "Imagine the torment—being surrounded by all those sweets and unable to eat anything."

They spent the rest of the walk home in a very interesting debate about who they would haunt if they were ghosts. Sareena wanted to spy on Prime Minister Laurier, while Grace liked the idea of haunting famous poets. She would whisper ideas in their ears, and they would put those ideas in their poetry, and although her name would be forgotten, her words would live forever. She thought there was something terribly romantic about being famous and forgotten at the same time.

To Grace's surprise, as she and Sareena ducked beneath the boughs of the witch's woods, they heard voices in the distance. Two men appeared on the path ahead, having obviously come from the depths of the forest, judging by the mud on their boots. One was carrying what looked like rolled-up maps under his arm, while the other had a compass, notebook, and pencil.

"You two," the first man snapped. "What are you doing here?"

His voice was so loud and mean that Grace fell back a step. Sareena gripped her arm and said bravely, "What are we doing here? What are *you* doing here?"

"Just a couple of village kids, looks like," the second man muttered.

"Well, clear out," the first man snapped. "This here's private land. No trespassers."

Grace's mouth fell open, and before she even knew what she was saying, she snapped, "This is the witch's forest!"

"The witch's forest?" the first man repeated. They exchanged looks, chuckling. "Sure it is, little girl."

Somehow, Grace mentioning the witch made the men lose all interest in her and Sareena. They tramped on by, heavy boots squelching in the wet earth, complaining about the cold.

"Go on home now, girls," the second man called over his

shoulder, like an afterthought. "It's not a day to be playing games out-of-doors."

Grace stared after them until they faded into the shadows. Once they were gone, she found it difficult to believe the men had ever been there, invading the witch's quiet woods with their stomping boots and loud voices. The forest was even quieter now, but it was an eerie, deadened quiet, as if the men had crushed some vital part of it under their boots. A chill scuttled down Grace's back.

"What do you think they meant?" she said. "About trespassers and private land? They're the trespassers! They're lucky the witch didn't see them."

"I bet they have these woods mixed up with a different woods," Sareena said. "Most woods *do* look alike, after all. But ask the witch to be sure."

Grace nodded, another little shiver going through her. Fortunately, her mood lifted as they reached the witch's cottage. It was just as eerily beautiful in winter as it was in summer, with the promise of warm fires behind the golden windows and a cozy curl of smoke drifting out of the chimney. Everything about the house beckoned you inside, especially when you compared its warmth and friendliness to the gloom of the forest, which seemed to be in cahoots with the witch and made itself even darker as you approached her house.

Grace always felt a thrill of happiness when she looked at the witch's cottage, and a small voice inside her whispered, *Mine. That's* my *house.*

But her good mood faded as they went inside. Sareena had permission from her parents to stay the night—which was the most wonderful thing imaginable—though, alas, she and Grace would not be staying up eating ice cream and telling spooky stories. They had finished spell number forty-three yesterday, and now had to solve the dreaded spell number forty-four.

How to stretch time by an hour? That was what they had to work out.

"Let's go through the instructions one at a time," Sareena said.

Grace groaned and flopped heavily onto a chair. "What's the point? There are simply too many impossible spells in that grimoire to finish in a lifetime, let alone half a year."

"Stop moping," Sareena said. "We're not doing too bad, you know."

Grace had to admit she was right. Over the past few months, they had solved quite a few of the grimoire's mysteries.

Gathering the three left footprints of a deer that the "For Ice" spell called for had been surprisingly easy. Sareena and Grace had melted beeswax and poured it into three deer prints in the forest floor, then lifted up the wax after it hardened. The sneeze of a sparrow ("For a Nice Smell") had been much trickier. With Windweaver's help, they had captured a sparrow in a cage, then sat it down next to the other spell ingredients. Unfortunately, birds did not often sneeze, and never on command. But again, Windweaver had come to the rescue. He knew many bird secrets, and as it turned out, birds sneezed for the same boring reasons that people did. Once they had gathered up a few handfuls of dust and blown it over the cage, the sparrow started sneezing away. The sound of a sparrow's sneeze was impossible to describe, but quite delightful.

But they had not worked out how to fill a pitcher with midnight, nor how to get their hands on a spiderweb woven during the new moon, for how did one compel spiders to make webs at a particular time? And on and on it went.

And they were still behind schedule. The spells were getting harder, and each one had been taking more and more time to work out than the last.

Grace rested her head on her hands. Her heart was making an odd *thump-whoosh, thump-whoosh* sound. "I might as well turn my magic over to the witch right now."

"Hush," Sareena said. "Can I move this?" She didn't wait for a reply, of course, and moved the witch's sleep potion to the back of the stove. She set another pot on the stove and went into the pantry.

"We have most of the ingredients," she said. "The lavender, thistle milk, lemons, honeycomb, pinecones." She set everything on the counter. "Even the black robin's egg."

"Well, we cheated on that one," Grace pointed out. Robin's eggs only came in blue, so they had dyed the shell with ink.

Sareena shrugged. "It's black, isn't it? The only thing we're missing is the pitcher of midnight."

"And the ability to change time," Grace said. "Nothing to worry about."

"I still think we should try the spell without the midnight," Sareena said. "We can use a substitute. And perhaps we can simply set the clocks back an hour after we begin the spell."

"I don't think magic is that easy to fool," Grace said. It was an old argument between them. "Besides, if we don't cast it properly, the witch might say it doesn't count. Then I'll have to do it again."

"Well—"

They were interrupted by the witch stomping down the stairs. She was wearing her nicest cardigan—white with lace and beading—and pearl earrings, which drew the eye to her furious expression. Grace knew without a doubt that it would be the wrong time to ask her about strange men wandering around in her woods.

Sareena ducked behind the door of the pantry, as if to shield herself. Grace said nervously, "You're off to Mrs. Crumley's, then?"

The witch made no reply, merely shoved her hands roughly into her silk gloves as if they had personally insulted her. She had been putting Mrs. Crumley off for months. The old woman seemed intent on befriending the witch, as she was the sort of busybodyish person who would not rest until she had made friends with everyone she knew. In that way, Mrs. Crumley reminded Grace of Priscilla, but Mrs. Crumley was playing a much more dangerous game. Though the witch never hexed the residents of Brook-by-the-Sea, Grace guessed that she would very much like to make a special exception for Mrs. Crumley. The witch had only agreed to have supper at Mrs. Crumley's after finally running out of excuses not to. Also, Mrs. Crumley had recently begun threatening to send an army of doctors to the witch's cottage, given how often the witch came down with the stomach flu.

"There is a chicken in the larder," the witch informed Grace. "As well as a fresh loaf from the baker's. And you know where the carrots and potatoes are. If you and your little friend burn the place down before I return, I will do whatever you are imagining that I will do to you, and then I will do something ten times worse. Do you understand?"

Grace nodded frantically. Sareena squeaked, "Yes ma'am." The witch swept another dark look over them, then stormed out.

"Whew!" Sareena leaned against the wall. "If the witch keeps that look on her face while she's having dinner with Mrs. Crumley, I doubt she'll have to worry about any more invitations."

"Shall we get supper started?" Grace said. She wanted to think about something that wasn't spell forty-four. "You'll have to be in charge—I can't cook without burning something. Mrs. Spencer used to say I could burn a meal just by looking at it."

Sareena nodded. Grace fetched the chicken and vegetables, and Sareena opened the oven. "Yuck!" she cried, recoiling. "There are *bones* in here!"

"I know," Grace said. "It would be nice of the witch to clean out her oven. I suppose she leaves it that way to scare the next person she puts in there."

Sareena sat down in her chair, looking faint. "Has she baked anybody since you moved in?"

"No, she's kept her promise. She doesn't seem to do much magic, on the whole. I suspect it's because she isn't well."

"Hmm," Sareena said. "Maybe she'll die before next May. You can keep living here, and you won't have to give up your magic."

"What an awful thing to say!" Grace exclaimed.

Sareena gave her a long look. She looked at the oven, full of bones, then back at Grace.

Well, Grace supposed it *was* silly to worry about the witch dying. But she just couldn't imagine it. She didn't *want* to imagine it. The witch had taken her in, after all. She had given Grace what all those ordinary, kindhearted parents who'd come to Rose & Ivy never had—a home. Not just a home, but a home with a perfect little bedroom with an every-flower quilt and a best friend next door. An evil witch who had tried to bake her alive and steal her magic had given her all that!

Also, the witch let her talk and talk without interrupting (though she did complain about Grace's noise on a regular basis), and she had begun serving biscuits and gravy at least once a week after Grace said they were her favorite. Of course, the witch claimed she was only doing so to keep Grace quiet, but it was still a kindness, no matter her reasons, and Grace had had so little kindness in her life that even scraps were precious.

"Well, we can't roast a chicken in there," Sareena said definitively. "It's horribly unsanitary. Come on." She found a dustpan and an old broom and scooped the bones out. "I guess we should bury them."

"We can't," Grace said. "The witch might get mad. We'll have to put them back after the chicken is done."

Sareena shuddered, but the witch's threats were still fresh in her mind, so she didn't argue. They found a nearly empty burlap sack used for potatoes, took the potatoes out, then filled the sack up with bones. There were four skulls and a variety of ribs, as well as some very small bones that were possibly toes, or perhaps fingers—Grace tried not to look too closely.

"This is the weirdest thing I've ever done," Sareena said as they took the sack out to the porch (it made a horrible rattling sound). She paused and thought. "No, actually, putting the bones *back* in the oven will be the weirdest thing I've ever done."

Grace agreed. She also wished they hadn't been talking about ghosts earlier. It was true that she had no evidence that the ghosts of all those unlucky people were haunting the witch's oven. It was also true that she had no evidence they *weren't*, which in a way was just as bad, wasn't it?

They felt better once the chicken was in the oven and filling the kitchen with lovely cooking smells. Grace decided to ask Rum about the pitcher of midnight. Even though they had a bargain, she still tried to avoid calling on him unless she had to. But if anybody was going to know about impossible magic, it was a fairy.

First, Grace spent five minutes explaining to Sareena again about Rum being a fairy, just to get it out of the way. She'd learned that it was easier for Sareena to believe this when Rum wasn't actually *there*—likely because when he was, he used his fairy magic to confuse her. But if Grace waited too long before she summoned him, Sareena would forget again, and she'd have to explain it all once more. None of this became any less irritating over time.

"Rum!" Grace called once she had Sareena sorted.

To her surprise, he didn't step sideways out of nowhere, but knocked on the front door. He looked resplendent in layers of winter gray, his crown a leafless band of twigs and icicles. His wings were white and very faint, like snow falling on a distant mountain.

"What are you doing?" Grace said.

He shrugged. "I thought knocking would be more polite." To her dismay, he held out another bouquet of flowers.

"I don't—oh, what does it matter?" she grumbled. "Find a vase to put them in, then."

Rum looked pleased, despite her rudeness. Usually Grace threw his flowers away—she had no intention of accepting flowers from her archenemy—but she couldn't quite bear to do that this time. The bouquet was made of midnight-blue lilies of the valley, holly berries, and violet mayflowers—Grace had a soft spot for mayflowers. It was a very unusual bouquet, and she thought the witch might like it.

"Would you like to stay for dinner?" Sareena asked Rum. "The chicken will be done soon."

Grace glared at her. Sareena gave her a look that clearly meant *well, he's helping us, isn't he?* Rum said, "Thank you. I like chicken."

Grace decided to get right down to business—she didn't want Rum thinking she wanted to make up with him. "If you needed to gather a pitcher of midnight, how would you do it?" she demanded.

"A pitcher of midnight?" he repeated, taking a vase out of the cupboard. "Well, I'd do it the easy way, of course."

"And what way is that?"

He shrugged. "There's a tree in Faerie called a midnight elm. We named it that because at midnight it opens its leaves and scatters these little flowers everywhere. You could fill a pitcher with those."

Sareena clapped her hands, looking delighted. Grace said, "But that's not—I mean, the spell calls for a pitcher of *actual* midnight. You know." She gestured at the darkness outside.

"You could use actual midnight, I guess," he said. "My way is a lot easier, though."

"Could you bring us the flowers?" Sareena asked.

"Easy," Rum said, looking annoyingly happy that she'd asked. Sareena handed him an empty pitcher, and he marched back out into the gloom.

"We can't use flowers from some fairy tree," Grace said. "It won't work."

"Why not?" Sareena said. "We used deer footprints made from beeswax, even though the grimoire didn't tell us to, and when the 'For Fishing' spell called for a thousand seashells, you got one and crushed it into a thousand pieces. Both those spells worked fine, especially the second one—the witch sure was happy when we brought her that big salmon, wasn't she? I think these spells are often a matter of interpretation. We could probably come up with several ways to gather a pitcher of midnight, and all of them would work. We could—oh, I don't know—fill a pitcher with pocket watches stopped at twelve, or find a cat named Midnight that's about the right size—"

"We're not putting a *cat* in the potion!"

"It was just an example, Grace."

They argued about it for a while, and by the time Sareena had Grace convinced—for she almost always won their arguments, being clever as well as brave and true—Rum had returned with the pitcher full of flowers, and dinner was ready.

They all felt better once they had eaten. Sareena washed the dishes and Grace began peeling lemon rind and measuring thistle milk and adding everything to the pot.

"Are you just going to sit there?" Grace said, narrowing her eyes at Rum.

"What?" Rum looked up from his third bowl of ice cream. Unlike Sareena and Grace, who took their ice cream plain or with cookies crumbled over it, he liked his heaped with salted peanuts and honey. "Oh. I'd rather not have anything more to do with that grimoire of yours, to be honest. Witch magic gives me the creeps."

"Well, I don't suppose you'd know where we might find an extra hour? I need twenty-five of them, you see."

"What would I know about mortal hours? I hate the way time moves in your world. It's so boring. I suppose it has to be, to match your boring lives."

He helped himself to more ice cream. "What?" he said as Grace continued to stare at him. "Did you want the last scoop?"

Grace could hear her pulse thundering in her ears. "Is it midnight in Faerie?"

"In some places it is. Time moves differently there."

"Yes," Grace murmured. "You said that before."

Sareena was watching her. "What is it?"

"Could we—" Grace swallowed. "Could we cast the spell in Faerie? Is there a place in Faerie where time is moving more quickly than it is here? Where a whole hour might pass there without any time passing here at all?"

Sareena let out a slow breath. "That's it, Grace! You've cracked it."

Rum didn't look at all impressed by Grace's brilliant idea. "You can't go to Faerie."

"Why not?"

"Because witches aren't welcome there. We hate witches." He added quickly, "Well, *I* don't hate *all* of them."

"Isn't there anything you can do?" Sareena demanded.

He drummed his long fingers on the table. "I suppose I could blur the worlds together a little bit. Your potion could be in Faerie, but you could be here, brewing it."

Grace's head spun. "What?"

"That sounds complicated," Sareena pointed out.

"It's not complicated at all," Rum said in an exasperated voice, as if they were asking him how to tie shoelaces. He walked up to the stove and gave the pot with the ingredients a shake, then lifted the lid to look inside. He wrinkled his nose. "I hate the smell of witch magic."

He put the lid back on. "There you go. That should work."

"What?" Grace said. "You didn't do anything."

"Yes, I did. Boy, you mortals are terrible at noticing things. How long does it need to brew?"

Sareena and Grace exchanged skeptical looks. "For a day with twenty-five hours," Grace finally said.

Rum nodded. "Well, you'd better get it going. Clock's ticking."

Grace still didn't understand what he'd done, but she and Sareena rushed to add the midnight flowers and the rainwater to the pot. The flowers were small and soft and sticky. They clung to her hands, looking like a strange sort of flour.

"This doesn't look much like midnight," Grace grumbled, because grumbling took her mind off the strangeness of it all.

Rum smirked. "Well, you can always go out and gather your own midnight. I'd like to see that."

She glared at him to hide how flustered she was. By now,

she was used to people helping her—Sareena was brilliant at solving the grimoire's mysteries, Daisy Bean could find pinecones in a willow grove, Poppy could pick leaves for hours without tiring, and Priscilla . . . well, the best you could say about Priscilla was that she was *there*, but just being there was something.

But Rum wasn't supposed to help her—not unless she ordered him to. Only friends helped you because they wanted to, and she and Rum were certainly *not* friends. She felt as if she was compromising her principles by letting him help.

Oh, how she hated to compromise her principles!

But what choice did she have? Give up and hand her magic over to the witch?

"All right," she said once the pot was bubbling away. She couldn't understand what Rum had been complaining about; the potion mostly smelled like the lavender they had added, with a hint of strangeness that probably came from the midnight.

Sareena wiped her brow and squinted at the pot. "I thought you were going to send it to Faerie somehow. It's still here."

"I suppose it is," Rum said. "You see, I just *blurred* the worlds together. That pot is in two places at once—here, and in another kitchen in Faerie."

Sareena made a garbled sound. "A *fairy* kitchen?"

Grace leaned over and held her ear close to the pot. There—she thought she heard something. A sort of distant murmur and *clink-clink* sound, the sort of sound you might

221

hear in a kitchen where several people were preparing a meal. Strange reflections moved across the pot—a pattern of light and shadow that had no connection to the witch's kitchen.

She drew back, feeling faint. She lifted the lid and gave the potion a stir, trying not to wonder if her hand holding the spoon would briefly be visible in Faerie.

"Do you want to play a game?" Rum said.

Sareena's face lit up. "Oh yes!"

Rum brought out a deck of cards—a very strange deck with a great many cards in it, with a leering jack and a fairy-winged queen and king.

"No magic," Grace warned him. "And no cheating, either."

"I wasn't going to cheat," he said, but he sulked a little afterward, so she knew he was lying.

Rum taught them a fairy game that Grace couldn't remember the next day, but she did remember having a lot of cards in her hands—more cards than you should have in a whole deck—and laughing a lot. Sareena laughed the most. She was closest to the bubbling pot, so she was the one to stir it, and once she laughed so hard that she splashed some of the potion on herself. The three of them ate their way through another bucket of ice cream—it kept much better in the cellar now that it was winter.

Grace was enjoying herself so much that she was almost able to forget about impossible spells and her terrible pact. Rum was in a better mood than Grace had ever seen him in.

"Where do you live, anyway?" Grace asked.

"With my uncle." Rum's face darkened.

"Is he a nice man?"

"No." He said it so vehemently that Grace and Sareena exchanged looks.

"Why do you wear that crown?" Sareena said. "Are you a prince or something?"

Rum touched the green jewel in the crown as if he'd forgotten he was wearing it. "What else would I be?"

Sareena's mouth fell open. Grace spat a mouthful of ice cream across the table.

"Yuck," Rum said, wiping his sleeve on a napkin.

"Are you serious?" Grace demanded. "You're a *prince*? Why didn't you say something?"

Rum rolled his eyes and tapped the crown again.

"Well, that's not fair," Grace protested. "For all I know, *all* fairies wear crowns. I've only met one of you."

He shrugged as if none of it mattered. "Does the witch have more honey?"

While Grace went to the pantry to fetch another jar, Sareena said, "What's it like being a fairy prince?"

"Awful," Rum said. "Somebody's always trying to murder me or lock me up so they can steal my kingdom. Well"—he poured half the jar of honey into his bowl—"'cept when I'm here."

"That's horrid!" Sareena exclaimed. "Aren't there any nice fairies?"

"Fairies are a lot of things. *Nice* isn't one of them." He shook his head. "You have no idea what it's like."

Grace was quiet. She knew a great deal about what it was like to feel alone. Not only that, but the witch had locked her up in her oven.

"Maybe you shouldn't wear that crown everywhere," Sareena suggested.

"My mother gave it to me," Rum said, and his grip tightened on his spoon. "I don't have anything else of hers. I'll *never* take it off."

Sareena opened her mouth again, but Grace caught her eye and gave a quick shake of her head. She thought of the photo of her parents, the only piece of them she had. She often felt that if she lost that photo, it would be as if they'd never existed, as if she'd never even had a mother or a father.

She felt an odd urge to touch Rum's arm, which she mercilessly squashed. *You're like me,* Rum had said—and he was right, wasn't he? As much as she adored Sareena, the other girl didn't know what it was like being a friendless orphan. The part of her that longed for friendship above anything else stirred as she looked at Rum—after all, while it was lovely to have friends who were girls, wouldn't it also be nice to have one who was a boy?—but she squashed that, too. Archenemies couldn't be friends.

After they were finished playing cards, they told spooky stories. They turned down the lamps and set a single candle in the middle of the table while the December wind rattled the windows. It was the most wonderful atmosphere for spooky stories imaginable.

Sareena told a story about the ghost of a woman in a white dress who lived in the birch forest between By-the-Sea School and the witch's cottage. It had Grace covered in goose bumps, which was proof of how good it was.

Grace told them a story she had heard at the orphanage, which she embellished a little to make it spookier. It went like this:

Once upon a time there was a graveyard in the middle of an old wood. It was a wood filled with strange creatures: foxes with the ears of hares and hares with ravens' talons. The graveyard was connected to a village by a little path too narrow for a cart and barely wide enough for a coffin. Everyone in the village avoided the graveyard at night, when, it was said, the ghosts came out to dance. This was an especially ghastly sight because some of the ghosts were headless or missing limbs, for the graveyard was on a cliff slowly eroding into the sea, and some of the bones had been jumbled around or lost. The graveyard was so very frightening that the villagers eventually stopped burying decent people there. Only criminals and those with cruel and selfish hearts went into the ground in that graveyard.

One night, a man named Johnny was drinking in the village pub. Those gathered there were talking of a strange light they had glimpsed in the graveyard through the boughs of the tree—a light shaped like a human head. It drifted from grave to grave and muttered about how inconvenient it was to have only a head and nothing else. A head was no good, it complained, for scratching itches, and it had a bad one on the left side of its nose.

Johnny laughed at the story. He wasn't from the village and didn't think there was anything scary about the graveyard. He was more afraid of the living, he said, than he was of the dead.

The villagers were annoyed at Johnny for laughing at them. They told him that if he was so brave, he should walk through the graveyard at midnight. Johnny accepted the challenge at once. To prove he'd gone all the way to the graveyard, he would stick a hayfork into the ground beside the oldest grave. He finished his beer and set out at once, still laughing.

The next morning, there was no sign of Johnny. The villagers went to his house and found his poor dog whining and scratching at the fence. Spooked, the villagers gathered up their weapons and made their way along the narrow forest path, one by one, to the old graveyard, trying to ignore the squirrels twitching their feathered tails and the sparrows watching them with catlike eyes.

Once they reached the graveyard, they found poor Johnny lying on the ground. Both his hands were missing, and he'd been impaled by the hayfork, which was stuck so deep into the earth, it took three strong men to pull it out. And what did the villagers see through the trees that night? Three drifting lights: a skull and two hands.

When Grace came to the end, Sareena let out a shriek, much to Grace's delight. Rum claimed not to understand about ghost stories, so when his turn came, he told a strange tale about a king and queen trapped in a tower by the king's wicked brother, and how every day the tower grew higher and higher until it reached all the way up into the stars, where-upon the king and queen were swept away to another world by meteorites. The wicked brother had declared himself king and adopted his nephew as his own son, only he kept trying to murder the little boy to get him out of the way. It was certainly scary, though it didn't seem like a story.

After that, though, Rum seemed to get the hang of things and told a wonderfully scary story that Grace also forgot about afterward, except that it had a possum in it. She told an even scarier one about a ghost ship, and suddenly it was a compe-tition between the two of them. She tried to stop herself from having too much fun, but it was nearly impossible not to have fun when ghost stories were involved. And Rum was an annoy-ingly good storyteller.

"I wonder when the witch will be home," Grace said. It felt late, close to morning, maybe, though the sky was just as dark as it had been when they started the potion. She looked at the clock on the wall, but for some reason, she couldn't read it. The numbers slid right out of her head when she tried.

Rum didn't seem to have any trouble reading the clock. "Your spell's done," he said, giving a great yawn.

"What?" Grace stared at him. "It's only been a few hours."

Rum laughed. "What are you talking about? We've been here all day! I—oh." He suddenly went pale. "Oops."

Grace stood up. Her legs felt strange and her rear end was numb, as if she'd been sitting in the chair for much longer than she remembered. "What do you mean, '*oops*'?"

"I should be going." Rum waved his hand. "There. I've unblurred the worlds. Have a nice day."

Grace grabbed him before he could fold himself away. "Rum, what have you done?"

Sareena gave a snort and lifted her head off the table, where she had fallen into a doze. "Whazzat? Timesit?"

Rum grimaced. "I may have blurred the worlds a little *too* well. It's hard to judge these things precisely. I meant to only affect the pot—but I may have accidentally let the whole kitchen drift into Faerie."

"*What?*" Grace exploded.

There came a frantic pecking at the kitchen window. She pushed it open, and Windweaver soared in, *crah*-ing frantically.

Where were you? he demanded. *I looked and I looked, and I couldn't find you.*

The door of the house flew open, and the witch stormed in.

"*There* you are, you utter disaster of a child," she snarled.

228

Grace was so shocked that she barely noticed how relieved the witch looked, underneath the anger. "Where on earth have you been?"

"Here," Grace said, giving Rum a poisonous look. She was still gripping his arm. "I thought I was here, anyway—"

"And my kitchen!" the witch exclaimed. She ran her hand over the counter as if it were a beloved dog that had returned home at last. "Good grief! You can't imagine how unpleasant it is to come home and find that your kitchen has gone missing."

She pressed her handkerchief against her mouth and began to cough. The witch's cough always seemed to flare up whenever she flew into one of her rages.

"It wasn't me!" Grace cried. Rum was squirming to free himself from her grip now. "It was Rum—he sent us all to Faerie, including the kitchen!"

The witch fixed Rum with a look so vicious Grace half expected him to burst into flames. "You let *that creature* into the house?"

Grace realized the witch had never met Rum before, and in the same moment realized that this had been a very good thing, for it was clear that the witch not only distrusted fairies, but hated them. Or perhaps she only hated Rum for stealing her kitchen—it amounted to the same thing.

"Well, you never actually said I couldn't," Grace babbled. "I mean, you said that Windweaver couldn't come inside—" She remembered in that moment that Windweaver was sitting on her shoulder, and the babbling grew even worse. "And well, this isn't, I mean, Rum wouldn't, um, Windweaver—"

At that moment, Rum finally wrenched himself free. "Sorry," he muttered to Grace, then stepped sideways and was gone, leaving her to face the witch and her fury alone.

Only, not quite alone. Sareena let out an unladylike *hiccup*. She was swaying a little in her chair as if moving in time to an imaginary song, and there was a broad smile on her face.

"What a marvelous nap!" she exclaimed. "I am so full of happiness that I could hug you all—yes, even that nasty witch!"

"Oh no," Grace whispered.

"What on earth have you done to her?" The witch glanced down at the grimoire. "'For Good Cheer'—oh, how foolish."

Sareena let out a peal of laughter so loud, it echoed off the walls. "What a beautiful night it is! And this is such a lovely house. Everything is lovely, and it makes me so happy that I could just start singing."

And then she did.

"Well, she's cheerful, all right," the witch said, raising her voice.

"I didn't mean to!" Grace cried. "Sareena only stirred the potion—I didn't know—"

Grace kneeled next to Sareena and gripped her hand. "Sareena! Do you know me?"

Sareena giggled. "Course I do!" She was talking too loudly and grinning from ear to ear. "You are my bestest friend ever, Grace, and I think you are sho brave and sho—"

"Wonderful." The witch's voice was ice-cold. "How will

we explain this to her mother? She's already come here twice looking for Sareena. She was supposed to be home hours ago."

"But—" Grace looked out the window. "But it's still night—"

"It's Saturday night, you fool. You two have been gone a whole day."

Grace thought about how Rum had said time moved differently in Faerie. Did time also *feel* different? It didn't feel as if they'd been sitting around the table for a whole day, telling stories and eating ice cream—but in another way, it did.

She felt faint.

"Oh, don't look like that," the witch said. Now that her kitchen had reappeared and she had an explanation for everything, she had calmed down. "These sorts of spells wear off after a while."

There came a rapping at the door, and the witch grimaced. "That will be Mrs. Khalil."

21

A BAD EXAMPLE

The humming-bird feeds upon honey; and so,
Of course, 'tis a sweet little creature, you know.
But sweet little creatures have sometimes, they say,
A great deal that's bitter, or sour, to betray!
—Hannah Flagg Gould, "The Humming-Bird's
Anger"

Grace was braced for a terrible storm.

But the storm never came, and afterward, she thought that she and Sareena were safe. That nothing would change between them.

The witch spoke to Mrs. Khalil. She explained that Sareena and Grace had mistaken the witch's currant wine for a bottle of raspberry cordial and hadn't realized their mistake until they were good and drunk. She would punish Grace soundly, of course, and offered Mrs. Khalil her sincere apologies.

Mrs. Khalil had seemed calm. She had taken Sareena by the hand and helped her to her feet, and had only paled for a moment at the sight of her daughter laughing and singing away like a wild thing. Mrs. Khalil had accepted the witch's apologies graciously, and then she and Sareena had left.

Of course, Sareena didn't behave as if she was drunk. According to the witch, drunk people didn't have Sareena's coordination—while she did trip over her own feet several times and sway when she walked, she did it in a dreamlike way, as if her happiness was so great that she couldn't care less about ordinary things, like walking in a straight line. And when she slurred her words or talked too loudly, it seemed to be for the same reason, as if happiness was burbling up inside her and pouring out as she spoke.

But of course, "drunk" was the only explanation that would make sense to a non-witch, someone who knew nothing about grimoires or "For Good Cheer" spells or kitchens that wandered off into Faerie.

Grace went to Sareena's house the next day with a basket of lemon cakes she had made herself and a jar filled with ice cream. She was prepared to apologize to Mrs. Khalil on her knees if need be—in fact, she hoped Mrs. Khalil would expect it, for that would lend a great deal of importance to the apology. Grace spent the walk imagining how it would go—she would throw herself at Mrs. Khalil's feet, for starters, and grasp the hem of her dress.

The door opened slightly at Grace's knock, and there stood Mrs. Khalil, staring at Grace through the crack. Grace barely had time to regret her inability to throw herself at Mrs.

Khalil's feet, for she would only bang her head into the door if she tried, before she saw that Mrs. Khalil's face was like stone.

Grace felt a whisper of dread.

She hurriedly dropped her gaze to Mrs. Khalil's shoes. "I—I'm sorry if I'm interrupting, Mrs. Khalil. I came to inquire after Sareena, and to offer you some cakes and ice cream as an apology for—"

"We're not in need of cakes," Mrs. Khalil interrupted, her voice like a knife. "And you are not to set foot on our property again."

At first, Grace thought she'd misheard. "I don't—"

"As I have told Sareena several times," Mrs. Khalil continued, still in that bladelike voice, "you are no longer friends. Please express my thanks to Miss Puddlestone for the gifts."

The door closed shut. It did not slam. It merely closed with a gentle *creak* like the sigh of the wind, yet somehow the sound echoed in Grace's ears like a thunderclap.

She walked home in a daze. Then she stopped and walked back to the Khalils' house. She snuck around the back to see if Sareena was looking out from her bedroom window. But the curtains were drawn.

She waited for an hour out there behind the hedge, until her fingers turned white from the cold and the cakes grew as hard as rocks. Then she went home.

She could not believe it. Surely Mrs. Khalil did not mean—no, it was too awful to contemplate. Surely she was only angry with Grace, and would forgive her when she calmed down.

Grace could only pick at her dinner, though the witch had made her favorite, biscuits and gravy, again. The next day, she waited in the lane by the willow, where she and Sareena always met to walk to school, but Sareena did not come. When Grace reached the schoolhouse, she saw her getting out of her father's wagon—he had driven her there, which had never happened before, even in the worst weather. She caught Grace's eye, and the most miserable look spread across her face.

That was when Grace knew.

Yet even as the despair sank its talons into her heart, she did not give up hope. She followed Sareena into the schoolroom, but Sareena didn't sit at the back in her usual place—she sat up front with Priscilla, who shot Grace a sympathetic look. Later, Priscilla passed Grace a note, which read:

> *I'm afraid that Sareena has been forbidden from speaking
> to you ever again. Her parents believe that you are a bad
> example and that you will make Sareena more unladylike.
> Shall I come over for tea today?*
> *Corjully,*
> *Your friend,*
> *Prissy*

Grace buried her head in her arms until Miss Gordon arrived and scolded her. The other students shot Sareena and Grace looks all day. Priscilla must have blabbed everything to them, though Grace didn't know which version of the story she had shared: the one in which Grace got Sareena drunk, or the one where Grace put a spell on her. Really, did it make a difference? They were both terrible things to do to one's best friend. Grace sank down into her misery and said nothing all day.

"Here," Poppy said softly at lunchtime. She set an apple on the edge of Grace's desk and went back to her seat. Poppy often bullied apples and other treats away from the smaller children. Everybody hated her for it, though most didn't know that Poppy had the worst lunches imaginable, usually consisting of a thermos of milk that was going sour and a pile of wilting green vegetables. Poppy's awful mother watched Poppy's figure like a hawk, claiming that vegetables were the best food for girls to ensure they didn't "grow up to be fat"—as if there was something wrong with that.

Grace opened her mouth to thank Poppy, but she was hunched over the grimoire, muttering to herself. Grace felt grateful for the gesture of friendship, so she ate the apple, although it tasted like dust.

22

THE MOST DREADFUL CHRISTMAS EVE

What saw you in your flight to-day,
Crows, awinging your homeward way?
Thieves and villains, you shameless things!
Black your record as black your wings.
—E. Pauline Johnson (Tekahionwake), "The
Vagabonds"

To Grace, Sareena's absence felt like a missing limb, or like the witch had carved out Grace's heart for one of her spells. She would have handed over her own fingernails if it meant having her dearest friend back. Worse, she did not even have time to mourn Sareena properly, for she could not take her attention off the grimoire and the ever-present threat of the loss of her magic. She had no choice but to keep working.

Her heart went very quiet, filled with that distant seaside roar, as if it knew she had no need for it anymore. Priscilla and Poppy came often to the witch's cottage, and Rum was there, too, when he knew he could keep out of the witch's way. She worked so hard that eventually there came a day when she finally cast spell number fifty, which meant she was halfway through the grimoire. And yet without Sareena to celebrate with, the victory felt hollow.

Grace had long feared that she would lose Sareena one day. She lost all her friends eventually, didn't she? But she had never imagined it would happen so soon.

"You look ridiculous," the witch said one day. It was Christmas Eve, in fact, not that the witch cared. Grace hadn't expected her to celebrate Christmas, but still, it made her feel low. At least at the orphanage there had been a tree in the dining hall and a present for every child, usually socks or something else useful.

"I am *pining*," Grace told the witch. "It's not ridiculous at all. I have lost my best friend in the whole world, and my heart is forever broken."

The witch snorted and looked Grace up and down. Grace had turned several of her dresses black ("For Black Roses" worked on other things besides roses, it turned out) so that her clothing would match her sorrow and despair.

"What a to-do," the witch said from her rocking chair, where she only sat on the days her cough was at its worst. She was gazing into the fire and fondly stroking one of the books of fairy tales, which she had opened to a story about a witch who curses a whole village with foot fungus. "Go have something to eat, you silly girl. I made your favorite, chocolate crinkles."

Grace's mood lifted an inch or two before crashing down again. "With all the baking you do, I'm starting to think you're fattening me up to eat me after all."

"Old habits," the witch said. "Wait until you try my blackberry tart. No child has ever been able to stop eating it, even if it makes them sick."

"Yuck." Grace slumped against the wall. "Though it's not as if I'll be here when your blackberries ripen. Surely I'm doomed to failure now, without Sareena's help."

The witch blinked, and a furrow settled into her brow. "Oh yes," she said quietly, and Grace realized that for a moment, the witch had forgotten about their pact, and about the fact that Grace might not be there in the summer. "Yes, of course."

The witch blinked again, and for some reason, her mood seemed to darken. She scowled at Grace and said tetchily, "The way you carry on about that friend of yours—it's too much. You would have lost her eventually. We lose everyone eventually, you know. If you live as long as I have, you will grow wise enough to stop caring."

"What do you know?" Grace demanded, her temper flaring. "I'll bet you've never had a friend in your entire life, or if you did, you ground them up and put them in a potion or turned them into something dreadful. Well, I'm not going to forget about Sareena the way you've forgotten about poor Patrick!"

Grace spun on her heel and thundered upstairs, then slammed the door with a satisfying *bang*. She realized afterward that this meant she would have no supper, and on Christmas Eve of all nights, as she couldn't possibly go back downstairs and eat with the witch after storming away so dramatically—that would completely undo the storming away.

She slumped onto her bed, certain that never in history had there been a girl more miserable than her.

Windweaver had been napping beside Grace's pillow. He fluttered up to her shoulder and plucked at her hair, crooning softly. She petted his silky black feathers. He was missing several from his tail, for those nasty pinecone-wielding crows had been bullying him again.

"You are my dearest, Windweaver," Grace said. "Without you, I would be completely alone. I love you very much."

I love you, too, he said sleepily. *Will you read tonight?*

Grace gathered her poetry books into her lap—for she had *three* books of poems now, an unimaginable wealth of words—and said, "What would you like to hear?"

"*The Duck and the Kangaroo*," Windweaver said. This was a favorite of theirs, one of those plain, hearty poems that Grace liked best. It was about a duck and a kangaroo and how they were the best of friends. That's it.

She found the poem and read:

> "*Please give me a ride on your back!*"
> *Said the Duck to the Kangaroo.*

"I would sit quite still, and say nothing but 'Quack,'
The whole of the long day through!"

Ducks are very noisy, Windweaver said.

"And we'd go to the Dee, and the Jelly Bo Lee,
Over the land, and over the sea;—
Please take me a ride! O do!"
Said the Duck to the Kangaroo.

The kangaroo is kind, Windweaver said, *to carry the duck every-where.*

"Well, they're friends, aren't they?" Grace said. "Also, everyone should be kind to birds."

Windweaver nodded approvingly.

As she read, Grace became aware of a chill breeze on her neck. She had left the window open a crack—she usually did, except on the very coldest nights—to allow Windweaver to come and go as he pleased.

She pretended to yawn and gave a great stretch. At the same time, she cast a quick glance over her shoulder.

Sure enough, there was Patrick, hovering outside her window. He had been listening to the poem.

It wasn't the first time Grace had caught him doing this. Usually he shuffled away if she noticed him, for if there was one thing she had learned about the witch's brother, it was that he was very shy. Grace thought that she would like Patrick, if he were a person; she liked most people who had a taste for poetry. Not that she *disliked* him as a cloud, but clouds were difficult to get to know.

She read a few more poems, trying to ignore the rumbling in her stomach. Windweaver fell asleep, and perhaps Patrick did, too. Finally, to her relief—for it had been the most dreadful Christmas Eve she had ever experienced—she felt her own eyelids drooping. She turned off the lamp and pulled the blankets over her head.

23

THE WEIGHT OF SHADOWS

Amid the flowers the woodpecker
Is seeking out a withered tree.
—Naitō Jōsō

S now fell overnight, as if to spite her. Grace gazed at that pale glitter, the trees draped in kingly white robes, the sky the color of a blushing eggshell, and could not enjoy a single thing about it. Not even the magic of a Christmas snowfall could lift her misery. In fact, all those drifting snowflakes put her in mind of the hourglass again, each one moving her closer to May-maybe-June and her doom.

She threw on one of her black dresses and over that a black sweater, and then to further emphasize her misery, she left her hair in disarray and did not even wash her face. Thus armored in her despair, she stomped down the stairs.

To Grace's disappointment, the witch was not in the kitchen. It was cold and dark, despite the late hour.

She was sorry she'd shouted at the witch. Not because the

witch hadn't deserved it, but because Grace had clearly made her angry, and now Grace would have to spend Christmas alone.

Briefly, she considered summoning Rum—that was how lonely she felt. But her principles were all she had now, she decided, and she would not compromise them.

She fixed herself a cheerless breakfast of scrambled eggs and toast, which she shared with Windweaver. The witch still did not appear.

Grace gazed out the window. Without an audience for her misery, she felt it lift a little. She knew she should work on the grimoire, but given that it was Christmas, Poppy and Priscilla would not be helping her today, and she couldn't bear the loneliness of working on it by herself. So she bundled up and went outside to build a snowman. It was a miserable one, of course—Grace made sure of that—with a huge frown on its face. Windweaver helped gather twigs and stones for its arms and features. She threw a snowball at him, and he let out a squawk. Then he rolled his own snowball with his clever crow talons, lifted it into the air, and dropped it on her head.

After an hour or so, she had to run inside, breathless with laughter—Windweaver's aim was much better than hers, and her hair was covered in snow.

Her laughter died as she crossed the landing. The kitchen was still empty, and the parlor, and the witch's bedroom.

This was very strange. The witch had never been gone

for so long. A fanciful thought came to Grace, that perhaps witches and other monsters ceased to exist on happy days like Christmas. But then of course she remembered that *she* was still there.

Grace decided that she would summon Rum after all. It didn't mean they were friends if she only wanted to order him around. That was their bargain, after all.

"Rum!" she called. She went to the door, but he wasn't there. But when she went back to the kitchen, she leaped backward in fright. He was sitting in a chair, looking rosy-cheeked and happy, watching Windweaver peck crumbs off a plate. Out of all of Grace's companions, Windweaver seemed to mind Rum's presence the least.

"Hello!" Rum said. "I'm glad you summoned me. I was worried you were upset with me for losing your kitchen. Do you want to play a game?"

"I—no," she said, though the idea was tempting. Rum was wearing a fine cloak that looked as if it were made of silver and snowflakes, and smiling at her with his mischievous fairy eyes, and overall looking like exactly the sort of companion she would wish for in her wildest daydreams. "I want you to help me make snowmen in the garden," she said, and then she stopped and made her voice sterner. "I mean, I *order* you to help me make snowmen."

"Snowmen," Rum repeated slowly. "What are those?"

"You don't know what snowmen are?" Grace couldn't

245

believe it. "You know—creatures children make out of snow. They have sticks for arms and a carrot for a nose and big mouths made of pebbles."

"Sticks for arms?" he repeated. "What about their legs?"

"Well, they don't really have legs," Grace said. "Just a big lump of snow."

Rum looked dubious. "*Children* make these?"

"Yes!" Grace exclaimed in annoyance. She didn't see what he was so confused about.

"All right, all right." He shrugged. "It's your garden, I guess."

They went outside. Rum picked up a handful of snow, and Grace, assuming he meant to throw a snowball at her, threw one at him first. It hit him square in the ear, and he stood there gaping at her in such astonishment that she realized that he *hadn't* been planning to throw one himself. Maybe fairies didn't know about snowball fights, just like they didn't know about snowmen.

Rum caught on quick, though, and soon there were snowballs flying in all directions. Rum turned out to be an excellent opponent for a snowball fight—he was easier to aim at than Windweaver but he had his fairy tricks to keep things interesting, like folding himself away unexpectedly and unfolding somewhere else. Grace retaliated by summoning the wind to blow his snowballs back at him whenever she saw them coming. Rum would shriek in fear at this, for he still disliked witch magic, but often there was laughter mixed up in the shrieking.

Worried that she was once again having too much fun with

her archenemy, Grace ordered Rum to stop throwing snow-balls and showed him where she wanted him to build his snowmen. She began rolling up snow to make the base of her own snowman, but she had barely finished smoothing it down before she heard a terrible squawking from Windweaver.

She turned, and let out a scream. Looming out of the snow was the most hideous sight she'd ever seen. Calling them "snowmen" was only true in the sense that they were made of snow—one had a long snake's tail and a yawning mouth filled with fangs. Another had three heads, each with its features contorted in horrible agony. The other two didn't look even a little bit like men, but something between a bear and a dragon, with fearsome claws and horns running down their backs.

"This is actually fun," Rum said, adding more snow to the closest creature.

"But—but—" Grace sputtered. "What have you *done?*"

His stared at her. "What do you mean? I made snowmen."

"Those aren't snowmen!" she cried. "They're—they're snow*monsters!*"

He threw up his hands. "I thought that's what you wanted! What sort of *man* has arms made of sticks and a carrot for a nose? It's grotesque."

"What is the witch going to say?" Grace shrieked. "The vil-lagers already think she's strange! We can't have these things in her yard!"

"Maybe the witch will like them."

She picked up a handful of snow and hurled it at him. "Just

go! You ruin *everything*—I don't know why I invited you! Go!"

"Fine!" He glared at her. "I have lots of important things to do in Faerie, you know. I didn't even *want* to come here." And with that, he vanished.

"Wait!" Grace shouted. "You have to get rid of them first!" But it was no use. Rum was gone.

Grace stormed up to the nearest snowmonster and gave it a vicious kick. She kicked and she kicked, but no matter how hard she tried, she couldn't topple it. Her boot sank into the snow, and when it came out, there was no mark at all on the snowmonster.

She kept trying until she exhausted herself. Grumbling furiously about Rum, she stomped up the stairs to the cottage.

But as soon as she was back inside, she regretted sending Rum away. The house was very quiet. Grace hadn't noticed it before, because the witch's cottage was usually quiet (though it rarely stayed that way for long when Grace was around). She knew now that this was a different sort of quiet. Quiet has *moods*—it could be comfortable, like the quiet between old friends. It could be angry, or sad.

The quiet inside the house now was *afraid*.

Something was wrong. Where was the witch?

Grace ran back outside. Windweaver caught her alarm and plummeted toward the ground in a dark arc like a bracket, landing on her shoulder.

What is it?

"I don't know."

Grace checked on the witch's horrible horse, but he was sleeping peacefully in his stall. So she hadn't gone out in the carriage. But as Grace ran back toward the house, she noticed a set of footprints that weren't hers. They were fainter, partly filled in with snow.

They led into the woods.

This way, Windweaver called. He flew ahead, weaving through the branches.

Grace ran after him. The witch's trail was harder to follow in the woods, for the snow was patchy there. But Windweaver always found the trail again.

They found her in the clearing.

She lay on her side with a little dusting of snow on her. At first Grace mistook her for a misshapen log, just a feature of the forest, because she was so still. But then Grace saw her cloak, and those painful-looking laced boots she always wore.

Grace fell to the ground and shook her. "Oh no, oh no, don't be . . . oh no—"

She knew she wasn't making much sense. "Miss Puddlestone," Grace finally cried, and the witch drew a rattling breath.

"Not—my name," she whispered. She began to cough.

Grace helped her sit up. "Patrick," the witch murmured between coughs. "Patrick—have to say—goodbye—"

"Oh no," Grace murmured. Was Patrick sick, too? Did clouds get sick? "Let's get you back to the cottage. I'll go look for Patrick afterward and see if he's all right. Oh dear, have you been out here all night?"

Grace helped the witch to her feet. The witch was surprisingly light, impossibly so—but then, she was made of shadows, wasn't she? Shadows weighed nothing at all.

The witch kept mumbling "Patrick," over and over, and once she let out a quiet sob. She didn't seem to know Grace was there.

"It's all right," Grace said in the soothing voice she used to use on the littlest children at the orphanage when they cried at night. "Let's get you inside."

Windweaver took flight, leading them on the quickest path, and they made their slow, halting way back to the cottage.

24

NOT A TERRIBLE CHRISTMAS

And now I see them peer and peep . . .
And then they drop their play,
Flash up into the sunless air,
And like a flight of silver leaves
Swirl round and sweep away.
—Archibald Lampman, "Snowbirds"

Grace got the witch settled on the sofa with cushions and blankets, then she worked the fireplace up to a fine blaze that soon had the house sweaty-hot. The witch seemed to revive after that, but her cough was still bad, so Grace made her pot after pot of tea with honey.

"Here you are," Grace said, adjusting the blankets around her. "Let me just fluff that pillow—"

"You will do no such thing," the witch snapped, but then she started coughing again, and Grace used the distraction to finish fluffing.

"You are a ridiculous child," the witch said a while later,

when Grace brought out a lunch of soft-boiled eggs, cheese, roast beef, and a baked apple. Grace ignored her and set the tray on the witch's lap.

"Windweaver, fetch the witch a clean handkerchief," Grace said. Windweaver obeyed, dropping the hankie neatly on the witch's head.

"I thought I warned you about that bird," the witch said, but the edge in her voice was wearing off. Grace handed her another cup of tea.

"Ridiculous," she muttered, though Grace could tell her heart wasn't in it anymore. The honey trick had greatly improved her cough.

"Now, are you going to tell me why you were out there?" Grace asked.

"None of your business."

Grace shrugged. "All right. Well, perhaps you could give me your opinion on an important philosophical question. You see, a while ago, my dear departed Sareena and I were having a debate about mayflowers and why they are so much lovelier than other flowers. I said that they must bloom only in places where angels have tread, but Sareena thinks that's too sentimental. Do you think a person can be too sentimental about mayflowers? I don't. Anyway, she thinks that they are the ghosts of the flowers that were snipped into bouquets that made people smile. Which I quite like, for they look like happy little ghosts, don't they? And then I said—"

"I was trying to visit my brother," the witch snapped.

Grace blinked. "You were *trying*?"

"He won't see me. After all these years, he still won't see me."

"Oh dear," Grace said, trying to sound sympathetic, though secretly she didn't blame poor Patrick one bit. "When was the last time you tried?"

"Oh—years ago."

Grace's mouth fell open. It was one thing to turn your brother into a cloud, but quite another to abandon him.

"There was no point," the witch snapped. "If he wants to mope and sulk and avoid me, what I am to do about it? I tried everything I could think of to turn him back."

Grace frowned. "Then what made you decide to look for him last night?"

The witch said nothing. She stared down into her teacup. Her gaze was far away and strange, as if she were reading a terrible book and was hardly aware of Grace at all.

Grace recognized that look all too well.

She shot to her feet. "You see them! You see the visions, too, when you look at me."

"Settle down," the witch snapped. "What do I care about a vision or two? A minor inconvenience is all it is."

Despite the witch's dismissive tone, Grace could tell she was furious. She hadn't wanted Grace to know that she could see her own regrets when she looked at Grace, and Grace

253

could understand why—the witch wouldn't want anyone to know she even *had* regrets.

"But why—" Grace stopped. "Why don't *I* see them, too? I see everybody else's regrets. Those who have them, I mean."

"I've closed my mind to you," the witch said. "Ordinary mortals don't know how to do that."

Grace shook her head, almost too astounded for words. "What do you see?" she said in a near whisper. There were so many dreadful possibilities, given the life of wickedness the witch had led.

"Don't look at me like that," the witch said with a snort. "There is but one memory that troubles me, and one alone." She added quickly, "And it is *barely* troubling at all. After all, it was an accident. Hardly my fault. Certainly not worth holding such a ridiculous grudge over."

Grace let out her breath. "Patrick."

The witch frowned into her tea. "He was always so sensitive," she murmured. "We were the best of friends when we were children. He was so quiet that the other children bullied him constantly—until I used my magic to put a stop to it. He liked that, but when he grew older, he began to lecture me. He told me I should simply avoid using magic, like our mother did. She believed magic was evil."

"I suppose your parents were horrible, were they?" Grace always imagined the witch with terrible parents. She supposed it was because she still saw the witch as a fairy tale, and there were no happy childhoods in fairy tales. Children were either tragically orphaned or left in the woods to starve.

"No," the witch said. "They were perfectly ordinary folk, apart from my mother's magic. Rich, too. My father was a businessman. He owned things—land, buildings, ships. We had a grand house in Massachusetts that my mother filled with books. That was unusual, I suppose. Women in those days weren't encouraged to read. Patrick spent most of his boyhood reading. He particularly loved poetry."

Grace thought about Patrick listening at the window as she read to Windweaver. She felt even more sorry for him then. There were no books up in the sky.

"Patrick didn't understand what he was asking me to do," the witch said. She was leaning heavily against the pillows, her gaze distant. "Magic gave me power in more ways than one. Magic gave me the world. With my magic, I could do anything—see everything. Without it, there was only one future for me—to marry and settle down, and disappear into a quiet life. And I didn't want to marry. Particularly after what happened with André."

"Oh no," Grace said, though her dread was coupled with a shiver of anticipation. She did love a good doomed romance. "Was André your suitor? Did he reject you? Did you transform him into something dreadful?"

The witch shook her head. "I should have, I suppose. This was a long time ago. I was a very silly girl back then—terribly sentimental."

Grace couldn't imagine this, but held her tongue.

"André was sixteen, like me, when he proposed," the witch said. "Just a boy. Though sixteen-year-olds were considered men and women back then. I took too long to think it over, I suppose—much as I liked him, I wanted to learn more about my magic, and how could I do that with a husband and a half dozen babies to look after? Eventually, André got tired of waiting and went to work on a trading ship. And I was furious. Not because he decided not to marry me. But because I could never do what he did. For me, there was no choice. Those ships were no place for a woman—that's what people always said. Watching him sail away to have adventures and see strange lands . . . that was when I decided that I would never live an ordinary life. Not I."

"Did you see the world?" Grace asked eagerly.

"Oh yes." The witch's voice was growing faint. "I made homes for myself in the forests of Germany and Russia, Romania and Turkey. I found many strange and wondrous ingredients for my spells, and grew more powerful with each passing year. And I left stories behind wherever I went. But I tired of moving around. I tired of many things, eventually."

Grace wanted to ask the witch a hundred more questions. What a fascinating life she had led! But the witch's eyes were closed, and her ragged breathing had grown even. So Grace simply took the half-empty teacup from her hand and tucked the blankets around her.

* * *

In the end, it was a good Christmas.

Not a perfect Christmas, nor even an entirely happy Christmas. But it certainly wasn't a terrible one.

The witch dozed, and Grace brought her a steady supply of tea and soup and sandwiches. She complained about it all, and called Grace ridiculous many times, and Grace ignored her. For supper, Grace served leftovers from the day before—baked ham, mashed potatoes with plenty of butter, cabbage rolls, and roasted mushrooms, managing to heat everything in the oven without burning one mushroom cap. And for dessert there was cherry ice cream.

Grace was extremely proud to have invented cherry ice cream. It was simply ice cream with tinned cherries mixed in until the ice cream turned light pink. Words could not express how divine it tasted.

"I don't see why you won't let me help with Patrick," she told the witch as they ate their dinner. "There's every possibility that I might be able to turn him back."

"There is no possibility, you silly girl," the witch said. "I never wrote down the spell I used—that is the problem. I can't remember any of the ingredients, which means I can't work out a counterspell."

Grace thought it over. "Still. I fixed your sleep potion, didn't I?"

"That was *barely* a second-order spell," the witch said dismissively. But she gave Grace a brief, thoughtful look. Grace resolved that she would try to turn Patrick back into a man as soon as she finished all the spells in the grimoire.

"He seems to like you," the witch said. "There have been times when I've found you so irritating that I considered breaking our pact and throwing you out, no matter what the council does to me, but each time I remember how much Patrick seems to enjoy your company, so I resist the temptation."

"That's a very cruel thing to say," Grace said. "Although given how wicked you are, I suppose it's halfway thoughtful. Thank you."

As Grace had guessed, the witch frowned at that. She was always so disappointed when Grace was not put off by her nastiness; it was the best way to irritate her. Grace chuckled to herself.

After dinner, the witch informed her that she had stored some of Patrick's old poetry books in a chest in the cellar, and that Grace could take them into her bedroom if she wished. The witch made it sound as if the books were in the way, and that Grace would be doing her a favor by moving them, of course.

Grace gawped at her. "A Christmas present! Oh, how wonderful! That was the very last thing I expected this year—I did not even imagine receiving an old pair of socks, let alone an entire library of poetry. I cannot imagine a better gift—it is beyond words!"

"Then let it stay beyond words," the witch said, uncovering

her ears. "And it is not a gift. I am merely informing you that—"

"Thank you ever so much!" Grace cried. "Thank you, thank you, thank—"

"Good grief!" The witch's hands were over her ears again. "I've had more than enough of your babbling today. Good night."

Her voice was gruff—but Grace had seen her blink several times, very rapidly. Still with her hands over her ears, the witch hastened out of the kitchen. If she had remained a moment longer, Grace would have hugged her—she suspected the witch was aware of this.

Of course, Grace went immediately to the cellar, where she found the promised poetry—two dozen books in all. They were yellowed with age, and some were falling apart, but most were in good condition. There were poets Grace had never heard of before, with amusing names like Donne and Chaucer, and unfortunately several volumes by dull Mr. Shakespeare. Still, now that she knew Patrick liked him, she thought she would read a sonnet or two whenever he came by her window.

She hugged the books to her chest. Yes, it had been a good Christmas indeed.

"Grace?" the witch called from the parlor, an odd note in her voice.

"Yes?" Grace dashed upstairs, happiness lightening her steps. She knew she shouldn't hold out hope for a hug, but that would truly complete the day, wouldn't it?

She found the witch standing by the front window, where she had gone to draw the curtains, staring out. "You called?" Grace said hopefully.

"Yes," the witch said, turning to glower ferociously at her. "What on earth are those *things* out on the lawn?"

25

MISS CORDELIA BURBAGE COMES TO TOWN

Oh! snowstorm, at whose blast the birds
Begin to cry o'er sea and hill!
—Kawai Chigetsu

The following week brought a not unexpected visitor to the witch's door in the form of Mrs. Charity Crumley, who considered herself the witch's dearest friend. (Grace did not like to think about how the witch viewed Mrs. Crumley, but she saw the witch's eyes stray longingly to the sack of bones Sareena and Grace had left on the porch.)

"There's that Grace girl," Mrs. Crumley said as Grace hurriedly hid the grimoire—she had been measuring sand for spell fifty-four, "For Lightening" (not to be confused with spell thirteen, "For Lightning").

Mrs. Crumley looked Grace up and down. "Politeness is not a skill of hers, is it, Evelyn? I've had no apology from her for ruining my dress the first time we met."

Grace didn't think it was very polite to talk about someone

as if they were a shabby piece of furniture, but she held her tongue. And anyway, she had completely forgotten that she had kicked a bucket of ice cream at Mrs. Crumley all those months ago, and that had certainly been rude of her. Grace looked at her feet and mumbled an apology.

Mrs. Crumley, to Grace's surprise, accepted the apology without complaint. "There's a good girl," she said warmly, and handed Grace her coat and gloves. Grace put them away in the closet, like a good girl, feeling more than a little ashamed of herself.

"Dear me, you are not looking well, Evelyn," Mrs. Crumley said. "Is it that cough again? You must see Dr. Herbert about it."

"I've seen numerous doctors, Charity," the witch said, which Grace doubted was true. How could the witch see a doctor? She had very little in the way of a body to examine. Even a doctor used to missing limbs and a variety of strange diseases would find that peculiar. "It's just the cold air."

Mrs. Crumley harrumphed. She had brought the witch some groceries, so that the witch would not need to go out in the snow. As Mrs. Crumley put everything away, she gave the witch all the latest gossip about who had fallen out with who and who was dying or getting married in Brook-by-the-Sea, which the witch did not seem very interested in. She said "quite" and "ah yes" in all the right places, though.

"I hope you're putting that girl of yours to work, Evelyn," Mrs. Crumley said. "She seems a willful child, but willful children can be tamed if you give them enough chores. Do you say your prayers every night, girl?"

"Not exactly," Grace said slowly. "But I do read poetry. I keep the window open, too, so that if God is listening in—as I suppose He must be—He can have a bit of entertainment. I expect it gets dull listening to prayers all evening long. For how many times can a person hear 'Now I lay me down to sleep' before they feel they are going batty? I would certainly welcome a distraction, if I were Him, especially if the poetry was by Emily Dickinson or Pauline Johnson or Edward Lear or Du Fu."

Grace smiled, pleased by her logic. Mrs. Crumley stared at Grace as if she'd kicked another bucket of ice cream at her.

"Poetry!" she exclaimed. "Poetry, instead of prayers! Now I've heard everything. Do you encourage this nonsense, Evelyn?"

"No, of course not," the witch said, shooting Grace a poisonous glare.

"I should hope you don't. Children shouldn't be allowed to read poetry—little girls especially. It fills their heads with all kinds of fanciful notions, which only sets them up for disappointment, for life is rarely as rosy as the poets say it is. But where is the child getting all this poetry from?"

"Well—my brother had a few volumes that he left in my possession. I didn't think—"

"Oh, Evelyn." Mrs. Crumley shook her head. "I'm sure it was kindly meant on your part, but a headstrong girl like this should not be allowed to clutter her head with such things."

Grace gaped at her. Poetry wasn't clutter! Clutter was old socks left lying around, or dishes not put away. Imagine putting poetry in the same category as socks! And Grace knew Mrs. Crumley could have read little poetry herself, for if she had, she would know that most poets were terribly mopey individuals who very rarely took a rosy view of anything.

The witch sent Grace away then, to prepare tea for herself and Mrs. Crumley. Grace was quite happy to be sent away from Mrs. Crumley. She could never be friends with someone with so little appreciation for beauty.

"That's a child that needs a firm hand," Grace heard Mrs. Crumley say in a voice that carried to the kitchen. "Does she often ramble on like that, Evelyn? How trying for you."

"Oh, I don't know," the witch said. "She is a ridiculous little thing, it's true. But there's nothing boring about her. And with a person that ridiculous, you can't help wondering sometimes what they'll come out with next."

Grace was so astonished she dropped the sugar. Was the witch *defending* her?

"I suppose," Mrs. Crumley said grudgingly. "We all need a little company, don't we? But still, there's something terribly unladylike about her."

"She's like my brother," the witch said absently. "He had a head full of daydreams, too."

For once, the witch didn't make this sound like an insult. There was something in her voice that, if she had been anyone other than the witch, Grace would have thought was sadness. She wasn't sure why, but it made her feel sad, too. She busied herself with the tea.

When Grace brought the tea tray into the parlor, Mrs. Crumley was delivering more gossip. The witch was barely listening as usual, until Mrs. Crumley said a name that made her sit up straight.

"*Who* has arrived in town, Charity?" she demanded.

Mrs. Crumley blinked. "A Miss Burbage—Cordelia Burbage. Arrived last month from Halifax—strange time of year to travel, isn't it? She's very tight-lipped, but I understand her visit has something to do with her father's disappearance. Frederick Burbage—do you remember him, Evelyn? Mrs. Fisher says he was rather dashing. He was a businessman from Charlottetown. I don't know what kind of business it was, but it brought him into Brook-by-the-Sea a few times about twenty years ago. It was quite a scandal when he vanished into thin air—some said he ran off to America with a mistress. Do you remember?"

"Yes," the witch said. "I remember."

Her tone was perfectly bland, but for some reason, Grace felt a shiver run down her spine. "That's right," Mrs. Crumley said. "You and Mr. Burbage were friends, weren't you?"

Grace eyed the witch with interest. She wondered if the witch had been real friends with this Mr. Burbage, or the sort of friends she was with Mrs. Crumley.

"I don't know," the witch said. "He—he stopped by a few

times, that's all. He owned part of the woods, and he would sometimes go for a walk—what are you hovering about for, girl?"

She said this last sentence sharply, and Grace jumped. Both the witch and Mrs. Crumley were scowling at her.

"Eavesdropping is not a virtue in a young lady," Mrs. Crumley said.

"Is it a virtue in an *old* lady?" Grace demanded, her temper flaring. "You seem to learn half your gossip that way."

Mrs. Crumley's mouth fell open in outrage. The witch let out a snort that she hastily turned into a cough.

"What a beastly temper this child has!" Mrs. Crumley exclaimed.

"You will apologize to Mrs. Crumley at once, Grace," the witch said.

But Grace had no intention of apologizing to the poetry-hating old woman, who was every bit as rude as she thought Grace was, just in a different way. Grace whirled on her heel and stormed off. It was one of her better storming-offs, she felt, for she was wearing her favorite black dress, which had a full skirt that swirled dramatically whenever she turned around.

"What a willful little thing," she heard Mrs. Crumley say as Grace slammed her way out the door. "I do hope you'll deal with her, Evelyn."

"Oh yes," the witch replied. "I'll deal with her, all right, Charity. Never fear."

26

THE MYSTERY OF FREDERICK BURBAGE

It can't be summer—that got through;
It's early yet for spring;
There's that long town of white to cross
Before the blackbirds sing.
—Emily Dickinson, "It can't be summer—that got through"

The witch did *not* deal with Grace. In fact, she spent most of supper chuckling to herself.

"The look on her face," the witch said happily as she stirred her sleep potion. "She *really* dislikes you now. I doubt we'll have any more unexpected visits from Charity Crumley."

Grace didn't laugh with her. The truth was, she was feeling rather guilty. Mrs. Crumley couldn't help it if she was old and sour and had no imagination. People who lacked an interest in poetry should be pitied, Grace had decided, not scorned.

She tried asking the witch about Cordelia and Frederick Burbage, but the witch just pretended not to hear. Well, Grace decided, she would ask around the next time they took the carriage into town. Surely there would be someone besides Mrs. Crumley who could tell her about the mysterious Frederick.

But she didn't have to wait that long. A few days later, in the middle of a winter Sunday, there came a knock on the door.

It was one of those January days that made the eye ache for the colors of spring. The trees were barren, and everything was shades of white and gray. Grace wondered if this was what living on the moon was like, the whole world gone pale and silent.

She was in the kitchen, chopping mushrooms for spell number fifty-eight ("For Illusions," a wonderfully mysterious-sounding spell) and thinking about living on the moon. Occasionally she tossed a scrap to Windweaver, who was perched on one of the cupboards out of sight of the witch, who was resting on the sofa. She had recovered much of her strength following her collapse in the snow, her face losing its grayish tinge, but she was still sleeping rather a lot. The house was filled with a sweet aroma, as, in addition to working on spell fifty-eight, Grace was baking cinnamon scones for their tea, which happily turned out only a little singed on the bottom, by far her greatest triumph in the cooking department. She banged about in the kitchen, reciting bits and pieces of new poems she had learned, just to enjoy how the words felt in her mouth. The witch occasionally called out complaints about the noise she was making, but Grace knew by then that she only did it because she enjoyed complaining, and that she actually liked the company of Grace's noise.

Grace chopped the mushrooms very fine, for she was worried the witch would not approve the spell; she had only been able to find fourteen foxchild mushrooms, not seventeen, as the grimoire called for. She hoped the witch wouldn't notice.

When the knock came she sprang to the door, expecting Priscilla or Poppy, for they had both promised to visit that day to help with spell fifty-eight. Instead she found a thin young woman of twenty or so dressed in severe blacks and grays. She was pretty, Grace thought, but she had a pale, sharp sort of look about her that made Grace think of a ghost. This made Grace warm to her instantly, of course.

The woman looked startled to see Grace. "Good day," she said uncertainly. "Is your—er—mother about?"

"Sort of," Grace said, meaning that the witch was only her mother in a very, very loose sense, but the young woman's expression grew cold, as if she thought Grace was being unhelpful on purpose.

"If she's at home, you will let me in," she said in a very high-and-mighty voice, as if she were royalty and Grace a servant. Then, ruder still, she barged past Grace without waiting for a reply.

"She's in the parlor," Grace called after her, not because she wished to be helpful but because she didn't like the idea of an unpleasant person like that roaming around the witch's house willy-nilly.

The young woman didn't barge any farther than the hallway, though, and stood there a moment, looking around as if expecting something to jump out at her. Her expression was a curious mixture of dread and dismay. A very reasonable reaction to a witch's house, Grace supposed, but she'd never seen an adult look at it that way.

"May I tell her your name?" Grace said, to remind the woman that there was such a thing as manners. The woman only looked more alarmed. She went into the parlor without saying another word.

The witch looked up and frowned. She hated callers, particularly unexpected ones. "Yes?" she said frostily.

"I—" The young woman looked as if she wanted to turn and run out the door. But she controlled herself and drew back her shoulders. A cold anger hardened her face.

"My name is Cordelia Burbage," she said. "I believe you knew my father?"

The witch's expression froze. "Freddy." She swallowed, and Grace gave a start, remembering the photograph on the witch's desk. *From Freddy, with love.* Freddy was Frederick Burbage! "Yes," the witch murmured. "You—you look a great deal like him."

Cordelia ignored this. "What exactly do you think you're doing here, Miss Puddlestone?"

This seemed to Grace a very strange question for a stranger to ask upon barging into your house. But the witch didn't seem to notice. There was a little silence, and then she said, "Nothing that should concern you. This land was not being used, technically, and so—"

"Technically?" Miss Burbage repeated. "You want to be technical, do you? Well, Miss Puddlestone, I can say that *technically* you are a squatter. This land does not belong to you—it never did. It belonged to my father."

Grace drew in her breath. She expected the witch to deny this, but the witch just returned Cordelia's look coolly.

"Your father wasn't doing anything with these woods," the witch said, "so I didn't see any harm in it. And neither did he—when he realized I was here, he was quite content to look the other way. For a time, in fact, we were"—she paused—"friends."

"Perhaps." Cordelia gave the witch a long, dark look. "But my father has been missing for two decades. He has officially been declared dead, and now that I am a grown woman, everything he owned has passed to me. Including this." She swept her hand out, seeming to encompass everything—the witch's house, the garden with the stream threading through it, the forest.

"I see." Cordelia could have been reading the weather report, for all the witch seemed to care. "Congratulations."

"'Congratulations'?" Cordelia repeated. Her hand clenched around her skirts. "Is that all you have to—"

"Those men," Grace said suddenly. "Those men who were

poking around in the woods last month. They said Sareena and I were trespassing. You sent them, didn't you?"

"I don't know that I like your tone," Cordelia said. "Yes, I sent a few surveyors to inspect these woods—*my* woods. And I had every right to do so."

She seemed to be making an effort to control herself. She fixed her gaze on the witch, and to Grace's astonishment, the witch flinched.

"My father may have indulged you," Cordelia continued. "He even let the villagers think you had a right to be here, that this land belonged to you. Yet none of them seem to have any memory of when, precisely, you came to Brook-by-the-Sea, nor where you were before that. Going by my father's records, you've been here at least fifty years. It's peculiar, isn't it?"

The witch shrugged. "Villages like this have plenty of peculiar characters, Miss Burbage."

The young woman's jaw tightened. "I have no intention of living here myself. But this land is mine now, and I will do with it what I please. My men tell me that these woods could easily be turned into profitable farmland, so I have already arranged to have the trees sold to a timber company. They will begin logging in the spring. I will not turn you out in the dead of winter—I am not so heartless as that. I shall give you six months to make your arrangements."

Grace looked from her to the witch, dumbfounded. Was what Cordelia said true? The witch wasn't denying it.

"You're wrong," Grace burst out. "This is Miss Puddle-stone's land. You can't force us out! This is our home."

"I certainly can." Cordelia's face darkened as she looked at Grace. "You're like her, aren't you? You have that same look—more goblin than girl. Am I supposed to feel sorry for you?"

Grace reddened with fury. She would have flown into a proper rage, but something in the witch's face stopped her. The witch still hadn't spoken—she was simply sitting there, face pale and eyes dark. Grace was suddenly filled with dread. Cordelia might be horrible, but Grace didn't want to see her cooked alive.

"You should go," Grace said, touching Cordelia's arm. The woman jumped as if Grace had hit her. Some of the confidence seemed to leak out of her then.

"Yes," Cordelia said. "Yes, I suppose I will. I've said every-thing I wish to say."

The witch sat with her dark eyes fixed on Cordelia's face. Cordelia took a hasty step back, as if finally sensing the danger she was in.

"Come on, come on," Grace said, nearly dragging her now. Grace opened the door, and Cordelia went out immediately. She gave Grace one last, puzzled look, and then she was hur-rying down the steps and along the snowy lane.

Grace went back into the parlor. "What was she talking about? Surely she's wrong about the forest. But if she isn't, I really hope you won't turn her into anything dreadful. There must be a spell that can simply send her away, mustn't there?"

The witch still didn't speak. Grace supposed she was too furious.

"Or perhaps we can make her frightened," Grace said. "So frightened that she leaves Brook-by-the-Sea at once and never—"

But at that moment, the witch fell back against the sofa in a faint.

27

TO TRAP THE MOON

She opened the cage, and away there flew
A bright little bird, as a short adieu
It hastily whistled, and passed the door,
And felt that its sorrowful hours were o'er.
—Hannah Flagg Gould, "The Bird Uncaged"

Grace stumbled over the snow, her breath hissing through the scarf she had wrapped around her mouth and nose. Her boots sank into hidden depths where there were roots and stones to trip her. She was shaking all over, but not from the cold.

She knew she had only an hour. The moon rose before five o'clock, and she had to reach the lake before it dipped below the trees again.

The witch had barely been breathing when Grace left her. If she had been any other old lady, Grace would have thought her heart had given out. But of course, the witch had no heartbeat, so Grace couldn't very well send for a doctor to check on it.

The only option was magic.

"For Strength," spell number sixty in the grimoire, was particularly tricky, so tricky that lately it had been giving Grace a stomachache from worrying about it. The trickiness was due to a single ingredient: a piece of the moon.

As the witch lay on the sofa, her eyes closed and her face pale as bone, Grace's panicked thoughts had turned to the grimoire, and she had remembered spell sixty. Surely strength was just the thing the witch needed. But how was she to find a piece of the moon?

The idea struck her with such force that she fell out of her chair. Windweaver, asleep by the fire, mumbled something but didn't wake.

Grace paused only long enough to adjust the blankets around the witch, then went crashing out the door, buttoning her coat as she plunged into the winter evening.

She reached the lakeshore at last. The lake was deep in the woods, and was perhaps closer to being a pond than a lake, but the water was clear and cold. Now, of course, it was covered by a layer of ice.

A fox eyed her sideways as it slunk back into the underbrush, a splash of red on the snow, and the lake shone in the purple twilight. Grace searched the sky for the moon, and there it was! Just peeking out through the bare branches, a jewel caught in a strand of wavy hair. She knew that once it rose above the branches, she would have only a few moments before it began to dip back down again.

Hesitantly, she stepped out onto the ice.

There was a slight creak, like an old house settling at night. She bit her lip, but she knew she had to keep going—if she didn't, the witch could die. She might *already* be dying. Grace couldn't let that happen—she couldn't be all alone again.

With her next step, the ice was silent. Slowly, testing each step as she went, she made her way across the lake.

There came another long, low creak, which echoed softly off the trees crowded against the shore.

For a moment, Grace froze, heart thundering, but the ice didn't shatter beneath her feet and swallow her into the lake. The moon was just above the branches now. It was between half-full and full, a waning gibbous. Crescents and full moons got all the glory, but Grace thought this shape was just as beautiful, like a sleepy eye. It cast its reflection upon the ice, between where Grace stood and the dark place in the middle of the lake.

She was so excited that she lurched forward, barely remembering to be cautious. Fortunately, there were no more ominous creaks.

She knelt beside the moon's reflection and drew a bottle from her coat. It held the remains of spell number ten, "For Making One from Two," which fortunately took the form of a potion. Potion spells could be bottled and used up later— the witch kept many of her potions in the pantry, shoved in among the flour and tinned preserves. It was not at all a well-organized pantry, and Grace supposed it could be quite a dangerous one for an unwary human.

Her hands were so cold that she nearly spilled the potion all over herself as she was undoing the stopper. Shaking, she poured the dark liquid over the ice and the moon's reflection.

"May it be, by sun and stars," she said. Then she held her breath.

The potion trickled over the ice. At first it looked like a wound leaking dark blood, but then the trickle slowed as the potion began to freeze. Little wisps of mist curled off the ice, and suddenly the potion vanished.

Grace picked up a broken branch she had found in the woods. Carefully, she banged it against the ice, forming a circle around the moon. Chips of ice struck her face, but she kept banging. And then—

The ice gave a groan, and a spiderweb of cracks began forming. She gave the ice one last bang, then she leaned against it. Her weight shattered the ice beneath her hands, and she drew back quickly before she fell in.

And there it was! Drifting among the shards of ice was a jagged sliver, rounded on one side, which held the reflection of the moon. That held it even as the moon began to dip below the trees, even as she lifted the shard out of the water and turned it away from the sky. Her spell had bound the reflection to the ice!

She let out a gasp of delight. She turned the shard this way and that, admiring how the moon hovered there within the ice.

It was the most beautiful thing she had ever seen.

Grace stood, grinning, and that was when the ice burst apart.

She screamed as she fell, and then there was nothing but the cold. Oh, but *cold* didn't begin to describe that water—cold was ice cream and snowballs, or the look on the witch's face when Grace wouldn't stop talking. This was the kind of cold that lurked in the black space between stars. The cold of nothingness.

She thrashed toward the surface, spots exploding in her vision. Her head struck a heavy shard of broken ice and she clawed at it, trying to find a way through. She was going to die, some part of her thought distantly.

Yet her panic gave her strength, and she punched at the piece of ice until it broke down the middle, and she shoved her head back into the night. She screamed again, or tried to—the air felt even worse than the water now, freezing her hair to her skin. She fumbled for the ice, trying to pull herself to safety— she couldn't feel it, even when a sharp edge jabbed her in the stomach. Choking and sobbing, she lifted an elbow onto the edge, then a knee—

The edge broke.

She sank back into the lake, and that distant little voice noted that she wouldn't have enough strength to pull herself up a second time. *What a silly way to die*, the distant voice observed. *Not very witchly at all, drowning. Now, being burned at the stake, or perhaps accidentally turning yourself into an asteroid and zooming off*

into space, that would be much more—

Suddenly, there were hands wrapped around Grace's shoulders, pulling her out. The ice broke around her as she was dragged backward toward the shore—how was her rescuer able to balance on breaking ice?

Grace didn't notice when she reached firm ground. Somebody was patting her face. A very strange somebody with wings illuminated by the moonlight, which traced little golden veins running through them that she had never noticed before.

"Rum!" she said, or tried to, for her face seemed to be frozen. It came out as "uhn." So he *was* following Grace around—there was no other explanation for it.

"What's wrong with you?" he demanded, his eyes wide and frightened. She tried to tell him that she was freezing to death, but all that came out was "uhn uhn uh eth." Somehow she was still holding the piece of ice with the moon in it.

"I'll take you home," he said decisively. "The witch will know how to fix you."

Then something very curious happened. Looking back on it, Grace realized that Rum did his folding trick again—but he brought her with him through the fold. For a moment, the world went green-gold, and there came the sound of rustling leaves and the smell of wet earth, that lovely smell of a warm spring day after a rain, but not *quite* the same, and she knew she was in another world. Then they unfolded or folded another way—fairy magic was terribly confusing—and they were back in winter by the old cherry tree. She didn't realize it at the time, for she was still clinging to her anger, but that was the moment when she really and truly forgave Rum. Not because he had pulled her out of the lake, but because he gave her a glimpse of that other world.

Rum dragged her inside the witch's house, and she collapsed on the floor by the fire.

28

INTO THE FIRE

The eggs that lay in the nest when I took to bed
Have changed into little birds and flown away.
—Po Chü-i, "Illness"

Being mostly composed of a mixture of tree roots and spices, "For Strength" was straightforward enough if you overlooked the impossibility of using the moon as an ingredient. When the ice melted in the pot, the reflection of the moon remained. Grace poured the potion into a bottle, and the little moon floated there among the roots and the dark flecks of spice.

"May it be, by sun and stars," Grace murmured, holding the bottle beneath the witch's nose so that she could breathe the peppery scent. The witch's eyes snapped open and she sat up with a snort.

"Spell sixty," Grace couldn't resist telling her, for no matter what crisis was at hand, there was still their bargain and the loss of her magic to worry about. The witch scowled and waved her hand.

"What happened?" Grace said. "When you fell over, I thought—I was so worried that—"

"Spare me the melodramatics," the witch said. "Cordelia Burbage is a witch, apparently. That's what happened."

"What—oh!" Grace said. "Then she—she made you see visions? Bad memories? What did you see?"

The witch made no reply. Grace worried she was going to faint again.

"That was terrible of her," Grace said. "To barge in here and magic you like that."

The witch shook her head once. "She doesn't know."

"Doesn't know—" Grace stopped. "That she's a witch? How can a person *not* know that?"

"It isn't so hard to believe," the witch said. "Most people don't drift through life with their heads full of fairy tales."

Grace was almost happy to hear the insult, for it meant the witch was feeling more herself. But she wouldn't answer any more questions about Cordelia Burbage, and this filled Grace with a terrible dread. Surely if Cordelia was wrong about the whole thing, the witch would have been bursting with threats and curses. But the witch was quiet, and after drinking some tea, she went to bed.

Grace was desperate for someone to talk to. She opened the window and called for Windweaver, and after a few moments, he came soaring in from the dark trees.

He was shaking, though not from the cold. Half of his tail feathers were missing, and he was balanced on one foot, the other curled up against him.

"Windweaver!" she cried. "What's happened?"

It's all right, he said. *It's not broken. I brought them a mouse, and they attacked me.*

Grace's jaw dropped in outrage. "You brought them a peace offering—such a thoughtful one, too—and they repaid you with an act of violence? Those rotten birds! I'll teach them."

Don't, Windweaver pleaded. *Just leave it. You'll only make it worse.*

Grace felt terrible for Windweaver. He so missed the company of other crows, of having his own flock to protect and be protected by. And yet every crow he met knew he was touched by magic, and despised him for it.

Grace hugged him to her chest, hating the cruelty of the world. She would always protect him, and they would never be apart—even if she did lose her magic, she swore to herself that she would find a way to keep him.

Windweaver felt better after she fetched him a raisin scone and some smoked salmon. They sat by the fire, Grace in her shift with a blanket wrapped around her, Windweaver curled up in her lap, sleeping off his meal. Grace supposed she must have fallen asleep, too, for the next time she opened her eyes, the fire was almost out and somebody was knocking frantically on the door.

She squinted at the grandfather clock. It was barely five in the morning! Who would visit at such an hour? Could it be the detestable Cordelia Burbage again? Putting on her sternest face, Grace pulled open the door.

It was Sareena. She stood there wrapped up in two coats and scarves but still shivering. At the sight of Grace, she burst into tears.

Of course, Grace burst into tears as well. Then they leaped into each other's arms and collapsed upon the landing in a heap.

"Oh, Sareena, I've missed you so much!" Grace cried.

"I missed you, too, Grace." She gripped Grace's arms. "These last few weeks have been utterly dreadful. I've been so worried about you and how you're getting on with your spells that I've barely been able to sleep! There were some nights that I woke up afraid that the witch would get fed up and decide to bake you after all, no matter what she promised."

Grace swiped a hand over her eyes. "But what are you doing here? Has your mother finally forgiven me? Do come inside and tell me everything."

But Sareena shook her head. "I can't—Grace, you must come with me. It's Daisy Bean. She's terribly unwell. My father has sent for the doctor again, but he wasn't any help at all yesterday, so I thought that you—maybe there's a spell—oh, Grace, I'm so scared."

No sooner had the words left her mouth than Grace was flying upstairs, Sareena at her heels. Grace threw on a dress and stockings and raced down again.

"Windweaver," Grace called, buttoning her coat, and he followed them into the darkness.

They talked incessantly as they hurried through the snow, breath rising around them in billowing clouds. Sareena told Grace how Daisy Bean had tripped and cut her arm, how she had seemed all right at first, until the fever set in. She told Grace other things, too—how her mother had forbidden anyone to mention Grace's name, how insufferable Priscilla was sometimes, and how she missed sitting next to Grace in their back-row desks instead of up at the front with Priscilla. Grace told her about her progress with the grimoire and babbled out all her fears about Cordelia and the witch's illness.

"Oh, Sareena, what if the witch *does* get turned out?" Grace said. "What if they cut down the forest? Where will I go? How shall I live with the memory of this wonderful place in my head all the time, knowing that I can never get it back again?"

"You can live with me," Sareena said. "I'll hide you in the attic until you're grown and can make your own way in life. You can wear a long white dress and veil, so that if anybody catches sight of you in the window, they will assume you're the ghost in the attic. It's perfect, because my mother already thinks there's a ghost up there."

"That's very kind, but—"

"I swear it would work," Sareena said, misunderstanding Grace's objection. "She spends half the day talking about cold spots and clanking chains. Daddy gets so desperate to get away sometimes that he goes out and washes the cows. Cows don't need washing, Grace."

Grace sighed, for Sareena had never understood her attachment to the witch's cottage, which Sareena had once referred to as "creepy" and thereafter kept her opinions to herself, having learned how much Grace loved it.

"Thank you," Grace said simply, and squeezed her hand. Sareena squeezed back.

"I'll bet the witch will hex that horrid Cordelia," Sareena said. "She'll send her somewhere far, far away and you won't have to go anywhere."

"I expect you're right," Grace said. She had assumed that the witch would do so when she recovered her strength, though as she thought about it, she felt a shiver go through her.

Surely the witch would recover her strength. Wouldn't she?

Sareena took Grace straight to Daisy Bean's bedroom. It was a small room filled—unsurprisingly—with green, which somehow made it feel bigger. The quilt was green, the curtains, the woven rug. The window was open despite the cold. Sareena's father sat by Daisy Bean's bed with a basin of water and rags, his sleeves rolled up past the elbow. He was a slight man with very bushy eyebrows and an impressive mustache. Both eyebrows and mustache twitched at the sight of Grace.

"It's all right, Daddy," Sareena said. "Grace has come to help."

Grace stepped inside. Daisy Bean, dwarfed even by her small bed, gazed back at her with the bright, unseeing eyes of fever. Her face was red, her hair plastered to her forehead with sweat. Her breaths were rapid and shallow.

"What is this?" A shadow fell across the door. Sareena's mother stood there, her face gone white. She started forward, as if to yank Grace away from Daisy Bean. "Get out."

"I—I can help," Grace stammered. "I know about infections. I nursed some of the little kids at the orphanage."

This wasn't true, but it made Mrs. Khalil stop where she was. Her husband went to her side. "Let her try," he murmured. "There's no harm in it. Until the doctor comes."

Mrs. Khalil made a noise that suggested she saw a great deal of harm in it. Mr. Khalil touched Grace on the shoulder— he had warm eyes, even when pinched with worry. "Sareena speaks very highly of you—she says you're a true friend. I think that's enough for us to trust you."

Grace swelled at this, her confidence rising. She could think of no higher compliment than *true friend*. "I'll do my best."

Mr Khalil nodded. "I'll fetch some more water and fresh cloths," he said, and left the room. Grace wished he would stay—now she and Sareena were alone with Mrs. Khalil, whose eyes, as she watched Grace, were decidedly *not* warm. Grace's hands shook a little as she drew the "For Strength" potion from her coat. She tried to look confident, for Sareena's sake.

"May it be, by sun and stars," she whispered. The moon trapped in the potion trembled a little. "May it be, by sun and stars."

"What is that?" Mrs. Khalil demanded.

"Mum," Sareena said. "Please."

Grace held the potion under Daisy Bean's nose for a moment, and then she poured a little into a cloth and wiped it over her forehead. Potions did not need to be drunk in order to work—in fact, many contained ingredients that would kill you if you tried. Grace didn't like to think what would happen if Daisy Bean swallowed the moon—perhaps it would get stuck inside her and leave her stomach aglow forever.

"What is she doing?" Mrs. Khalil cried. "I won't stand for—"

Her voice died as Daisy Bean gave a cough and lifted her head a little. "Mummy?"

"I'm here, darling." Mrs. Khalil flew to her daughter's side. "Oh! Her color looks better."

Grace felt Daisy Bean's forehead. The little girl *did* look better—but that was only compared to how she had looked before. She was still terribly sick. "For Strength" had given her strength—but that wasn't enough, if the illness was still inside her.

"I'm sleepy," she complained. She drank a little water that Mrs. Khalil offered her, then closed her eyes and was instantly asleep.

"Do it again," Mrs. Khalil commanded. There was no fear in her eyes now, only a desperate intensity. "Whatever you just did—*do it again.*"

"It's not enough." Grace searched for a way to explain it to her. "It's as if—"

289

"Grace, we don't have time," Sareena said. "Is there anything else that might work? What about 'For Ice'? To take the fever away?"

Grace shook her head slowly. "For Ice," spell twenty-eight, wouldn't work, she was certain of it. She felt a calm confidence settle over her, the same thing she had felt when she had burned the roses for the witch's sleeping potion, or found her way to the moonweed.

And then she knew what to do.

"I need lemon peel and mint," she said. "And thistles. And—Windweaver!"

The crow alighted on the windowsill. Mrs. Khalil started, but didn't cry out.

"Do you remember where you found that beehive last summer?" He nodded. "Show Sareena."

Grace turned to her friend. "You'll need to fetch a piece of honeycomb as long as the dawn—that means a small piece. Like this." She held her forefinger close to her thumb. "That's about as much as bees can make in that time. I'll go back to the cottage for the rest of the supplies."

Sareena nodded and hurried out the door.

"When will you be back?" Mrs. Khalil demanded. She seemed not to notice the strangeness of the question—after all, barely a moment ago she had been ordering Grace to leave. But Grace could see now that she was a practical person—that must be where Sareena got it from. And if there was a chance that Grace could help Daisy Bean, Mrs. Khalil would take it, even if it meant putting up with crows who nodded their heads. She had a pale, grim look that suggested she was trying her hardest not to faint.

"Soon," Grace promised. "Daisy Bean will be all right for a while."

She had no idea if that was true—Daisy Bean's breathing was shallow, her cheeks red as apples. But Mrs. Khalil seemed to calm a little, and Grace saw her watching from the window as Grace and Sareena raced across the snow in opposite directions.

By the time Grace returned, the doctor still hadn't come. He had likely been called to one of the distant farmsteads, Mrs. Khalil said. Mr. Khalil had gone to search for him.

Grace put the mint, lemon peel, and thistles in a pot with several handfuls of snow, and set the pot over the fire that crackled in the parlor. Snow, she'd found, worked just as well as rainwater.

Sareena and Windweaver returned with the honeycomb. Grace put it in the pot, stirring as she absently licked the stickiness from her fingers.

"Bring her in here," she told Mrs. Khalil.

They settled Daisy Bean in the armchair closest to the fire. She didn't stir, and seemed to be barely breathing now. Mrs. Khalil kept swiping her hand over her eyes in an almost violent gesture, as if she was furious at her tears for distracting her.

"All right," Grace said. The potion filled the parlor with a clean, crisp smell. "That should do it."

"What do you need?" Mrs. Khalil said. She seemed to have completely forgotten that she hated Grace—or at least, she had put that aside for now. Grace decided that Mrs. Khalil was not horrible after all. Yes, she'd thought Grace was wicked, and Grace *was* wicked, so how could she blame Mrs. Khalil? Grace might be her enemy, but she wasn't Grace's.

"Move her closer," Grace said. "She needs to be as close to the smoke as possible."

The "For Clarifying" spell (number twenty in the grimoire) was a little different from the others. Once brewed, the potion had to be poured over a fire to produce smoke—it was the smoke, Grace supposed, that carried the clarifying magic. When she had cast the spell the first time, nothing much had happened. The world had seemed sharper than before, and somehow less cluttered, as if only the essential parts were still there and everything else had been washed away. Grace couldn't have said why she thought it was the spell to help Daisy Bean. But the witch had said in one of her few helpful moments that many spells had more than one use. Since then, Grace had come to think of magic like poetry—a poem, after all, could mean more than one thing, or mean different things to different people.

Grace drew a shaky breath. Mrs. Khalil crouched before the fire, Daisy Bean cradled in her lap. Sareena hovered nearby, clenching and unclenching her hands.

"May it be, by sun and stars," Grace said, and emptied the pot over the fire.

Smoke filled the room. They all started coughing—Mrs. Khalil doubled over, for she'd inhaled a lungful. But through the tears streaming from her eyes, Grace saw that Daisy Bean wasn't coughing. She lay on the carpet, quiet and still.

Her stomach gave a lurch. "May it be, by sun and stars," she said again, or tried to, for her throat was raw from all the smoke.

She grabbed Daisy Bean by the shoulders. "May it be, by sun and stars," she cried, louder this time.

Daisy Bean didn't move.

Sareena was crying. Grace shook Daisy Bean. The little girl's head fell back, her dark hair trailing on the carpet and the ashes strewn across it.

The ashes. Yes, that's what was needed—ashes. The thought didn't make any sense, but Grace didn't pause to question it. She lifted Daisy Bean, then threw herself and the little girl into the ashes and charcoal and flickering embers of the fireplace.

It should have been hot. After all, the fire had just been put out—it was still lurking there, beneath some of the larger logs, ready to spring up again the moment it caught a breath of air. But it *wasn't* hot. And the smoke wasn't sharp and painful in Grace's throat anymore, either—it went down like cool water. There was quite a lot of it, more than had been pushed out into the parlor, for most of the smoke was being drawn up the chimney. Grace breathed it in, and so did Daisy Bean, great gulps of it.

And then Daisy Bean began to cough.

Mrs. Khalil let out a shriek. Daisy Bean gave another delicate cough and blinked up at Grace.

"Why am I in the fireplace?" she said. "Does the witch want to cook me?"

29

THE WIND OF THE STARS

Fly away, fly away over the sea,
Sun-loving swallow, for summer is done;
Come again, come again, come back to me,
Bringing the summer and bringing the sun.
—Christina Rossetti, "Fly Away, Fly Away Over the Sea"

"Well, you've really done it now," the witch said.

The witch had just shooed away their latest caller. She set a jar upon the kitchen table—a table already laden with jars, and tins, and scones, and cookies, and handmade mittens and scarves and every other item that can be made from wool, as well as a new gown for Grace from the dressmaker (lacy, with five flounces in the skirt!) and a new hat for the witch from the hatter.

"What is this, anyway?" the witch said, squinting at the newest jar. "Mrs. Barrett brought it over—blueberry preserves?"

Grace unscrewed the lid and stuck her finger in. "Plum," she said, licking the finger clean.

"Ugh," the witch said. "I detest plums."

"I don't," Grace said. "They're exquisite with ice cream. I can't think of a better pairing—except ice cream and strawberries, perhaps. But plums! They lend such a sense of luxury to everything, with their purple jackets wrapped around all that velvety orange pulp. And as for spiced plums—well, spiced plums are almost *too* magnificent. I sometimes imagine that if there is a dessert best suited to emperors and kings, it must be spiced plums. Though I wonder if they would serve it with ice cream? They must, for emperors would know which desserts go best together, wouldn't they? If I were an empress, I would—"

Grace felt the weight of the witch's glare boring into her, and closed her mouth.

Mrs. Khalil had told everyone in the village that Grace had healed Daisy Bean. Now they were all bringing presents to the witch's cottage, which the witch viewed as a terrible burden, for it meant she had to put up with unexpected visitors at all hours.

Mrs. Khalil had decided that Grace had healed Daisy Bean using a folk remedy. Mrs. Khalil, who was every kind of superstitious, from believing in ghosts to being afraid of breaking a mirror, was also a great believer in folk remedies.

"She's always complaining about modern medicine," Sareena told Grace the day after she cast the spell on Daisy Bean. "She believes doctors don't know what they're talking about, and that most things can be cured with the right herbs. She's managed to convince herself that what you did wasn't magic. Isn't that incredible? I mean, she was *there*. She saw what you did—I think she even believed it for a while."

Grace didn't reply. Yes, it was incredible—but she couldn't stop thinking about what the witch had said, about grown-ups being too scared of magic to believe in it. *Oh, Sareena*, she thought, *please don't ever forget about me.*

Sareena was no longer forbidden from visiting the cottage. In fact, Mrs. Khalil seemed to be encouraging it—every time Sareena came to see Grace, she brought with her a basket of scones or namoura, a delicious Lebanese cake beloved by Mr. Khalil.

Sareena and Grace were wandering the woods one February day, hunting for roots for a spell and chattering away with the delight of two friends separated for years rather than weeks, when suddenly Grace grabbed Sareena's arm.

"Look," she whispered.

Sareena drew in her breath. There among patches of melting snow was the most fearsome thing Grace had ever seen: a purple snowdrop.

Spring was almost upon them—and they still had thirty-one and a half spells left.

Grace's hands had gone clammy, and she squeezed the handle of her basket. She saw that hourglass again, trickling away, only now it was not falling leaves or snowflakes that measured the passing days, but tiny flowers lifting their heads above the snow.

And yet even that—*that* meaning Grace's looming failure, loss of magic, and exile from the only home she had ever known—couldn't dampen the spark inside her.

She had done real witchcraft.

Not practice. Not casting every spell in the grimoire so she could prove herself to the witch. Real witchcraft, the kind that helped people. Not just once, but twice—first to awaken the witch, then to heal Daisy Bean.

And it had felt good. Wonderful, even—it gave her a warm, clean feeling, as if she'd just had a good long soak in a bubble bath. Grace realized that although she'd always wanted to learn more about magic, she'd never really given much thought to what she might do with it. She'd loved having magic because it made her feel as if she were in a story, and she'd always felt at home in stories. If she'd imagined doing magic at all, she'd pictured herself striding about in a billowing cloak with lightning bolts dancing about her, summoning meadows of flowers in the dead of winter or raising ancient ghosts to learn their secrets. But perhaps she could *also* use magic to help people.

She had never thought of magic like that before. When she did, it was as if a whole world opened up before her, one every bit as interesting as Faerie or the Land of Sleep.

Sometimes Grace felt so filled with happiness that she

couldn't help dancing over the forest floor, though Sareena and Windweaver both told her she looked very silly when she did. She had Sareena back. She could do real magic. It was perhaps the happiest time in her life.

Until the witch disappeared.

It was a day like many others. Sareena, Poppy, and Priscilla came home with Grace after school. The late February afternoon was cold but clear, and if the chill wind bore no hint of the coming spring, the lengthening sunlight did.

"How about 'the Young Ladies of Whimsy'?" Priscilla said as they cut bark from one of the birches for spell number seventy, "For Peace and Quiet."

"Gag," Sareena said.

"What do you think, Grace?" Priscilla said politely, ignoring Sareena. "You are our leader, after all."

"I'm just not sure we need a name for ourselves, Prissy," Grace said. "This isn't a club, you know." Grace kept to herself the fact that she quite liked "the Young Ladies of Whimsy." Priscilla had a way about her sometimes that was essentially bossiness hidden behind a sickly amount of politeness, and it made you want to disagree with her about everything.

"Also," Grace added, because Priscilla's face had fallen, "'the Young Ladies of Whimsy' leaves out Rum."

The others looked puzzled. "Who?" Sareena said.

"Do you have any ideas, Poppy?" Priscilla said, trying to

take charge in the conversation again as usual. "Daisy Bean? I think we *must* have a name."

Daisy Bean, lurking a few paces back as usual, shuffled behind a stump.

Poppy was quiet for a moment. Then she said, "How about 'the Seaside Circle of Sorcery'?"

Priscilla's eyes widened. "That's *brilliant*."

"Not bad," Sareena said, nodding.

"I thought you didn't want us to have a name," Grace said. Indeed, Sareena had been strongly opposed to the concept on the grounds that it put her on the same level as Priscilla and made her feel less important.

Priscilla was clearly angling to be at least as important as Sareena, if not more. She had read through the grimoire cover to cover several times, and often tried to politely dictate which spells they worked on and where they looked for ingredients. It would have been annoying if Priscilla was still the same annoying Priscilla, but she was much less annoying these days. She no longer picked her way through the woods like a duchess walking through a filthy alley. Just that morning she had been splashing around in a puddle with Daisy Bean.

Sareena frowned. "I don't. But if the others *must* have a name, then it might as well be interesting. I've been thinking, Grace. We need some new members for our group."

"You mean for the Seaside Circle of Sorcery," Priscilla trilled.

"New members?" Grace said. "Why?"

"We need as much help as we can get," Sareena said. "You still have over thirty spells to cast, and they're all head-scratchers. I think my cousin would help, if I asked him."

"Elizabeth S. and Elizabeth E. would help too," Priscilla said. "They're always asking me about you and the witch. They'd love to know what we're up to."

Grace nodded slowly. "It's a good idea. Perhaps we should come up with a list of people who might help us. They would have to be fairly brave, so as not to be terrified of the witch." Grace thought for a moment. "I suppose they could also be stupid instead of brave."

"Good," Sareena said. "Let's all put our heads together and—"

Grace let out a gasp and dragged Sareena and Priscilla behind a tree. Poppy was quick-witted and hid herself without needing to be dragged.

"What is it?" Priscilla whispered, peering through the branches. "What did—oh!"

She saw what the rest did—a little knot of men standing in the clearing, squinting at the trees. One held a map. They were dressed in rough clothes and big boots—working men. Standing with them was Cordelia Burbage, looking both rich and pretty in a stylish woolen coat with fur trim.

"Is that—?" Sareena began. Grace nodded, frantically motioning for her to be quiet.

"What are they doing in the witch's forest?" Priscilla whispered.

"It isn't the witch's forest—it's *hers*," Grace whispered back, gesturing at Cordelia.

"Well, why hasn't the witch hexed her yet?"

Grace couldn't answer that. She'd been wondering the same thing herself, as spring crept closer and Cordelia's deadline loomed.

"I'd have thought the witch would have baked her by now," Sareena said. "Like she did to that Frederick Burbage."

"Do you think she baked him?" Priscilla said, pressing a muddy hand to her cheek. "Maybe she cut out his heart. It sounds as if he and the witch were in a star-crossed romance. Cutting his heart out would have been more appropriate."

"We don't know that they had a romance," Sareena said scornfully. "Star-crossed or otherwise."

"Well, he let her stay on his land, didn't he? Why would he have done that if he wasn't desperately in love with her?"

"Good grief," Sareena said. "I wish you'd go back to reading fairy tales instead of those silly romances you're always carrying around."

"There's nothing wrong with romances," Poppy said, surprising everybody. Poppy was usually the quietest of them, but every once in a while, she would pipe up to defend Priscilla when Sareena was cruel to her. Like most people, Poppy seemed to have a soft spot for Priscilla and her sunny personality, though Grace still found it strange that Poppy, a bully through and through, would want to protect anyone. Grace wondered if everyone had such contradictions inside them, places where the pattern of who they were skipped a stitch or went a bit lopsided.

"Thank you, Poppy," Priscilla said with her sunniest smile, and threaded her arm through Poppy's, something she often did with her other friends, and sometimes with Grace, but had never once done with Poppy. Grace didn't think *anyone* had ever taken Poppy's arm. Poppy stared at their linked elbows, looking slightly stunned but also pleased.

Sareena glowered. "Well, *I* think—"

Grace hushed her. One of the men looked in their direction, but they were well hidden by the shadows. After a moment, the men moved away.

Cordelia paused for a moment, though. She pushed back the fur hood of her coat and peered into the forest. She shouldn't have been able to see Grace, and yet Grace was certain that their eyes met for one long moment. Her heart thudded in her chest like an ordinary girl's. Cordelia's mouth became a thin line, and then she pulled her hood up and followed the men.

When Grace got home, she didn't even bother removing her coat and scarf. The witch had been wont to sit by the fire in the armchair lately, but she wasn't there now. Grace dashed upstairs, but the witch wasn't in her bedroom, either. Her red cardigan with the mother-of-pearl buttons was laid out on her bed, as if she had been in the middle of getting dressed.

Where on earth had she gone? Grace paced the kitchen, knotting and unknotting her fingers as she watched the hands of the clock calmly circling its face.

But the witch didn't return that day. Nor the next day, nor the next. To distract herself from her worry, Grace threw herself into the grimoire and its spells, but she could barely focus. The cottage was silent and still in a way it had never been before. Sometimes the shadows flickered in the corner of Grace's eye and her heart leaped, but they weren't the witch— they were only shadows.

Finally, nearly a week after the witch vanished, Grace came home from school to find her sitting in the armchair with a blanket wrapped around her as if nothing had happened.

"Fetch some tea, Grace," the witch said in a quiet voice. She looked thin and terrifyingly pale.

"Where have you been?" Grace demanded.

"The tea," she said. Grace went to get the tea, adding plenty of honey and lemon. The witch drank most of it down as soon as Grace brought it to her.

"That's better," she said, gazing into the fire.

"That woman was here again," Grace said. "Cordelia Burbage. Poking around in your forest."

"It never belonged to me." The witch let out her breath. "The world was a different place once. People didn't *own*

forests when I was a girl. Forests simply *were*. We witches could drift from place to place, from wood to wood, weaving cottages from magic and whatever bits of the forest were handy, and nobody would burst in demanding to see evidence that we owned anything. The world was . . . *bigger* then. There's not as much room for people like us anymore."

Grace bit her lip. "I thought you would have cast a spell to send her away."

"I'm afraid such spells are beyond me now," the witch said.

Grace felt cold. "What do you mean? Where *were* you?"

"Nowhere," the witch said. "And everywhere. I'm afraid that I will be disappearing more often. It has been happening slowly but surely these last few years. But that visit from Cordelia—" She shook her head almost ruefully. "I'm afraid it sealed my fate."

"Cordelia." Grace's hands clenched into fists. "That awful woman—"

"There's no point in being angry with her," the witch said. "She's upset about her father."

This only made Grace angrier. She was upset about her parents, too, but she didn't go around kicking other people out of their homes. "What happened to him? Did you—did you put him into your oven?"

"No," the witch said, her face hardening. "Though he would have deserved it. He told me that I was the love of his life, but he *didn't* tell me he was already married—with a baby on the way, to boot. When I found out, I turned him into a tree."

"Which one?"

"You know which one."

"Oh," Grace breathed. The old cherry tree.

"Nobody suspected me," the witch said. "Except Cordelia, apparently. She's actually been in town a few times these past few years, poking around for clues. Clearly, Freddy's daughter has a witch's intuition."

She gazed into the fire for a long moment. "I didn't think I regretted what I did to Freddy. And I still don't think I do— but I find myself wearied by it all."

Grace bit her lip. "But you're a witch. Wickedness is what you live for!"

"One gets tired of everything eventually," the witch said. "Even wickedness, Patrick."

Her voice was faint. A shiver went down Grace's spine as she turned, half expecting to see Patrick hovering there, but of course there was no one. The witch was gazing at Grace, and also *through* her. She blinked.

"Grace," she said. "Of course. Forgive me. I see him often, when I look at you. I see what I did. All these years, I've almost been able to forget. But now—" She finished in a whisper. "Well, I wish I could forget again."

She faded into the shadows of the couch. For a moment, she was just a shadow with eyes and a yellow cardigan, and then the shadow became the witch again. But Grace didn't think she'd meant to become a shadow this time, and she felt an icy panic seize her.

The witch was fading away.

"You can have my magic," Grace said recklessly. "My magic will heal you—that's what you said before. I'll simply quit then. The grimoire will probably prove to be too much for me anyway." Grace added quickly, "Of course, I must be allowed to stay here. Alive and unroasted."

The witch stared at her for a very long time. "You would give me your magic freely?" she said slowly.

Panic rose in Grace again—a different panic, this time. What was she doing? She didn't want to give up her magic— she loved magic. She wanted to learn more, to see all the paths her magic could take her down.

And yet didn't magic bring sadness of its own? What if Sareena forgot her? Would she eventually become like the witch?

She felt the panic ebb. It would be wrong to let the witch die if Grace's magic could help her. Grace didn't *want* her to die. She didn't want to be all alone in the cottage without the witch to scowl at her noise or call her impossible, or bake her favorite chocolate crinkles, even if she pretended it was just to keep Grace quiet.

The witch shook her head. "Why?"

"Because you gave me a home," Grace said. "Nobody else ever did that."

She felt the truth of the words in her bones. A home was

what she'd always wanted. She would give up her magic for that. She would give up anything.

"Hmph," the witch said. "Still—that isn't enough for me to deserve such kindness."

"That's true," Grace said. It *was* true—and yet she felt her heart lurch at the sight of the witch sinking into herself, thin and pale, all that fiery wickedness reduced to a few flickering embers. "But some people who deserve kindness never get it, so I suppose it must work the other way around, too."

The witch shook her head. "You care too much. About everything. You will learn to be more sparing with your feelings one day."

"I *hope* not," Grace said fervently. "I don't want to end up like you."

The witch gave a surprised snort of laughter.

"It's all moot, anyway," the witch said. "I don't believe your magic will be enough to heal me anymore." She gave Grace a long look. "But there is something . . . "

Grace sat up straight. "What? A healing spell? I can start on it right away—"

"No," the witch said. "You must finish working through the spells in the grimoire. Once you do, according to our pact, you will officially become my apprentice. That means you will have access to all sorts of higher magics."

Grace stared at her in rapt attention. "Really? Like what?"

The witch gave her a serious look. "Like the Wind of the Stars."

Grace let out a slow breath. "The Wind of the Stars," she said softly, savoring each word. "How wonderful! The name alone gives me the shivers. But I can summon wind already."

"That's completely different," the witch said. "Only witches and their apprentices have the power to call down the Wind of the Stars. Even then, the Wind doesn't respond to just anyone. But if you should succeed in summoning it, the Wind will heal any wound and cast out any illness."

Grace was so enthralled that she gasped. "Then that's it! I knew there must be a way to help you! But I can't call the Wind if I'm not your apprentice?"

The witch shook her head. "A witch's apprenticeship is a magically binding thing. It would allow you to draw on my own magic in times of need. You are not strong enough to call the Wind alone—not yet. Do you understand?"

"Yes," Grace said. It all made sense—indeed, it made for the perfect quest, as good as any story. Yet something nagged at her. "Why didn't you call on this Wind of the Stars before, though? Why not when you first got sick?"

The witch drew a slow breath, which ended in a cough. Grace handed her a handkerchief. "The Wind won't listen to me," she said finally. "I—I did something to hurt it. It was a long time ago."

"I can believe *that*," Grace said, shaking her head.

The witch set the handkerchief aside. "Calling down the Wind of the Stars is not an easy task. Think carefully before agreeing to this."

"I don't have to think about it." Grace drew herself to her feet. She was going to use her magic to help people—she had already decided that. And she would start with the witch.

The witch gave her an unreadable smile. "Thank you, child. You don't know what this means."

30

THE SEASIDE CIRCLE OF SORCERY

"Hope" is the thing with feathers -
That perches in the soul -
And sings the tune without the words -
And never stops - at all -
—Emily Dickinson, "'Hope' is the thing with feathers"

A few days later, Grace was wandering through the woods, searching for a particular moss for spell number seventy-two and thinking of nothing in particular. Well, that was not entirely true—she was full of dread and mulling over all her worries about the witch and Cordelia and the mysterious Wind of the Stars. The grimoire tucked in her pack felt like it was made of lead.

A dark shape exploded through the bare boughs ahead, and Grace started. But it was only Windweaver.

Don't go any farther, he said. His feathers were ruffled, his small chest rising and falling rapidly.

"Why not?"

It's—it's bad, he said.

Well, that got her running. She started forward so fast that Windweaver lost his grip on her shoulder and went tumbling over backward. When she reached the birch grove, she froze.

What should have been a gentle valley clothed on both sides by birches was now a barren, empty landscape. An acre of stumps stretched out before her, eerily silent. Birds and other small creatures crept around the edges of the emptiness, puzzled and uncertain. She thought of those proud birches with their rustling leaves that always sounded like an exchange of secrets. Just days ago she had noted the first buds appearing on their boughs.

Sareena found her lying in a heap later that afternoon—Grace had barely moved all day.

"Oh, Grace," she said as she surveyed the devastation. "Isn't this dreadful? But don't be too sad—the forest will grow back, you know. It's just a few trees."

"But it isn't," Grace sobbed. Sareena didn't understand—Grace's tears weren't for the trees, not entirely. The trees were *home.* The forest was where she had met Sareena, where they had roamed for days, searching for spell ingredients. If Cordelia could take a piece of Grace's home from her so easily, she could take the rest. She *would* take the rest.

Sareena held her as she cried. She looked sad, but also thoughtful.

Grace was late to school the next day—Sareena had already gone ahead without waiting for her. This was unusual, though not out of character, and Grace didn't think much about it. Miss Gordon scolded Grace as she took her seat.

After Miss Gordon had turned her attention back to the lesson, Sareena passed Grace a note.

Meet me at the Keep after school.

Grace frowned. She and Sareena usually met at the Magician's Keep on those days when Sareena had to help her mother with something and couldn't come straight to the witch's cottage. Yet there was something very solemn about the way she had written this particular note.

It was a strange day. More students than usual seemed to be looking at her and whispering, which made her nervous. Rum appeared out of nowhere, as he often did, and then Sareena beckoned to him at lunch and they spent several minutes muttering together. Sareena wouldn't tell Grace what they were muttering about.

"Oh—this and that," she said vaguely. They were seated outside on the moss by the brook, for the day was clear and almost warm, if you were in the sunshine.

"Well, he'd better not be trying to put another enchantment on you," Grace said.

"An enchantment?" Sareena's eyes widened. "Rum is a witch, too?"

Grace gave a tremendous groan and lay down on her back, covering her eyes with her arm. Her sandwich was not sitting well in her stomach today. "Yes, he's a witch. A very nasty witch who I hope will become covered in warts one day. How I wish the grimoire had a 'For Warts' spell—I'd hex him ten times over."

She spent the rest of the day alternating between pleasant daydreams about cursing Rum with warts in inconvenient places—elbows seemed like they would be a particularly vexing location—and pure misery. Then it was time to go home and begin again the impossible task that was spell seventy-five. She had been stuck on it for days. The chief problem with spell seventy-five was that it called for seven hundred leaves of a plant called Queen Anne's lace. This was a problem because they had managed to find not even one leaf of Queen Anne's lace. It wasn't a magical plant—it simply wasn't very common on the Island.

When Grace came through the door of the cottage, she was surprised to see the witch standing by the front window wearing a magnificent glare—even by her standards. She was draped in a blanket and clutching a cup of tea.

"Shouldn't you be resting?" Grace scolded. "Here, I'll make you a fresh pot of tea, and bring in a few more logs for the fire—"

"What on earth is wrong with you?" the witch demanded.

Grace sighed. "Since you are forever coming up with things that are wrong with me, you'll have to narrow your question a bit."

"Don't be smart with me. You know exactly what I mean.

You expect me to believe you didn't notice them as you came up the lane?"

Grace frowned. She had been gazing at her boots all the way home, too full of despair to admire the day. She went back outside and looked around. It did not take much looking to discover the cause of the witch's displeasure.

The entire student body of By-the-Sea School was waiting at the Keep.

Little Henry, whose dreams Grace had stolen, was splashing through the stream in his rainboots with a few of his friends, parting the grasses as they hunted for frogs. Elizabeth E. and Elizabeth S., Priscilla's friends, stood with her in a little knot, gazing around them with anxious excitement. Even the older boys had come—Amir and Roger and John and Michel, who seemed to be pretending to ignore the prettiest of the older girls, Charlotte, who was wading about with the younger children, her skirts hiked up and her pink ankles fully exposed. Even Rum was there, lounging on the bank with his shoes off and his crossed feet dangling in the water, the very image of a mischievous fairy up to no good.

Grace walked toward them as if in a dream. Pausing, she glanced back at the house. There was the witch in the window, a terrifyingly spectral figure at this distance with her hollow eyes and her glower fixed upon the children. Sareena hurried up to Grace.

"Isn't this wonderful?" Sareena said. "I wasn't expecting them *all* to turn up."

Grace realized her mouth was hanging open, and she closed it with a snap. "I thought—I thought we were going to make a list of people who might help us, and you were going to—"

"Oh yes," Sareena said. "I decided not to wait to do all that. I thought, why not just invite everybody, and see who shows up? And it turned out well, didn't it?"

Grace stared at her. She was used to Sareena's impetuousness, but this was too much.

"You've got to send them away," she said. "At once. The witch will kill them!"

"She hasn't killed anybody yet," Sareena said. "So far she seems content with a great deal of scowling. Really, Grace, the witch isn't in a state to send that Cordelia Burbage off with her brains addled; I doubt she's up to shoving an entire schoolroom into her oven."

"I don't know—" Grace began.

"Besides, they all want to help. Don't you?" Sareena said, raising her voice.

Reactions were mixed. A few students cheered. Henry beamed and waved a stick in the air like a wand. Priscilla elbowed her friends until they joined her in applauding, dubiously. The rest gave a mixture of mutters and hesitant nods. Grace suspected that some of them had only come out of curiosity, or because they didn't want to be left out.

Still—they were there. *All* of them. The whole school, come to help her.

"What did you tell them?" Grace demanded, trying to

cover up the wobble in her voice.

"Everything," Sareena said. "Or everything about the grimoire, anyway, and your pact with the witch. They know about Cordelia, and that she wants to turn the witch out and cut down the woods, and that she'll succeed if you can't finish all those spells and heal the witch."

"If she tries," Michel said, "she'll have to go through us first. I used to love playing in those trees as a kid. It was a game, sneaking into the witch's woods."

Several of the older students nodded.

"And we know about Daisy Bean," Henry said. All eyes turned to him, and he flushed red, but pushed on bravely. "How you saved her."

Even the children who had seemed unenthusiastic were nodding now. "We like Daisy Bean," said one of Henry's friends, a girl of six or seven. Daisy Bean, who was standing with Poppy by the cherry tree, drew her green blanket over her head.

Grace gazed at them, speechless. None of the children looked back at her with fear. There was plenty of curiosity, and some doubt, but mostly she saw determination.

"Khalil," Roger called. "When are we getting started?"

"Right now," Sareena said, turning. She pulled out the witch's plant book, a notebook, and a pencil, which she tucked behind her ear. Beside her, Grace noticed, was a pile of baskets and burlap potato sacks. "Now, we have a long list to get through today. First things first—Marie-Jeanne. You said you know where to find Queen Anne's lace?"

Henry's friend nodded. "It grows in the meadow behind Tubman Beach."

"Good. That's a long walk—take the older boys with you. We need bags of the stuff." She tossed the boys four potato sacks. "The rest of you, I want you working through this list. Anything you don't recognize, look it up in the book."

There was an astonishing lack of argument. The children passed the list and the plant book around, muttering among themselves. One of Priscilla's friends declared herself an expert on mushrooms, as her father was a mushroom picker, so they picked up a basket and set off into the woods, Priscilla dashing ahead. It wasn't long before the other items on the list were claimed, even the spider's eggs and the stinging nettles. Then the children wandered off into the woods, some alone and others in twos or threes. Some cast worried looks back at the cottage, where the witch still stood glaring at them from the window like a nightmare. Then they vanished beneath the boughs, and the witch's woods came alive with the voices and laughter of children.

Rum, Poppy, and Daisy Bean remained behind. "I thought the four of us could help you cast spell seventy-six," Sareena said, "while the others are doing the grunt work. Then when we have the Queen Anne's lace for spell seventy-five, we'll—"

Grace burst into tears.

"Oh dear," Sareena said. "Well, I planned for this, too. Here you are." She handed Grace a handkerchief. Grace blew her nose noisily.

"Do they really believe it?" she said. "About the grimoire, and me being a witch? Everything?"

"We-ell," Sareena said. "I'm not sure they *all* do. But enough of them believe, and the rest seem happy to go along with it. Even if they think you're mad, they still want to help you."

Grace continued to sniffle. Sareena watched her, not understanding, but sympathetic. Because how could she understand? Before coming to Brook-by-the-Sea, Grace had never had even one person show her such kindness.

"Come on," Sareena said, taking her arm. "Let's get to work."

31

PETALS ON THE STREAM

Birds in my blossoming orchard,
Chaffinch and goldfinch and lark,
Preen your bright wings, little happy live things;
The May trees grow white in the park!
—Edith Nesbit, "May Song"

"It's like a riddle," Sareena said.

"It's nothing like a riddle," Grace replied. "Riddles have answers. This is just impossible."

They were arguing about the last spell in the grimoire—the incomplete half spell. Grace read it aloud:

101. FOR WISDOM
12 handfuls worrywart mint
3 crystals
1 fox claw
Blood from a stone

Dash of salt

18 leaves

"Did you hear that?" Grace said. "Eighteen *leaves*. How many kinds of leaves are there in the world? How are we supposed to guess the right ones? And that's on top of everything else."

"You know, I remember you calling spell forty-four impossible," Sareena said. "But we still cracked it."

"That was regular impossible. This is impossibly impossible."

"If something is impossibly impossible, that means it's possible. It cancels out."

Grace let out a groan and flopped onto her back. Usually she appreciated Sareena's logic, but sometimes it felt like throwing yourself against a wall.

"Anyway, we're good at impossible things," Sareena said calmly. She passed the bowl of ice cream they were sharing back to Grace. "Here. Stop moaning and finish this off. If I eat any more, I'll burst."

Grace sat up grudgingly. The rosy sky was cooling into blue twilight, and they were lounging at the edge of the forest, dipping their feet in the creek as the drowsy murmurings of late spring floated by. May had arrived in all its terrifying glory, sprinkling the grass with clover and bumblebees and flooding the witch's overgrown garden with color. Fortunately, the month had started out rainy, and the old cherry tree was still bare, waiting for whatever secret signal trees wait for before they bloom. But every branch was dotted with buds that could any day burst into flower.

"What do you think?" Sareena asked, knitting her fingers nervously. Grace didn't have to ask what she meant.

They had reached spell number one hundred. The last whole spell.

"I'll check," Grace said, trying to sound ordinary when it felt like her insides were one big knot. She fished the pot out of the stream. It was full of dried flower petals and a dozen other ingredients that had been horribly complicated to find. The instructions for spell one hundred, "For Turning Things to Glass," had said to *brew ingredients in a stream*, so that was what she had done, setting the pot in a fast-moving channel and sur-rounding it with stones so that it couldn't drift away.

"I think I might be sick," Grace said.

"Don't you dare," Sareena said. "Or I will be, too."

"It's just—this is the *last one*," Grace said. "Apart from that horrible half spell, of course."

"I know," Sareena said.

"What if it doesn't work? All this work, all this time, what if it was all—"

"I know!" Sareena said. "Just check, Grace, all right? My stomach is gurgling like anything. I'm so nervous I think I might *actually* be sick."

Grace drew a long, slow breath. With the help of the other children, they'd moved through the hardest spells more quickly than she had expected. Even though they were hard, and frequently nonsensical, something about the casting itself felt easier to Grace. With each spell, she doubted herself a little less.

"Well?" Sareena said.

Grace peeked in the pot. In truth, it looked like a lot of sludge, the dried flowers turning brown and soggy in the muddy stream water. "Only one way to find out," she said. She dropped a freshly picked daisy into the pot and waved her hands over it. "May it be, by sun and stars!"

What followed was disappointing. The daisy grew water-logged and sank to the bottom of the muddy pot. A little bubble went up, and then the water was still.

"Maybe it didn't brew long enough," Grace muttered.

"It looks like the mud is forming a pattern. See?" Sareena pointed, but Grace knew she was just trying to be kind.

"Oh well." Sighing, Grace lifted the pot, planning to put it back in the stream.

Clink.

She and Sareena stared at each other. Sareena reacted quickest, shoving her hand into the muck and fishing around for the source of the noise. She dipped her fist in the stream to clean it, then opened her hand.

Cupped in her palm was a glass daisy. The stem was bent

a little, just like the real daisy's had been, and a few petals were missing. Somehow, the imperfections made it even more beautiful.

"Pretty!" Sareena exclaimed. She held it up to the light, which shone through and splashed a little green reflection on her cheek. "That's it, then. That's really it, Grace!" She was grinning from ear to ear. She threw her arms around Grace's neck with a whoop. "We did it!"

"Yes." Grace felt a curious sensation. She had expected to be happy like Sareena was, or at least relieved, that the last full spell was done. After all, it had taken months of work, months of fearing she'd never finish at all. And she *did* feel relieved—a little.

She looked around, but there was nothing in the landscape of flowers and unfurling shadows to explain it.

It's that half spell, of course, she told herself. *Any witch would be nervous about that.*

Henry wandered over, carrying a basket of leaves. "Here's the last of the trees," he said proudly, setting the basket at Grace's feet. "Larch and trembling aspen."

Grace examined the leaves. As they didn't know which sort of leaves were required for spell one hundred and one, it being an unfinished spell with an unfinished list of ingredients, Sareena had assigned the children to gather up as many kinds of leaves as they could think of, in the hope that one of them would speak to Grace.

"Thank you, Henry," Sareena said, glancing up from the

grimoire. "Would you like some ice cream? There's a strawberry tart to go with it that my mum made."

Henry nodded, grinning, and dashed over to the porch, where several other children from By-the-Sea School were lounging. Most of them had been spending every weekend at the witch's cottage helping Grace with the spells, and some had come every day after school, too. Sometimes they'd had more helpers than Grace could find tasks for. Now, even though they were nearing the end, many of the children had returned to help with the half spell, including Priscilla's friends and two of the older boys, who Grace could hear bickering over the classification of an ivy deeper in the forest.

She gazed at the neat row of baskets lined up in front of her, filled with leaves of every description. They also had several sacks of mushrooms, feathers, pinecones, and other odds and ends stored in the cellar, for the children of By-the-Sea School had found enough ingredients to cast the spells twice over. Looking at it all, Grace felt dizzy, as if the slope of the world had changed slightly and she hadn't yet found her footing. She could never have finished the grimoire without the help of the other children.

She glanced back at the cottage, hoping to spy the witch in the window, glowering at them all. But the witch had been bedridden for the past month—when she was corporeal, that is. There were also her drifting days, when she wasn't there at all. Those days frightened Grace more than any others, for she could never be certain if the witch would come back.

We're almost there, she thought at the dark window.

Sareena and Grace had gone over the half spell dozens of times, with Sareena making lists of possible ingredients and telling Grace to read them through carefully. Her theory was that Grace knew, deep down, how to finish the spell, just as Grace had known how to fix the witch's sleep potion. The problem was that Grace didn't know how to draw that knowledge out of herself—the other times, it had just *happened*.

Sareena handed Grace another list. "I still think ivy leaves are likely," she said. "They're in quite a few of the other spells, and they're wise, the way they can climb up anything to get to the light. They're well suited to a wisdom spell."

Grace bit her lip, trying to hide her disappointment as she read through the ingredients. She knew almost immediately that they weren't right. Slowly, she shook her head.

Sareena looked like she was trying to hide her disappointment too. "Oh well," she said. "We'll try again in the morning. I'll be here first thing."

Grace nodded, though she didn't want Sareena to leave. She didn't want any of them to leave. "Those men were here again," she said worriedly. "Poking around in the forest. I think Cordelia's planning to cut down more trees."

"Ugh, that awful woman," Sareena said.

"She's only angry about her father. Really, this is all the witch's fault—she's the one who went around turning people inanimate."

"I don't care whose fault it is—we still can't let that Cordelia

Burbage win. And why are you sticking up for her, anyway? She was horrid to you."

Grace sighed. "She was only horrid because she knows I'm wicked. I'm a witch, after all. I make people remember bad things. Plus, there's my temper and my wild imagination— Mrs. Spencer always said my imagination would be the death of me one day, if it wasn't the death of somebody else."

"You're not wicked," Sareena said heatedly. "You know what you are, Grace? You're a girl who takes care of people."

"I'm—what?"

"You took care of Daisy Bean, didn't you?" Sareena said. "You even take care of the witch, though she doesn't deserve it. Maybe you are a wicked witch, but I don't see any reason why you can't also be a kind one. Who says you can only be one thing?"

Grace felt her eyes well—fortunately, Sareena didn't notice. "Anyway," Sareena said, standing, "I'll see you tomorrow."

She strode off through the tall grass, leaving Grace staring after her.

Grace watched the sunset through the leaves a little longer, then tramped back to the witch's cottage, breathing a sigh of contentment. No matter what was to come, she would always love the cottage. She paused to give the stair railing a friendly little pat.

"Grace?"

She turned. It was Poppy, hovering awkwardly in the shadows. "What is it, Poppy?"

"Well—I just wondered." Poppy looked down at her big hands. "Will you still need help with spells after you finish the grimoire? Or do you—do you not need us anymore?"

Grace knew that when Poppy said *us* she really meant *me*. She also knew that Poppy's parents were intimidated by the witch, which was the only reason they let Poppy visit so often.

"Definitely," Grace said. "In fact, I might need *more* help— if I become the witch's apprentice, I mean. I'm sure being a witch's apprentice is very hard work."

Poppy flashed Grace one of her rare smiles. Grace smiled back, then went up the stairs to the cottage. Little Henry was awaiting her by the door, his hands clasped in front of him.

"I did the washing-up, Miss Witch," he said.

"Thank you, Henry. But remember, you can just call me Grace."

"Can I see the magic flower?" he said shyly.

Grace held out the daisy. He took it gingerly, tracing the glass with a fingertip, his eyes round.

"Would you like to keep it?" Grace said suddenly.

He stared at her. "I—I couldn't—"

"Course you can," she said, smiling. "I can always make another. I could make a whole glass garden, if I wanted to."

He looked like he might refuse again, but his hand was already tightening around the daisy. He stammered out a thank-you, his eyes lingering on the glass flower as it sparkled in the twilight.

"Magic," he whispered. Then, giving her a final shy smile, he dashed home up the lane.

Grace stood for a moment in the doorway, watching the light fade and the cherry trees whisper together, including the cherry tree that had once been Frederick Burbage. The forest was wrapped in a summer hush, and she felt a little prickle at the back of her neck. She closed the door and went to see if the witch wanted more tea.

She knew something was wrong before she opened her eyes the next morning. It was the silence.

The silence had changed. The night before, it had been a hush, as if a crowd of people was holding its breath. Now it was an emptiness.

She leaped from her bed so quickly that she tripped over the every-flower quilt, and Windweaver gave a dismayed croak as the covers slipped out from under him. Grace threw her coat over her nightgown and thundered down the stairs, yanking the door open with a *bang*.

The cherry trees were gone.

At first she couldn't understand it, and ran her gaze over the forest, as if the trees had simply picked up their roots and wandered off.

Then she saw the stumps.

She didn't remember crossing the lawn or wading through the stream. When she came back to herself, she was standing next to the stump of the tree that had been Frederick Burbage, her hem wet and her bare feet aching with cold.

There had been eleven cherry trees, tall and regal, some of them beginning to flower, leaning their boughs over the stream as if to admire their lovely reflections. They followed the curve of the water like a sister stream, rippling pink instead of silver. Now there were stumps, the felled trees lying behind them—*the men must be planning to return later to collect the wood*, some distant part of her thought. Most terrible of all was the stream, which was still dotted with pink and white blossoms, tiny ghosts slowly being swept out to sea.

Grace noticed, also distantly, that she could see the dawn star on the brightening horizon now. Before, it would have been hidden behind a curtain of blossoms.

There was a flicker of movement in the cottage. The witch came through the door, draped in a shawl and holding tight to the cane she had begun to use on the rare occasions that she ventured from her bedroom.

The witch paused for a very long time on the porch. She was too far away for Grace to make out the look on her face, but after a moment, she walked slowly across the lawn. Windweaver fluttered around the witch, croaking. She reached the stream and paused as if considering how best to cross. Then her cane fell to the ground, and she collapsed.

Grace let out a wordless cry. She splashed through the stream and rolled the witch onto her back—she weighed less than a leaf now. For a moment, the witch seemed to vanish, cardigan and all, and there was only a darker shadow against the shadowy grass. But then Grace blinked, and the witch was back.

"What should I do?" Grace demanded, tears rolling thickly down her face. She didn't know if she meant about the witch or the cherry trees.

"There's nothing you can do," the witch said, her voice as faint as breathing. "Our pact was tied to the tree's blooming, and now the tree is dead. It will never bloom. Therefore, our pact is dissolved."

"But then—" The words choked her. "But then I can never be your apprentice! And I won't be able to call down the Wind of the Stars."

"It doesn't matter," the witch murmured. "Ridiculous child. Go back inside. I don't want you here, do you understand? I never wanted you."

Grace began to sob in earnest now, because she could see the witch was lying, and after a moment, a tear trickled down the witch's face, too. They sat there until the sun pulled itself up over the horizon.

The witch seemed to realize that Grace wasn't going anywhere, no matter how cruel she was, or perhaps her mind was wandering. "Grace," she said in a distant voice, "find Patrick. Ask him if he'll see me." Her heart was making a very strange sound—it was not quite a heartbeat, but there was a faint pounding sound amid the ocean roar, as if it were *trying* to beat, but not quite remembering how.

Grace nodded, dashing the tears away. She crossed the bank, trying not to look at the cherry trees, but she couldn't help herself.

She froze.

There upon one of the lowest boughs of the old cherry tree was a splash of pink. One of the buds was just beginning to open, its petals stirred by the wind. And yet she knew—she *knew*—that it hadn't been there before, when she first came upon the fallen tree. All the buds had been closed tight against the chilly dawn.

"It's still alive," Grace murmured.

And so it was. Somehow, the tree hadn't realized what had been done to it yet, that the water it had drawn up through its roots in the night would be the last it ever drank. Despite the ungainly sprawl the woodcutters had left it in, its branches could still feel the sun. And as it tasted the warmth of spring, it was preparing to bloom.

Grace held the flower in her palm, and then she closed her trembling fist around it.

They still had a chance.

32

THE WISDOM OF DRAGONS

Far and beyond in blue deserts of sea
Where the wild winds are at play,
There may the spirits of sea-birds be free . . .
—Lucy Maud Montgomery, "The Gulls"

Grace plunged back into the woods, tripping a little in her haste.

"For Wisdom," she murmured over and over again. "For Wisdom."

She hadn't had any big ideas about how to finish the spell. She had simply decided that she wasn't going to wait for big ideas anymore—she couldn't. Time was running out.

So she was simply going to make it up.

She had the salt, the crystals—which Sareena had purchased from a shop in Halifax—and everything else, though not the blood from a stone. To get that, she was going to have to walk far—several miles each way.

Rum stepped out of nothing and a cluster of oak trees. "Where are you going?"

Grace shook her head. "No time to explain. Can you keep everyone away from me today? Even Sareena?"

He blinked. "What?"

"Like you did before. If anyone gets close to me, blur the worlds together a bit. Or send me to Faerie for a moment."

"Of course I can do that," he said. "But why?"

Grace bit her lip. "The others have helped me so much," she began. "Even you, Rum."

He shrugged, though his face reddened a little. It was a pinkish face already, for spring. "Well—I like helping." He looked down at his feet. "Not because I like *you* or anything."

He said it quickly, as if to get out ahead of Grace's temper. "It's all right if you like me," she said grudgingly. "I guess."

He looked up and gave her a fairy-quick smile. "Good. Because I *like* liking you. I miss my parents, and I hate living with my uncle. Being friends with you is like—it's like having a place I can go where I can forget about all the bad things."

Grace thought *friends* was a little presumptuous of him, when she'd only said it was all right for him to like her, but she kept that to herself. There didn't seem to be any trickery in his words. And she understood what he meant—being friends with someone *was* like having a safe, happy place you could visit when you needed to.

"Fine," she muttered.

"Fine what?"

"Fine, we can be friends," she said.

Rum's grin was broad this time, and to Grace's horror, she found herself blushing. "Good," he said. "We were always meant to be best friends, you know, Grace. It's destiny."

"*Best!*" she exclaimed, before she remembered she didn't have time for arguments. She drew in her breath. "Rum, I have to finish this last spell by myself, and I have to do it today. By sundown, if I can manage it."

He stood up straight. "I'll keep them all away."

She nodded, and hurried into the deep woods with Windweaver at her back.

Beyond the witch's forest was an old farm with open pasture for a herd of cows. And beyond that was the sea.

It rolled out and out, blurred with morning fog. She crossed the pasture and clambered down the dunes that lined the shore, then turned her face west.

It was rough going in places. Sometimes she had to scramble over slippery dunes or wade through streams. The reddish sand was hot from the sun and got inside her shoes, rubbing uncomfortably against her skin.

At last, she reached her destination. It was a cove lined with soft sandstone cliffs that blazed red against the green of the trees above—the effect of the iron woven through the rock, though Grace had always thought it looked like something out of a fairy tale. Surely some great sea monster had been slain here, and as it died it had sworn that its blood would never be washed away.

Grace found a slab of stone that had fallen off the cliff. It

335

was a dusty, sooty red. But when she snapped it in half, the broken side shone crimson as the iron inside tasted the air.

Blood from a stone, she thought. The fourth ingredient in the half spell. It wasn't *really* blood, of course—but you could certainly imagine it was. And that would have to be enough.

Her head pounded with thirst, and she was sweaty despite the sea breeze, but she didn't pause—she turned to begin the long journey home.

Back in the wonderfully cool shadow of the witch's woods, Grace heard distant voices—she thought one was Sareena's, calling her name—but they never drew any closer.

What about the missing ingredients? Windweaver said. Loyal Windweaver had been following her all this time, sometimes resting on her shoulder when he tired of battling the sea wind.

She drew herself up straight, willing away the pounding headache. "That's next."

She led him to the witch's garden, casting a hopeful look up at the cottage as she did. But of course, the witch wasn't watching from the window—she'd barely been able to stand when Grace had helped her back to the house.

She paused for a moment amid the rambling garden, overwhelmed. Wisdom—what plants could mean wisdom? What ingredients had the witch chosen all those years ago when she was only a little older than Grace, and then forgotten to write down?

Then Grace drew a breath and simply let her imagination run wild. She plucked any flower that reminded her of wisdom.

In particular, she was thinking of one of her favorite fairy tales in one of her favorite books at the orphanage. It was about a girl captured by a dragon—the dragon was planning to make a meal of her, but he was still full from the last girl he ate, so he simply held her prisoner in a cave until his appetite returned. The girl escaped and brought him a bouquet of the most fragrant blooms from the forest—honeysuckle, roses, lavender, sweet peas, and lilac. Dragons loved flowers, in the world of the fairy tale, and the girl promised to bring the dragon a fresh bouquet for every day he refrained from eating her. Eventually, after the girl filled his cave with flowers, the dragon saw the wisdom in eating only other, less helpful girls, and spared her life for good.

Grace grabbed the honeysuckle, the lilac, the lavender, the sweet peas. She remembered what the witch had said. *"Magic does not have a single path. It is like a vast wood with a thousand paths."* She could almost *see* the path in front of her, winding through the witch's garden.

She added dandelions to her basket—surely the cleverest flower of all, as they had learned to grow everywhere—and also trilliums, which were among the first flowers to recognize spring. She fetched eighteen ivy leaves from one of the baskets the children had filled the day before, because Sareena had suggested ivy, and it was wise to listen to a dear friend's advice.

The sun was setting as she made her way to the little lake deep in the woods where she had trapped the moon, the spell's ingredients filling the basket over her arm. She had always loved the lake—it was so still that it was a perfect mirror of the sky. Now it showed a dreamy masquerade of clouds arrayed in golds and pastels from the setting sun.

Grace had been walking all day. She was so weary that she was dizzy, but she would not rest until the spell was finished. She flung the basket into the lake, sending flowers and salt and crystals in every direction, a dramatic burst of color that struck her as perfect, though she could not have said why.

And then she began the incantation.

The witch's spells didn't really have incantations—apart from "May it be, by sun and stars." But Grace liked the idea of incantations very much, so she recited several of her favorite poems—as much of them as she could remember. Then she waved her hands over the dark waters in a very sorcerous manner, waggling her fingers.

That's a weird spell, Windweaver commented. *None of the others went like that.*

"None of the others were mine," she said. "They were the witch's. And *I* think spells should have a bit of poetry to them. It creates an atmosphere of—oh!"

It was in that moment that she felt wisdom settle over her like a cloak.

33

THE THING IN THE DARKNESS

"Tshirr!" scolds the oriole
Where the elms stir . . .
"May's here, I cannot rest,
Go away, tshirr!"
—Sophie Margaretta Hensley, "Song"

G race found being wise very disappointing.

She was expecting to learn the secrets of the universe—or at least a few of them. But all she got was a worse headache than before and an awareness of how little she knew about anything.

She didn't know where magic came from, or why she was magical.

She didn't know anything about Faerie, or the Land of Sleep, or any other Lands that might exist somewhere.

She didn't know how stars were made, or forests, or clouds, or mountains, or what lay at the bottom of the sea.

Now, she had already known she didn't know these things.

But suddenly she was *very* aware, painfully so, and also aware of other things she had never thought of. She had always admired the sound of crickets, for instance, but never realized that she had no idea how they made such a sound, or where they slept at night, or how they settled arguments among themselves, or a thousand other things.

Being wise, apparently, was not knowing a lot of things, but knowing all the things you didn't know. It was dreadful. She felt very sorry for all the wise people of the world.

She wanted to stand there by the lake and sulk, but there was one more task she had to do before she could return to the cottage. So she hurried deeper into the woods, trying very hard not to think about how little she knew about woods, and trees, and the nature of frogs. The nature of magic, and the nature of nature—oh, what a nightmare.

The witch lay in her bed beside the window, which was open to admit the mild spring night. She had even put on a cardigan, a black one with green flowers, which Grace took as a good sign.

"I cracked it," Grace told her. "The last spell. The unfinished one."

She had been hoping to surprise the witch with her astonishing success, a feat she had not once achieved, and to Grace's delight, the witch raised a single eyebrow one-quarter of an inch. "How?"

Grace told her. She snorted.

"Childish stories and ridiculous fancies—I should have guessed," the witch said. "Any spells you invent are going to be very silly."

"That's it, then," Grace said, far too excited to be hurt by the witch's insults. "I can call down the Wind of the Stars to heal you. How do I start? Do I simply look up at the stars and wave my hands about?" She demonstrated, making sure to let her sleeves flutter. Sleeves were an important part of witch-craft, she'd decided.

"There is no Wind of the Stars," the witch said. "It's an old folk tale that I heard somewhere a long time ago, back when I was a girl and it seemed like every glade and meadow had a folk tale attached to it, with more cropping up all the time like toadstools. There was a wind that blew down from the stars, and a witch who could summon it." She frowned. "I don't remember the rest."

There was a long silence in which Grace stared at the witch and the witch sipped her tea, nonchalant as anything.

"I don't understand," Grace said finally.

The witch sighed. "I made it up, because I knew you'd latch on to a fanciful story like that. I wanted you to finish that grimoire—if you didn't, then you would have had to give up your magic. It was a binding pact, after all."

Grace's thoughts were a tangle, but the wisdom spell smoothed them out. "You—you did it to be kind."

The witch shuddered. "Yes, isn't it ghastly? But it wasn't *much* of a kindness, really—I wasn't lying when I said that your magic couldn't heal me. Well, perhaps it could have given me another year or so. But what's a year? When you've wandered the earth for more than two centuries, you find—"

Her voice became faint, as Grace had thrown herself into the witch's arms, her sea-tangled hair muffling the witch's face.

The witch gave an exceptionally grumpy sigh, even by her standards, but she didn't shove Grace away. After a moment, she said, "Did you find him?"

She didn't sound hopeful. Astonishment dawned in her eyes as Grace nodded.

Grace pushed the window open all the way, and a tendril of fog drifted in. It was not fog, of course, but the edge of a cloud.

"As well you should," the witch said with asperity, in response to something Grace couldn't hear. "You were always one for grudges—quite unfair. You know that I tried everything—that if there was—"

She stopped, as if someone had interrupted her. "Oh, confound it."

But beneath her annoyance, the witch's eyes were bright with tears. The cloud gave a rumble that sounded like quiet laughter. It retreated and hovered just beyond the window, as if waiting for something.

"That's that, then," the witch said as she lay down again, in a tone so matter-of-fact that Grace didn't realize, at first, what she meant.

And then she did.

"No," she whispered. "No, you can't."

"I certainly can," the witch said. "And I will. Don't worry—I haven't forgotten our pact."

"What?" Grace stared at her. "How can I be your apprentice if—if you're—"

"Death does make things more complicated," the witch murmured. Her voice was growing faint.

"What about Cordelia?" Grace demanded through her tears. Blast her leakiness! She was crying so hard she could barely see. "And what about *me*? I don't wish to be alone again—I won't be able to bear it. Please don't go, *please*. There must be something I can do."

"As to the second problem," the witch said, "I can provide no help at all. I always preferred my own company. As to the first, you already know the answer, you ridiculous girl. You are an exceptionally talented witch for your age. You'll work it out."

Grace stilled. "I—I am?"

The witch rolled her eyes. "Naturally you are. You found moonweed and witch's helper without any effort. You fixed my sleep potion, which I had been working on for years. And you've solved my grimoire, which I did not complete until I was a grown woman of twenty. You shall be a truly fearsome witch one day, girl."

Grace's tears were falling again. Surely her heart would

burst from all the sadness and delight and terror filling it. "Why didn't you tell me that before now? You always said I was useless."

"Plenty of talented people in this world are useless," the witch said. "It's what you do with your talent that matters."

For a moment, the witch looked as if she didn't know what to say or do next. Then, in the most awkward way imaginable, she patted Grace on the head. She closed her eyes.

"I have lived a good long life," she said, and Grace had the impression that the witch wasn't talking to her anymore, but rather concluding an old argument with someone. "Well, I suppose it would be more accurate to say that I have lived an *enjoyable* long life. A life of wickedness and adventure. I have been the thing in the darkness that people fear. I would not have changed a thing."

There came an odd sound from the cloud outside— something that was almost a snort. And then the cloud rippled through the window and gently folded itself around the witch. The wind lifted Grace's hair from her face, bringing with it the smell of rain and high, distant places.

And then the witch was gone.

34

THE HAUNTED WOOD

A robin in the morning,
In the morning early,
Sang a song of warning,
"There'll be rain, there'll be rain."
—Duncan Campbell Scott, "Rain and the Robin"

The men came before dawn.

They came up the lane and across the witch's lawn as if they owned it all. Their axes were slung over their shoulders and their voices were gratingly loud against the misty pre-dawn hush. Cordelia rode up on a horse as they waited by the trees, looking a little nervous about entering the forest.

Grace watched them greet one another from her hiding place behind a stump, trying to ignore her heart thundering in her ears. She knew which trees they were planning to cut today—a cluster of big oaks by the marshy pond where she had found the moonweed and Patrick had rained on her that first time. One of the men had tied red ribbons around them.

Cordelia patted her horse kindly before leaving him tied to a branch. Grace felt a little flicker of guilt. Cordelia had been rude to her, it was true—but that didn't mean she deserved what awaited her in the forest. In fact, with her dark hair shining in the dim light and her long creamy dress, she looked more like the hero than the villain. And she was, wasn't she? She'd defeated her enemy, the witch—she'd stolen her home and driven her away.

And now Grace had to defeat Cordelia. What did that make her?

Sareena had said that Grace was good at taking care of people. Well, Grace thought, Sareena had to be right about that, because she was wise and clever and right about almost everything.

But now, Grace had to be good at being wicked.

Shadow shifted along the path, and one of the men started. The others laughed at his skittishness, but they didn't laugh long.

Out of the darkness came a horrible moan.

It sounded like a creature with a terrible stomachache, a towering thing with a great fanged mouth. You could *hear* the fangs in that moan.

"The wood's haunted," one of the men murmured. Nobody laughed.

The men backed up, and as they did, the underbrush began to snap and crunch beneath something that was at least as large as a bear, if not larger. Whatever it was, it was moving toward them.

That was enough to make two of them turn tail and run. The remaining five pressed together, while Cordelia stood frozen in front of them. The shadows shifted madly now, moaning and growling. Suddenly a dark shape erupted over the path, swarming the men and then fading back into the darkness.

One of the remaining men screamed. It was a sound that likely would have embarrassed him if he'd been in a state to be embarrassed, which made it all the more satisfying. Soon he was crashing after his companions. The shadows in the trees began to twitch like spiders, dropping on the men's heads. That did it—the rest ran, too, leaving only Cordelia, who seemed too stunned to move.

Grace smiled quietly to herself. For the witch had been right.

She *did* know how to deal with Cordelia.

Her tears hadn't even dried on her cheeks as she sat by the witch's empty bedside when that pesky wisdom had begun nagging at her. As it turned out, wisdom wasn't *only* about knowing what you didn't know—the world wasn't quite so miserable as that. It was also good for sizing up problems and finding solutions.

At least, Grace *thought* it was the wisdom spell that had given her the idea. She supposed it could have been her own wisdom—wouldn't that be something? She could have told the witch that she had practical ideas in her head now, in addition to the fanciful ones the witch was always complaining about.

Grace's hand tightened on the tree. But of course, she

couldn't tell the witch that, or anything else. She had gone where Grace couldn't talk to her, or harass her with her noise, or roll her eyes when the witch tried to frighten her.

It hadn't been difficult to gather up children's nightmares—no harder than it had been to gather their dreams. They'd fit neatly in a jar, little shadowy things that fluttered like dark moths. Grace had released them in that oak grove, and they had melted happily into the darkness as if they'd been there many times and knew their way around. Perhaps the children *had* visited the forest when they were asleep. Perhaps it had been woven into their nightmares—it was a witch's forest, after all.

And what were witches, if not scary?

Cordelia stumbled backward along the path. But before she could flee, Grace stepped out into the gray light of the forest.

"Stop," she said to the nightmares, and they listened. The shadows stopped their growling and moaning, though they didn't settle, but paced back and forth along the path like caged beasts.

Cordelia seemed to think Grace was one of the nightmares at first, and she gave a choked cry. But she was braver than the big men she'd brought with her, or maybe just more used to nightmares. She stood her ground.

"What was that?" Her voice was hoarse, and she cleared her throat. "What happened to these woods?"

"That's not for you to know," Grace said, relishing the mysteriousness of the words. Because the witch deserved mystery, didn't she? All stories did. And though Grace had stopped seeing the witch as a story, she knew Cordelia still would. Let her think the witch had magicked the forest from beyond the grave, filling it with monsters. Let her marvel at it and be frightened.

"The witch is gone," Grace told her. "She's—" She couldn't say the word without getting teary again, and she needed to be frightening now, so instead she finished, "She's not coming back. So you might as well leave."

"Why would I leave? This is my land."

"You'll leave," Grace said, emphasizing each word, "because you got what you came for. You wanted to destroy the witch, to chase her from her home. You came here for revenge. Well, you've had your revenge. You don't need this land—your father was rich without it, wasn't he? So rich he didn't care who lived on it, witch or not. From now on, if you keep cutting down these trees, or if you send men to pull down the cottage, you'll become more and more like the witch—doing things for the sake of cruelty."

Grace was walking toward her—mainly so that Cordelia could hear her properly, but with every step she took, Cordelia fell back the same amount. Her face was so pale it nearly glowed. "I'm not like you," she whispered. "I'm not like *her*."

Grace shrugged. "I think you know exactly what you are, deep down."

Cordelia shook her head as if to clear it. "Then she's—dead?"

Grace's hand clenched around her skirts, and she nodded.

"Good," Cordelia whispered. "*Good*. I wish I could have seen it. I wanted to be there, I—I admit, I wanted to do it myself. She deserved it, and then some. How can you be sad for her, you strange, wild little thing? Am I supposed to feel sorry for you?"

Grace gazed at her, and in that moment her anger fell away and she saw Cordelia for what she was. Frightened. She had been frightened for a very long time, so frightened that it was almost all she was now. Grace felt sad for her. Cordelia was half an orphan, and Grace knew well what a dreadful fate that was.

"Killing witches doesn't make you different from them," Grace said.

She backed up further. "I don't—I'm not—"

"I can help you, you know," Grace said. "I don't know much about magic, or being a witch. But I know a little. I can help you control your powers, or even use them, if you—"

But this kind gesture, which Grace considered very noble indeed, was what did it for Cordelia. A whimper escaped her, and she stumbled back into the trees. Grace heard her staggering about for a while, shrieking as the nightmares converged on her. They couldn't hurt her—at least, Grace didn't think they could. But Grace didn't like to think about what they showed her. Eventually Cordelia seemed to regain her senses, and she too fled from the forest.

35

BY SUN AND STARS

Strange black and princely pirates of the skies,
Would that your wind-tossed travels I could know!
—E. Pauline Johnson (Tekahionwake), "The Flight of
the Crows"

The wisdom spell wore off soon after that.

Most of it, anyhow. Grace sat on the front steps of the cottage, watching the dew flicker and flash in the dawn. A few stars hovered in the pink sky like pearls on a string, ready to slip off. Her mind was a haze of weariness, except for the occasional annoying burst of wisdom, where she would look at a beetle in the grass and realize that she knew nothing about where the beetle was going or why it seemed in such a hurry.

She had solved the grimoire. She had scared Cordelia away. On the surface of things, all was well. But she didn't *feel* well. She missed the witch.

Windweaver settled on her shoulder, plucking at her hair

and making that curious *purrr* sound that crows can make when the mood takes them. She petted his head.

You don't need to run off to live in the woods now, he said.

"Yes." She kept petting him, and a terrible certainty settled over her.

"I think it's time that I let you go, too," she whispered.

What? Windweaver said. Grace's voice wasn't cooperating, and he hadn't heard her.

"Windweaver," Grace said. "I know how to put you back the way you were. I think I could have done it before, except that I love you so, and didn't want to."

Windweaver stilled. *What are you talking about?*

"The witch said that I summoned you to be my familiar, even though I didn't know it. So surely I can un-summon you, if I try hard enough."

No. He sounded frightened. *No, I don't like this. Stop it.*

"You could live with the other crows again. That's what you want, isn't it?"

Windweaver shifted his weight from foot to foot, a sign of agitation. *I want to be with you.*

"Me too." Grace hadn't thought she had any tears left, but she was wrong. "But it makes you unhappy—I know you need to be with the other crows. It would be very selfish of me to keep you, Windweaver. I didn't see that before, but I do now."

He clicked his beak. *I—*

He stopped, and gazed out over the forest. Dark shapes fluttered among the boughs. And even though he was a crow, and showed none of his feelings in his face, she could feel the longing rolling off him.

All right, he said quietly. *Yes! Yes, of course. But we need a poem first.*

Grace nodded solemnly. "We do."

And so she went through "The Duck and the Kangaroo" again, and she didn't need the book, for they had read the poem so many times that she had it memorized. Then they sat there for a while, Windweaver nestled against her neck, and watched the light pierce the treetops.

She gave him a final pet. Then she let her mind drift back to the moment she had found him lying in the grass. He had been small and shivering in the damp—his coat was only soft down back then. He had seemed like the most precious thing in the world, particularly to a girl who was friendless and alone.

The wind lifted leaves and the petals that clung to the fallen cherry trees. They made a swirl of green and pink flickering in the sunlight like the memory of a dream. Windweaver pressed up against her, his heart going very fast, and her hair danced, a wild tangle. She closed her eyes, not wanting to see the moment when it happened, wishing that they could stay there like that forever.

Windweaver gave a sudden croak. He leaped off her shoulder, coming to rest in the nearest oak tree. He flapped his wings a few times, as if testing the air, and croaked again. Several crows alighted beside him. One edged toward him very slowly, as if afraid, and then some signal passed between them and they all flew off together.

"Windweaver?" The last of her wisdom was leaking away with the sun, and she felt a sickening surge of regret. "Windweaver!"

She raced to the edge of the forest, desperately calling him. But all she did was scare away a family of robins hunting for worms in the grass. The crows had gone, back to their secret hideaway deep in the woods, and Windweaver had gone with them.

Grace went back to the cottage and threw herself down on the stairs, where she buried her head in her knees and cried without ceasing. She didn't hear the hurried footsteps. She didn't even know Sareena had sat down beside her until she put her arm around Grace's shoulders.

"Isn't this dreadful?" Sareena said, scowling at the cherry trees. Of course, she thought that was why Grace was crying, and Grace didn't have the heart then to tell her the truth. "But we'll plant new trees, Grace, and they'll grow just as big one day, truly. Oh, if there ever was a person who deserved to be baked in a witch's oven, it's that Cordelia Burbage. I hope the witch makes her into a pie."

At that, Grace burst into a fresh river of tears.

"Oh dear," Sareena said, looking alarmed.

"Here." Rum unfolded himself from nowhere and handed Grace a fairy handkerchief. And what a ridiculous accessory it was, scratchy and cobweb-thin. But when Grace blew her nose in it and wiped her tears, the moisture seemed to vanish, so she supposed it wasn't as pointless as it looked.

"Th-thanks," she said with a hiccup.

"So!" Sareena said, with the grimness of someone steeling herself for bad news. "The witch is gone then, is she?"

Grace nodded, sniffling. Rum let out a sigh of relief, opened his mouth, and then, to her astonishment, closed it again. Perhaps the wisdom spell had rubbed off on him. Or perhaps he had simply learned to be a little less awful. Either way, Grace supposed it was all right to be friends with him. She would regret losing an archenemy, but perhaps he could be that, too; there were stories of heroes who ended up befriending their archenemies, weren't there? Indeed, she loved those stories best of all.

"Where did you get to yesterday, anyhow?" Sareena said. "I was calling and calling."

"Rum hid me with fairy magic," Grace said.

Sareena's mouth fell open. "Rum is a *fairy*? Why didn't you tell me?"

Grace buried her face in her hands. Rum smirked.

They sat there as the dew melted under the morning sun, filling the air with the lovely jungle smell that always accompanied the best spring days.

"It's a pickle, isn't it?" Sareena said. "Even if the witch stops by as a ghost every once in a while, it's going to be hard for you to stay here alone. Children aren't generally allowed to look after themselves."

"Perhaps you can say the witch is traveling across the sea," Rum suggested.

Grace sighed. "That might work for a while. But Sareena's right—eventually the villagers will find out. And then what? I won't go back to the orphanage."

Sareena squeezed her hand. "You can live with me. My mum likes you now. Look at all those strawberry tarts she baked for you and the witch."

"She's very generous when it comes to strawberry tarts, it's true. But taking in a child who doesn't belong to you is generosity of a different kind."

Sareena looked downcast. "Well. We have time to think of something else."

Grace scuffed her toe through the dirt. She didn't say that she was dreading going back into the cottage. She still loved it, and knew she would do so until the end of her days, but the cottage was empty now. The witch was gone. Her Windweaver had left. She was dreading walking through that door and feeling the emptiness all around her.

"Would you like some pancakes and ice cream?" she asked Sareena and Rum hopefully. To her relief, Sareena nodded and Rum said, "I hope you have plenty of honey," and they made their way up the steps. Later there would be more tears—the cleaning out of the saucepan that had held the witch's sleep potion; going to bed and finding the little nest of socks still next to her pillow. But now, at least, there were only pancakes and her two best friends.

"By the way," she said. "Don't go into the forest if you can avoid it."

"Why not?" Sareena said.

"Let's just say that I've turned it extra-spooky."

"Oh boy." Sareena paused on the porch, shading her eyes. "Who's that?"

Grace turned. A man had wandered out of the woods— *wandered* was really the only word for it, as he approached the cottage weaving this way and that, occasionally scratching his head and turning to look back over his shoulder.

She thought at first it was one of the woodcutters. But those had been large men with great quantities of graying facial hair. This man was slim and young—no more than nineteen or twenty, Grace guessed. He had dark hair and a daydreamer's face, with large eyes and soft features. And there was something else—something about those eyes, that long curving nose, that was familiar, though Grace was used to seeing them twisted into a scowl.

"Oh my goodness," she murmured. "Patrick. Patrick!"

She shouted it the second time, and the young man looked up.

"Oh," Sareena said, pressing her hand to her mouth. "*Oh.*"

Rum gave them a puzzled look. "Well, what did you expect?" he said. "The witch is dead now, isn't she? So her spells are broken. I thought you knew how magic worked."

Grace stared at him, mouth agape. Patrick had reached the cottage steps and stood looking up at them in puzzlement. His clothes were old-fashioned, and he was absently twisting a hat in his hands.

"I beg your pardon," he said. He had a strange accent, and his voice was hoarse, as if it hadn't been used in a very long time. "I—I seem to be not quite myself. That is—" He looked up at the cottage, and then at Grace. A smile flickered across his face. "I remember you. And your—your poetry. And I remember this place—bits and pieces of it. My sister, and the accident." He looked down at his hands. "But I'm afraid the rest of my memories are a terrible jumble. How did I come to be, ah, myself again?"

Sareena and Grace exchanged looks. Sareena's eyes were alight with excitement and scheming. "Why don't you come inside?" Grace said. "I'll make you some tea."

"Thank you," he said, sounding genuinely relieved, as if he'd been half expecting her to turn him away. "That would be lovely."

"Do you like ice cream?" A smile was growing on Grace's face, a hopeful one.

"Ice cream?" He pronounced each word carefully. "Oh dear. I'm afraid I don't know what that is."

"I think you'll like it," Grace said. "Everybody does."

She held out her hand. After a moment, he took it shyly, and she drew him toward the door. "Come in."

FROM THE WITCH'S GRIMOIRE

9. FOR BLACK ROSES

½ cup charcoal

6 handfuls red clover

4 black spruce cones, or 3 large

4 white spruce cones, or 3 large

6 appleseeds

Roses

Bury the ingredients together on the night of a new moon in a hole as deep as the night is long. Place roses on top.

May it be, by sun and stars.

18. FOR SNEEZES

6 silver maple leaves, dried and crushed

5 oxeye daisies

3 handfuls sea lavender

15 cobwebs (large)

8 dust bunnies

27 grains of pepper

1 cat's claw tip, newly shed

Mix well and scatter in a strong north wind.

May it be, by sun and stars.

77. FOR FINDING THE WAY

1 handful white cedar bark

3 bunches white pine needles

3–4 pinecones

1 handful dried dogberries

6 handfuls aspen leaves

1 witch hazel bough

1 beechnut

6 wild cherry stones

1 shadow of a raven

1 wild rose, crushed

7 fireflies

If lost at sea, add 1 crushed seashell (clam for best effect)

Set the ingredients alight and follow the embers.

May it be, by sun and stars.

ACKNOWLEDGMENTS

Huge thanks to my wonderful editor, Kristin Rens, as well as the team at Balzer + Bray, and to my ever-supportive agent, Brianne Johnson. Thank you to Nan Lawson for the beautiful cover, Ivy McFadden and Danielle Matta for their immensely helpful feedback, and to my amazing beta readers.

The ghost story told by Grace in chapter twenty is based on a local tale, which is recounted in Julie V. Watson's *Ghost Stories and Legends of Prince Edward Island* (Dundurn Press Limited, 2018; chapter twelve: "The Fork in the Graveyard"). Thank you to Julie V. Watson and Dundurn Press for granting permission to include this wonderfully spooky story here. Thank you to the staff and volunteers at Green Gables Heritage Place for answering my many questions about bedroom placements, wallpaper patterns, and so on. Many details were altered, as the witch's cottage is not Green Gables, but Green Gables was the rough pattern upon which the cottage was based. Other sources of inspiration included *The Landscapes of Anne of Green Gables* by Catherine Reid (Timber Press, 2018); *Anne's World, Maud's World: The Sacred Sites of L. M. Montgomery* by Nancy Rootland (Nimbus Publishing, 1997); and *The Annotated Anne of Green Gables* (Oxford University Press, 1997).